Wild With All Regrets

WILD
WITH ALL
REGRETS

E.L. Deards

SHE WRITES PRESS

Published 2023
Printed in the United States of America
Print ISBN: 978-1-64742-487-9
E-ISBN: 978-1-64742-488-6
Library of Congress Control Number: 2022915564

For information, address:
She Writes Press
1569 Solano Ave #546
Berkeley, CA 94707

She Writes Press is a division of SparkPoint Studio, LLC.

To EL, who largely inspired this work.

Foreword

The title of this novel is taken from a poem by Wilfred Owen, written for Siegfried Sassoon in 1917.

When I was around fifteen years old, I found myself sitting in my 10th grade English class, wondering how anyone could bear to study nothing but poetry for an entire semester. I was about to escape into the realm of the daydreamer, when I was asked to read the following poem, written by Wilfred Owen and published posthumously.

Dulce et Decorum Est

Bent double, like old beggars under sacks,
Knock-kneed, coughing like hags, we cursed through sludge,
Till on the haunting flares we turned our backs,
And towards our distant rest began to trudge.
Men marched asleep. Many had lost their boots,
But limped on, blood-shod. All went lame; all blind;
Drunk with fatigue; deaf even to the hoots
Of gas-shells dropping softly behind.

Gas! GAS! Quick, boys!—An ecstasy of fumbling
Fitting the clumsy helmets just in time,

But someone still was yelling out and stumbling
And flound'ring like a man in fire or lime.—
Dim through the misty panes and thick green light,
As under a green sea, I saw him drowning.

In all my dreams before my helpless sight,
He plunges at me, guttering, choking, drowning.

If in some smothering dreams, you too could pace
Behind the wagon that we flung him in,
And watch the white eyes writhing in his face,
His hanging face, like a devil's sick of sin;
If you could hear, at every jolt, the blood
Come gargling from the froth-corrupted lungs,
Obscene as cancer, bitter as the cud
Of vile, incurable sores on innocent tongues,—
My friend, you would not tell with such high zest
To children ardent for some desperate glory,
The old Lie: Dulce et decorum est
Pro patria mori.

For the first time in my life, a form of literature beyond the novel, play, or short story had spoken to me. The grim and bloody tapestry Owen was able to weave before my eyes left me dumbstruck— the casual attitude around death, the grim normalcies of the terrors that surrounded them, the bitter, miserable acceptance.

I wanted to know more about this man, about the war he fought in and protested against.

Wilfred Owen was born in 1893, the eldest of four children born to a middle class family in Shropshire. He discovered his love of poetry when he was eleven, but was unable to afford the university of his choice. He took courses in botany and English, and eventually moved to France to teach.

He enlisted to fight for England in World War I, and initially couldn't empathize with his fellow soldiers, finding them to be boorish and plain. After witnessing the horrors and trauma of war, and after being wounded badly himself, Owen's thoughts on the war began to change. He was diagnosed with shell shock, and was sent to recuperate in Edinburgh. There he met Siegfried Sassoon, who would change the course of his life.

His feelings towards Sassoon were close to that of hero worship, and he felt unworthy to even light his pipe. Sassoon in turn held a warm affection for Owen, and introduced him to a circle of gay and bisexual artists in Scarborough, who influenced him greatly. Wilfred Owen was himself a homosexual, and incorporated elements of homoeroticism into his works at the encouragement of the writers and artists he had met. Much of the written evidence of Owen's homosexuality has been lost, as his brother Harold removed and likely destroyed any parts of letters or diaries which he thought might be questionable.

Owen returned to the front after Sassoon was badly injured, as he felt that it was his duty to add his vocal opposition to the war now that Sassoon was unable. He wanted the truth of their misery to be shared with the world. Sassoon threatened to stab Owen in the leg if he returned, but Owen kept his plans secret until it was too late to change his mind.

Wilfred Owen was killed one week exactly before the Armistice, and was buried in a cemetery in France.

Sassoon waited for news of Owen's return, only to hear about his death several months later. Sassoon had likely never engaged in a romantic or sexual relationship with Owen, but mourned his loss for the rest of his life.

I've always been deeply inspired by stories of LGBTQ+ people. Of having to hide such an important part of yourself, of having to lie in order to exist, of finding a love worth risking absolutely everything over.

Wilfred Owen's story is beautiful, tragic, and his death was pointless and terrible. His life, his works, his journey of self discovery, and his great love of exposing the blood and filth beneath the surface were huge influences in writing this novel. I hope to honor his memory with this work.

1928

Lucas Connolly cleared away some of the gold and crimson leaves which cluttered the grave, and let his fingers skip along the smooth marble. The stone felt wet against his skin, and the chilly air cut through the thin fabric of his jacket. Grangegorman Cemetery was nearly empty, and Lucas was relieved for the privacy. This place had a beautiful silence to it, Lucas felt at peace here—Jamie would have liked it. He'd struggled with loud noises after being in the trenches, even when they were safe and away from the battlefield.

"I miss you," Lucas whispered to Jamie's grave. He never answered, obviously, although sometimes Lucas would shut his eyes and imagine that he had.

"*Y'aright, boyo?*" Jamie might ask, and Lucas would bump their foreheads together affectionately.

"Mm. Bit cold out though." The soft thump of fabric as Jamie's arm fell over his shoulders.

"*It's bloody October, you tit.*" And he'd smile, Lucas would, too, and they'd marvel at how it felt like no time had passed.

The anniversary of Jamie's death was always the hardest day of the year for Lucas, but never in his life had he felt as fragile as this: Jumping at noises in his home, seeing bloody Jamie in a crowd, and waking up in the night sweating, screaming, grasping at nothing. He'd attributed

1

it to stress, but deep down that seemed an insufficient answer. There was no number of confessions in the world that could absolve him or wash away the sticky black tar that encased the shreds of his heart.

It never got any easier. None of this ever got any fucking easier. Even now, Lucas still found himself a wandering stranger in the world, chasing ghosts and clinging to memories. This time, somehow, it felt different. In one week, it would be ten years, and Christ, Lucas had somewhat expected to be *better* by now. Jesus, the fucking ten-year anniversary. If his grief was a marriage, it'd be doing great. All around him the world was bloody changing. And yet Lucas was still . . .

Fuck.

"Lucas?" A piercing call cut through the crisp air of the cemetery.

Ugh. Angela's voice. What the hell was she doing here? He hugged his shoulders and prayed the grave was large enough to hide him from her hawkish eyes.

"I thought that was you!" She trotted over and waved at him, her slender hands wrapped up in black leather gloves. "You're late, you ass! You were meant to meet me at the pub!"

Lucas glanced at his watch. Good lord, he was very late indeed. "Most people would have gone home to teach their tardy friends a lesson."

She sat next to Lucas, her bottom squishing in the wet grass. "Yeah, well. Most tardy friends can't be shamed into buying drinks. Besides, I already know you're hopeless."

"How'd you know I'd be here?"

"Mm, knowing you, I figured this was a safe bet. Unless you got tied up with the blokes at the docks but, it's not sailing season, so. . . "

Lucas glowered at her. He hadn't traded at the docks in years.

"Plus, it's soon, right? The anniversary." She shivered briefly and stuffed her hands into her pockets. "You need a minute?"

"Yeah, Ange. Just give me a second."

"Lucas . . . don't take too long, all right? You spend too much time here as it is."

The sound of her footsteps softened as she stepped away from Lucas. He shook his head, narrowing his eyes—she'd still be in earshot, surely. Angela had no fucking business telling him how to spend his time, it wasn't her life that was withering away in isolation. To be fair, she was the closest living friend he had these days, but that didn't give her the right to tell him how to waste his own time.

Jamie was dead. He'd been dead for a decade. Their old flat in Dublin was long sold, and Jamie's clothes and possessions largely missing, stolen, or sent back to some unknown grieving loved one. Jamie's body was in a mass grave somewhere in the shell-torn fields of Belgium, never to be recovered. The tomb Lucas took so much comfort in was empty, but it hardly mattered. He'd saved up money for months to get the stone erected for Jamie; he'd even had the local priest check over his letters to make sure that the inscription would be perfect.

James A. Murray, Lieutenant of the Thirty-Sixth Ulster Division, killed in Belgium October 14, 1918. Honors include the Allied Victory Medal, the British War Medal, and the Victoria Cross, awarded for his death in the Battle of Courtrai and his bravery and tenacity in the Battle of Passchendaele.

Jamie's face flashed in his mind, flesh rotting, bones cracking through skin, and a hollow laugh echoing between his ears. A bony hand reached out to cup Lucas's cheek, his voice hollow, echoing . . .

"*Help me, Lucas. Jesus Christ, help me.*" Lucas's eyes snapped open, and he tried to catch his breath.

Jamie wouldn't want to see him like this, breaking down in the middle of a cemetery. Jamie would chuckle softly, clap him on the shoulder, and tell him to keep his head on straight. *"You're better than this, Lucas,"* he'd say, and Lucas would believe it, somehow.

Jamie's had been an easy existence leading up to the war, maybe he hadn't been ready for the horrors that faced him. The bombs, the shells, watching men being blown apart right in front of his eyes. Lucas had occasionally found Jamie alone in his hollowed-out room in the trenches, head in his hands, eyes glinting in the soft light of the lantern as he stared out into nothing.

"Jamie?"

A quivering silence. Hackles raised in anticipation. It was starting again; Jamie always got worse before he got better.

"Jamie." Lucas had placed a hand on Jamie's shoulder and flinched when those wide, manic eyes whipped around at him. "Jamie, it's me. I've got you."

The bombs fell anew, and Jamie flailed away from Lucas's solid hand.

Boom. Boom. Screams in the distance, dust shaken free from their makeshift rooftop, Jamie covered his head with his arms. Before the shell shock. God, Lucas didn't even like to think about it. Jamie would have run out to protect the others, would have covered Lucas with his bigger frame and stayed steady, stayed focused.

"Lucas . . . please . . . Jesus, help me. Help me!"

His pleading, desperate voice—begging him for help, those strong fingers digging into the fabric of his shirt. *It isn't real, it isn't real.* Lucas fingered the button that he kept in his pocket and tried grounding himself, hoping to prevent this little blip from turning into more than it was. *This isn't happening. Jamie's dead, he's dead. He's dead and he can't talk to you, can't see you, can't touch you. You can't help him now, idiot. Ground yourself. Lucas Connolly, it's your fucking fault he's dead, you're suffering because of your own fucking choices.*

"Lucas?" Angela called out, rushing over to him.

You deserve this. You deserve worse, you fucking coward.

"Lucas!" She shook his shoulders. "You're all right, I've got you. We're in Dublin, you're safe, okay?"

Lucas was suddenly aware of the way his whole body was shaking as he gasped, how his fingernails were caked in dirt from where he'd clawed his way through the earth beside him. He found himself coughing, and he pulled Angela close, shaking his head as reality settled in. Jamie wasn't dying. He wasn't in danger. It had all happened already. It was too bloody late.

"I'm sorry." He gasped, clutching at her coat, his hands slick with mud. He wasn't sure if he was speaking to her or to Jamie, shit— he wasn't sure of anything at all.

"I know." Angela whispered, stroking his back. "S'why I don't think you should be out here alone, okay? Come along, poppet. We were going to the pub, remember? Are you still up for it, or do you want me to take you home?"

Christ, he must have been in awful shape if Ange was willing to forfeit the alcohol he'd be expected to buy her. "It—I'm fine," He muttered, pushing himself away from the grave. Lucas's hand lingered, as it always did. He patted the stone and tipped his hat slightly. "I'll see you," he said softly.

Angie pulled him into a quick hug and held him there until his breathing slowed. "Y'aright, Lucas? You wanna talk about it?"

Lucas shook his head, eyes drifting to Jamie's name. "Don't worry. I think I've stewed in my memories long enough." Besides, the clouds were clearing up, and Lucas strongly preferred to suffer poetically when the weather matched his mindset anyway.

Angela kept hold of his elbow until they reached the pub, her broad smile reassuring in the face of Lucas's outburst. He truly appreciated her dedication to keeping things chipper.

"Rude bastard you are," she said lightly. "Standing up a beautiful lady like that! The bartender couldn't believe it—gave me a free round, he did!" She pulled off her coat as they arrived at the bar, plopping down in a comfortable booth. "So, guess what, smarty boots? Next round is on you. That, and you owe me for getting mud all over my lovely coat!" She kissed his cheek and fluffed up his hair. "Aw, that face! You're like a little kitten! Careful now, or I'll put you in a box and drag you home with me."

"Jesus Christ, Ange," Lucas mumbled, somehow feeling hungover already. "You ever figure out how to bottle that energy, you'll make a goddamn fortune."

"Don't need it! Tom proposed finally!" She raised her glass to him and chugged her beer. "You'll be my bridesmaid, right? I'll get such a dress for you!"

Despite himself, Lucas smiled. "Gonna make an honest woman out of you, then?" he asked, signaling the bartender for another round of beer.

"Ah to hell with you, ya bastard," she said, nudging him with her elbow. "Oh, you shoulda seen it, Lucas, he took me out to the garden, near the rosebushes—you know, the ones I planted with his mum last summer. And he took my hand and said, 'Angie, my father's going to disown me if I don't marry you, so I'd best do it before such a time as he starts to think poorly of me!'" She paused, downing her beer. "I slapped him right on his cheek, so I did! Then he showed me this lovely ring, and I didn't slap him again." She laughed and shoved her hand in Lucas's face so he could see it; a mischievous smile played over her lips. "He's such a cock, bless me for loving him so."

"And such a catch you are, Angie, I can't believe no one's snapped you up sooner," he said over the brim of his glass.

"You had your chance, you little buggering bastard!" she teased back, pushing her thick glasses up her nose. "Least I didn't have to get pregnant to get him to finally pop the question, which would've been quite undignified. Christ, what a proposal. He's lucky to have a woman as understanding and sweet as I am!"

Lucas frowned at that, but he knew Ange had no way of knowing how his own parents had met. She wasn't one to judge anyway, not even for his colorful social life. Truthfully, he was glad for her, glad that she'd managed to find happiness after the war.

She'd been an army nurse and patched Lucas together once or twice when he was in the trenches with Jamie. They'd go out sometimes when they were on leave; Jamie would come, too. They liked each other, they'd been a nice little group, but she'd always been much closer to Lucas. Maybe she just clicked better with Lucas, or maybe it was because—even then—Jamie had lost so much of himself. Lucas wondered if she even understood what all the fuss was about.

Lucas had admired Angie's guts more than anything else. Her unwavering ability to sift through mounds of flesh and blood and shards of bone, somehow managing to rip life away from the jaws of death. Her love had been killed in the war, though they hadn't even been stationed near each other. She was in Belgium, and he was in Germany. They hadn't exchanged a word in person for years by the time she got his death notice. Angie had mourned, tied back her hair, finished the war with a black band around her arm, and somehow moved on with her life. Lucas liked to tell himself that she probably hadn't loved Euan that much, considering the ease with which she'd gotten over her fiancé, but deep down, he knew that the abnormal behavior was his.

In ten years, Angela had furthered her career, made the world a better place, and now she was about to start a family with the man she loved. In ten years, Jamie had rotted away to bones in the earth, and Lucas had done nothing.

He and Jamie had never been lovers, had never even kissed. Hell, Jamie probably had no idea how much Lucas had obsessed and agonized over their relationship or . . . whatever the hell it was. Lucas sometimes wondered what the hell was wrong with him; he could probably move on if he would only allow himself to.

Angie finished her beer just as a man who could easily be mistaken for Jamie entered the pub. Lucas shut his eyes, turned away, and finished his beer. *Was he seeing things?* Jamie's stupid twins wandering around the city like they had nothing better to do than drive Lucas mad.

"How's Jamie?" Angie asked, an expert at catching Lucas in his moments of over-reflection. "Still as talkative as ever?"

"He's fine, thank you." Lucas set his glass down with a firm, definitive clunk. "Government isn't paying enough for the upkeep; I had to clear off the leaves again."

"They should pay you to do it! You're there often enough. Hell, you could probably give tours out, if you wanted to."

Lucas knew she was holding back. He'd been known to be quite sensitive over the matter of Jamie's grave, and neither of them wanted this to turn into a heated argument.

Angie took off her glasses and polished them, her warm brown eyes shining beneath her thick eyelashes. "Have you been able to work?"

It didn't matter, really. Jamie had made Lucas the beneficiary of his pension. He'd trade every last penny for the man who'd left it to him.

"Have you tried speaking to anyone real this week?" Angie followed.

He was silent, and Angela sighed.

"It's not healthy, Lucas. I don't know how many more times I can tell you that it's not healthy to have a dead person be the most prominent figure in your life."

"What about priests?"

She frowned. "What *about* priests?"

"Well, they devote their entire lives to a dead person. In fact, they get paid a living wage to do so."

"Technically, our Lord and Savior isn't dead, he's resurrected and immortal, ass. If you end up taking up the cloth, I'll eat my shoe. And technically, some pretty boy you had a hard-on for in the trenches isn't on the same level as our Lord and Savior, either. Checkmate."

"That all you've got?" he smirked, finishing his beer.

She reached over and grabbed his hand, placing it in her mouth and nibbling on it harmlessly.

"Honestly, Ange, I can't believe it took Tom this long to propose. I mean, you are the epitome of womanhood and class." He rolled his eyes but smiled, watching a little drop of condensation descend down the side of his glass.

Angie chewed on him a little longer and released his hand, seemingly sated. She passed him a kerchief for the saliva, and Lucas frowned at her.

"Lucas? I know this time of year is hard for you. I'm only trying to help."

"I know that, Angie. For what it's worth, I'm sorry that I cause you so much grief. I know it's not easy being my friend."

"No, but you make me laugh, and that's worth something. Why don't you try something for me then, boyo? Just for one month, don't visit the grave. Get up in the morning, eat your breakfast, go to work, and then at the end of the day, you go home. I bet you'll find that the world keeps spinning, eh? You might even find you get rid of that little wrinkle between your eyebrows." She pressed on it with her index finger and laughed. "What do you say?"

He considered it. Finding a job, a lover, and never visiting Jamie again. It might be a nice wee life actually, where he could be a man instead of a tattered wandering spirit. Let Jamie go, just . . . live? But that beautiful smile came unbidden to his mind, melting away seamlessly into blood, screams, and terror. His heart sped up as he relived Jamie's last moments anew, and he imagined Jamie's spirit waiting for him at the graves. He seemed cold; he seemed frightened. *No. I can't leave him like that. He deserves better.* And Lucas certainly didn't.

"Angie, please let me have this." *Visiting Jamie is one of the only things that brings me any peace, it's one of the only things that makes me feel like my soul isn't dying.* "You think I don't know how odd it is? How unhealthy it is? I need this. I need him." *And he needs me.* His voice cracked, and Angela took his hand. "If I forget about him, if I move on, it's like he never even—I don't want to lose him all over again. He's all I have."

Angie frowned a little, perhaps hurt by his words. She'd been his friend for a long time, and seemingly, it still didn't matter.

"I'm sorry. I didn't mean it like that, I just—"

"You know I love you, right, Lucas?" Her soft hand moved to cover his, her eyes were warm and gentle. "That I only want what's best for you?"

He swallowed, snatching his hand away as he angrily avoided her gaze. "I know what's best for me." *And he's dead and buried.*

1904

It was freezing. Then again, it was always bloody freezing. There was no fucking escaping from it. His mother couldn't afford to keep the stove going all the time, nor keep her children in warm clothes all winter.

Lucas did his best to build up a fire in their house with any scraps he could find. In his efforts, he'd inadvertently incinerated one of his father's betting slips, a fact which was not particularly well received.

Lucas could see the white of Mick's eyes as he staggered forward, grabbing at his son with one hand. "You cocksuckin' piece o' shite!" He punctuated his anger with a swig of liquor, the brown glass of the bottle shimmering in the warm light of the fire. "I paid good money on that bloody horse!"

He drained his alcohol and smashed the bottle on the nearest wall, leaving a sharp and jagged threat that he brandished at his son. Through his swelling eye, Lucas made out the deadly shards that stank of whiskey.

"Mick!" Lucas's mother, Molly, tried to get between them. "It was an accident only! He's tryn'a help the other children!"

Da' Connolly dropped his son and swatted his wife to the floor, looking down his nose at her. "He cost us a fortune!"

Lucas swallowed, heart beating frantically in his chest. *Stay away from her. Leave her alone!* He shifted nearer to the door, maybe he could get his father's focus away from his mother. "Y-your stupid horses never win!" He cursed his voice for trembling. "At least one of us can keep the family warm!" *You bloody fucking useless coward.*

"You miserable shit," Mick hissed. "The family's gonna starve because of you. We're all gonna freeze because you lost my winning ticket. C'mere boyo, I want you to watch while your fuckin' sister dies."

Mick lunged at Lucas, his whole body nearly quivering with rage as he lashed out. Lucas didn't want to stick around and squeezed through the door to get away from his father. He had no shoes on, but it didn't seem to matter. Lucas ran. He ran, and he ran, and he kept running until he didn't know where he was anymore.

"*You've murdered your family, Lucas.*"

He imagined his mother crying, trying to get the baby to feed. Mick'd be screaming his damned head off, hopefully taking his anger out on the furniture rather than his family. Damn it. Lucas's lip was split, his eye was throbbing, he was lost and cold, but anything was better than facing the wrath of his Da' again tonight. He was a coward, right? He'd left his mother alone with that monster.

"*It's your fault. You ruined us.*"

Shit. Why did people even have children, if they knew their whole lives were going to be terrible like this? It was his own fault, really. His Da' loved to remind him of the night he messed around with the lovely Molly O'Leary, with her sweet little bum and her bright little eyes—oh her hips, Lucas, her legs went so long, her body was so lush . . .

A spark formed between them that culminated months later, when Molly's father dragged old Mick Connolly out of the tavern and into a church to make an honest woman of his steadily broadening daughter. What followed were four months of drunken abuse, and a somewhat premature Lucas. His mother tried her best, she did, but money was

scarce, food scarcer, and her milk wasn't great. Lucas struggled, survived, and one year later, Jim was born. The story played out once
more, and—just as well, really, Jim died of the crib death before he
could learn the words "fuck," "you," and "whore."

Every year another wee Connolly was expelled to the dirty floor
and given a swaddling cloth and a swollen breast, with the best of luck
from Da'. Mick wasn't always horrible, really—it was just when he was
drinking, which was more often than not these days. Sometimes, Lucas
and his father would spend time together. Mick would try and teach
him about life or work, he'd put his son on his knee and tell him about
football. Lucas liked it when it was like that. He liked his shiny silver
eyes, he liked the soft rumble of his voice, how strong and warm his
hands were. But the more time passed, the more Mick's back ached, the
less he could work, the more he drank. It was getting harder and harder
to remember a time when they had been happy together as a family.
Lucas, being the oldest, was proud to take the brunt of his father's
anger. His siblings didn't know any better, and hell—it was Lucas's fault
two incompatible people had had to get married in the first place.

Mick blamed Lucas for everything, and loved to put his uppity near
bastard of a son in his place when required. A swift hand across his
face, swiping food off his plate, or locking him out for days at a time.
It was a harsh fucking world out there, but sometimes Lucas liked
to take his bloody chances. He pulled his collar up against his neck
and pretended the icy rain wasn't bothering him. *Shit. Might actually
freeze to death at this rate.*

They'd find his frozen little corpse wrapped in wet newspapers in
the middle of some piss-reeking back alley in the middle of Dublin.
Maybe they'd dig him a nice grave—more likely they'd ignore him 'til
he started to rot. Little beggar boys were hardly worth a second glance,
after all.

Lucas's lips were a bit blue, and he shivered, trying to stay awake as long as he could to stave off death just a little longer. After a time, his eyes slipped closed, his mind grew light, and the cold stopped bothering him as much.

A hand on his shoulder; a small hand, a boy? His eyes flickered open and, kneeling above him, illuminated by the glow of the streetlight, was an angel.

"Are you all right? Oh heavens, you're freezing!" The angel pulled off his own jacket and wrapped it around Lucas's shoulders, his silky blond hair kissed with raindrops. "My papa's only nearby, you wait here—okay? I'll be back in a tick."

No, he couldn't have been an angel. Angels didn't run in the puddles with their knees slicked with mud. Just a boy, then? Maybe a few years older than he was. Ech, how boring. *You idiot. Why would a fucking angel come to rescue you?* Still, the coat was nice and warm, and he liked the way it smelled. Lucas buried his head into the fabric and shut his eyes, wondering if he would die tonight after all.

"He's just here, Papa!" The lad ran back toward him, his fancy button-down shirt nearly soaked through from just that short amount of time in the rain. An older man was with him. He had the same blond hair, a short beard, and eyeglasses. Christ on the cross, what now? The man who he presumed to be his angel's father knelt down and looked Lucas over from top to bottom, gently wiping some blood away from his face.

"Oh, son," he said softly, his brows pinched together. "Where are your parents?"

What could Lucas say to that? 'My Da' beats me 'til he's too drunk to care, and my Ma's too scared to get him to stop?' He avoided the man's calm blue eyes and sniffled a little.

"Why don't you stay with us tonight? I'm in town on business. We're staying at my parents' house and there's plenty of room. What do you think?"

Lucas looked away. He didn't need these fuckers' charity.

The boy smiled at him. "Please? It's so boring while my dad is working. Plus, we can play together while we're waiting for the weather to clear up! My gran's got some nice dinner on the stove, too, I bet it'll be really lovely." He grinned. "I'm James, by the way. Most people call me Jamie, though. You're really brave being out here all on your own. I'd be so frightened."

Jamie had pretty hair, nice clothes, and a laugh that cut through the cold. It was hard to say no to him, and Lucas found himself nodding and following the strangers toward Jamie's granny's house. He hoped they weren't planning on selling him into servitude or something, but it might even be a step up from his current home life. Jamie put an arm around Lucas's shoulders and chatted to him about this and that, like they'd been friends their whole lives and were just catching up.

"My papa's real nice. He's a barrister! I mostly stay in our house down south, but sometimes I come up here to do business with him! We're getting books for our library at home! Do you like to read?"

Lucas wasn't sure what to make of Jamie's seemingly endless energy, and merely nodded and bit his lip, trying to figure him out. Jamie didn't seem to *want* to hurt him at all. He seemed incapable of it. "You talk a lot," Lucas said eventually. "It's annoying."

Jamie laughed at that. "I'm sure some people find it endearing. Ah, we're here!"

Jamie's father—who eventually introduced himself as John Murray—escorted the boys up to Jamie's room and let Lucas get settled. "Jamie, why don't you run your wee friend a bath, and I'll let you both know when dinner is ready."

Jamie smiled and nodded. "Righto, Papa! What's your name, anyway?" He smiled, offering to take Lucas's wet garments away so he could hang them up near the fire.

"Lucas," he muttered, glancing down at his raggedy clothes as they came off layer by layer.

"I like that name." Jamie clapped him on the shoulder. "C'mon, I'll draw you a bath and get you nice and warmed up. You can borrow some of my old clothes while yours dry out, okay?" He went to the kitchen and heated up some water to put in the tub. Lucas had never seen a water pump in a house before and was fascinated by it. He watched Jamie work and obediently stepped into the warm water once it was ready.

"Atta boy, Lucas! I'll leave out a towel and some soaps, you come out when you're ready, pal." He went back up to his bedroom, leaving Lucas bewildered and blushing from his nose to his ears. *The hell was wrong with this kid? Fucking nutter.*

The bath was absolutely heavenly. He'd always been a fastidious child, likely a result of living in squalor his whole life, but he'd never had the chance to have a nice, warm bath like this. On Henrietta Street, the cold sank into his bones and was impossible to shake. Lucas was accustomed to his fingers being so cold he couldn't feel them, to falling asleep to the sound of his teeth chattering. The water warmed him all the way to his core, and he felt himself relaxing in the gentle heat of it. Still, it would hardly do if he drowned in the tub before supper, really.

Lucas scrubbed himself clean, toweled himself off, and pulled on some of Jamie's too-large clothes. He realized with mild surprise that the home itself was warm too, that he didn't need to worry about the chill setting back in now that he'd gotten out of the water. He went searching for Jamie, still feeling ill at ease in this beautifully gentle space. His new companion greeted him with a smile and clapped him on the shoulder.

"Come on, my gran'll want to meet you!" He grinned again, and Lucas made a mental note about how white and straight his teeth were.

He followed Jamie through the halls, pausing at the threshold of the living room. Lucas wasn't really sure where to place himself—he didn't want to get in the way. He was used to making himself small and staying out of range of projectiles.

"He was just out in the rain by himself, poor thing. Jamie was so worried, and I couldn't in good conscience leave him, I— ah." John looked up, his glasses slipping down his nose. "Lucas, I take it you enjoyed your bath, then?"

God, Lucas hated it when people fucking pitied him. He knew he looked like a washed-up piece of shit, he didn't need some plump little grandma praying for him every night.

"Are you hungry, sweetheart?" Granny Murray asked. "You're all skin and bones, love."

He crossed his arms over his chest and refused to make eye contact despite the little granny's best efforts. His stomach ultimately betrayed him, however, as the whole house had the beautiful aroma of lamb, vegetables, and potatoes wafting through the air. The growling of his innards shook the floorboards, and Granny Murray smiled and guided him to the dining room.

Why was hunger so damned painful? John put a hand on his shoulder, and he flinched away, shaking his arm free from the gentle grip. John seemed to hesitate as he drew his hand back, his movements slow and deliberate.

"Come on, Lucas, let's all sit down for some dinner, hmm?"

Lucas was finding it hard to stay angry with the whole family for their stupid pity. John said grace, and Lucas waited for permission before he started eating. It was difficult. He wanted to dig in and gorge with abandon, but his dignity wouldn't allow it.

"Go on, it's okay."

Lucas peered over at Jamie, who had already begun to eat. Lucas cleared his plate much more quickly than he meant to, eating so fast and so much more than he was used to that his stomach began to cramp up. He put down his fork and hunched over a little in his chair, trying to hide the pain.

"Are you okay?" Jamie asked. "Do you want some tea or something? I get a tummy ache too, when I eat too fast."

Lucas scoffed. *Like this spoiled little brat knew what it was like to be starving, like he knew how it felt not to have had hot food for over a week, like he'd experienced the agony of your body digesting itself.* He knew Jamie didn't mean anything by it, he knew his heart was in the right place, but goddamn, this was humiliating.

Jamie's granny made some tea for everyone, and Lucas silently offered a prayer of thanks that the Murrays weren't drawing attention to his agony. She busied herself in the kitchen, and John went to help her with the dishes.

"C'mon, why don't we go sit by the fire?" Jamie asked, his stupid face too pretty in the dim light of the dining room. "Maybe if we get hungry later we can see if granny made any pudding for us." He led Lucas to the living room, which had two enormous bookcases filled almost to bursting with leather-bound volumes. Lucas had never seen anything like it. Jamie pulled one off the shelf and sat down on the comfortable couch in front of the fire, gesturing for his guest to join him. "Want me to read to you? I really like this book, it's called *Treasure Island,* and it's my favorite! It's tremendous fun, and I want to go on adventures like this one day!"

Lucas sat next to Jamie, letting their shoulders touch ever so slightly. He wanted to keep his distance, not to let this perfect boy into his heart, or under his skin . . . but his stomach was full, and Jamie was warm, and it wasn't long before he drifted off to sleep, nestled into the soft wool of Jamie's jumper.

John must've carried him to bed at some point, as Lucas woke up with a start in an unfamiliar room on an unfamiliar mattress. It was dark, but he soon determined that it was a child's bedroom, with a few modest toys and a sensible wardrobe near the wall. Jamie snored quietly in a bed on the opposite side of the room, and Lucas sat up, trying to decide what to do next.

His parents were probably worried sick about him Well, his mother, maybe, his father was probably unconscious in his chair.

You'd better get home soon, or there'll be hell to pay, boyo.

He shut his eyes and snuggled up into the blanket. Yeah, better to get home before he caused trouble . . . then again, he quite liked it at the Murray's house. Would it be so terrible to stay here a little longer?

But his family, his mother, his little brothers and sisters relied on him, and he couldn't bear to think of them struggling alone. Shit, he could steal all the silver and feed his siblings for a month. That granny probably had some jewelry knocking around somewhere as well. He hardened his resolve, justifying his actions in his head. Stealing was a sin, but his father had left his family starving, and it wasn't fair for Jamie's dumb family to have so much when his had so little.

Rain pelted the windows, and he shivered a little, despite the abundant soft blankets and pillows. His father's voice echoed in his mind.

Worthless parasite. Ruined the family. We're worse off because of you!

People said they looked alike. Sometimes, when Lucas looked in the mirror, he caught his father's eyes looking back at him. Saw the sharp little sneer he feared and loathed etched forever on his face.

His father might not be so angry anymore if Lucas was out of the picture. Maybe they'd be better off without him. Lucas made a little noise and burrowed into the blankets.

No. I don't want to go back. Please, please don't make me.

Jamie stirred in his little bed and yawned, his bright blue eyes lighting up as he realized he still had his new companion there with him. "Can't sleep? It's weird in a new place, isn't it? You can come lie with me if you want, I get scared in new places, too. It's nicer with a friend, I think. Plus, the storm's really loud tonight, huh?"

What a fucking joke. Lucas wasn't scared of storms; he had bigger problems to deal with. Thunder cracked outside the window, and he jumped a little, hugging his blanket to his chest. He hesitated for a moment, but made his way over to Jamie's open arms, tucking his head under Jamie's chin and trying not to cry. *When was the last time his mother had held him like this? When was the last time he'd gone to bed warm and with a full belly?*

Jamie stroked his back, seemingly unaware of Lucas's distress. "How old are you? I'm ten," He seemed to be very proud of the fact. "Papa says I have a long way to go before I'm grown up, but I like to help around the house anyway. I want to be a barrister when I get older, like Papa!"

Christ on the cross, he talks a lot. Lucas had half a mind just to let him babble on until he fell asleep again. But gradually, Jamie paused, perhaps realizing that he hadn't allowed his guest to get a word in.

"I'm eight." Lucas said eventually. "I don't know what I want to do when I grow up."

His father always told him he was worthless, that he wouldn't amount to anything. Work in some low-paying, no-education job, probably, whatever he could get as soon as he was old enough to take some of the burden of feeding his siblings away from his mother. If he lived that long. Christ. He almost hoped he didn't. His worst nightmare was ending up like his father, drinking himself into a stupor and destroying the people he loved.

"You have lots of time, pal. Papa says Ireland will be free one day, and when the day comes, we'll need people to help make life good and safe for everyone."

Lucas was starting to like it when Jamie spoke, his voice was gentle and comforting. Jamie was an annoying little chatterbox, but he was sweet, and he was gentle, and Lucas felt safer with him than he did in his own bed. Lucas didn't have many friends; his family's reputation made it difficult. He wondered idly if this was the start of something special.

"What's your mum like?" Lucas prompted, wanting to hear more. He didn't care about Jamie's mother in particular, but he was enjoying the steady rumble of the older boy's voice over his hair.

"She's really nice, she likes to make pies and things. Papa doesn't like to bring her with him when he goes to Dublin, since she's prone to getting herself ill. She's at home with Fiona just now. My little sister. She's only small, but she gets into all sorts of trouble, so she does."

"Does she look like you? She must be pretty." *Oh goddamn it.*

Jamie laughed. "I don't know about that. She has the same color hair and eyes as I do, though. My whole family sort of looks like we fell out of a wheat field. I think Mama has roots in England, but she doesn't talk about it much."

Lucas imagined the whole family sitting together in a brightly lit meadow, maybe picnicking on a checkered blanket under an ancient tree. John probably had Fiona resting on his lap, while Jamie was digging into a homemade lunch and talking about school. His mother would listen attentively, maybe stroke his silky blond hair and tell him to elaborate. And of course, he would, because he was happy, because he was secure, because he knew he was loved.

Lucas wondered if his own smoky gray eyes ever sparkled. He'd never been much of a smiler; his mother gave him a hard time about it. *"They'll think me a bad mother, Lucas. They'll think you're touched in the head. Normal children smile."*

Maybe Jamie thought he was strange.

"What's your family like, Lucas?"

"I'm really tired. I don't want to talk anymore."

Jamie was silent for a beat, and Lucas regretted the sharpness of his words. He certainly hadn't meant to hurt him but . . .

"Okay. Goodnight, Lucas, I'll see you in the morning."

"G'night. M'sorry."

Lucas seriously doubted that Jamie would be able to keep his fucking mouth shut for the rest of the night, but somehow, he found it very endearing. He buried his face in Jamie's chest and was surprised how easily sleep found him again.

1912

Lucas shut his eyes and steeled himself, his slender back pressed up against the wall of the alleyway. He hated doing things like this, but he didn't have any money, and he wasn't sure what else he could do. His father had left and never come back about three years ago, and once Lucas had grown old enough to work, he'd become the main provider for his ailing little family.

He supposed Mick was probably dead and, in his heart, Lucas genuinely hoped it was true. His Ma' turned a blind eye to his doings, knowing that Lucas probably had to break the law, and at least one of the Ten Commandments, to make ends meet now and again. No one wanted to hire the eldest son of Mick Connolly for anything serious; that horrific reputation dogged him throughout his childhood and beyond. He managed to secure odd jobs now and again doing construction or ditch-digging or filth-clearing—he had no skills and was at the mercy of whoever was handing out the work. More often than not, the job went to whoever would accept the lowest pay. It wasn't enough to keep his four little siblings fed, clothed, and educated, which had always been his main priority. Lucas didn't want any of them to turn out like him, to drop out of school too young and wind up as a criminal or a failure. Boys from his year would see him from time to time as he toiled in the dirt, ankle deep in grime, and he'd narrow his eyes as they snickered behind their hands at him. It was so easy to be cared for, wasn't it? He hated his work, but at least it was honest.

The seasons were changing though; the nights were longer, the days colder, and most of the construction jobs had dried up for the season. Lucas's sixteenth birthday was approaching, and he obviously needed his strength, but he tried to make sure his family was fed before he was. Lucas knew his mother was slipping him extra food when she could, probably out of fear that if he got too weak, he wouldn't be able to provide.

"Lucas?" Wee Jessie stared up at him.

"Yes, little fish?"

"What time are you coming home today?" She was terribly thin, and it made her eyes seem all the larger.

"As soon as I can. I won't be more than a few hours, kiddo. I'll bring something nice."

"Can you bring home lots of stuff? Can we have enough so we can share?" She was bouncing on the balls of her feet. "Can we get something with potatoes? Can I have a big piece?"

Lucas ruffled her hair and smiled. It killed him when he hadn't made any money. It killed him to tell this sweet little girl that once again, he had nothing. Today, it wasn't gonna be fucking like that.

He'd found he was good at two things: stealing, and letting perverts do what they wanted with him. Stealing, obviously he'd been doing since he was a young man: a hand in a pocket during a crowded event or grabbing some groceries while the shopkeeper wasn't paying attention. Lucas was small for his age; he moved quickly, and he blended into a crowd. As far as pickpocketing went, he was a goddamn natural.

As for letting perverts do as they wished with him . . . he'd been doing that with great success for the last four years. It was a discovery he'd made when he was about twelve, when Father Doyle had taken a shine to him. It had been a great honor for his family, actually, for one of their own to be selected and favored by a well-regarded priest like that—especially with his father flitting in and out of their lives as he did.

Lucas had glowed under the attention, feeling big and important for the first time in his life. Maybe he wasn't going to end up a broken failure like his father, maybe he really could take up the cloth and make something of himself one day.

Father Doyle took all of Lucas's confessions, and eventually they moved from the confessional to his private office. It was filled with old books and manuscripts, and Lucas had always thought that the chairs in his room looked very comfortable. He liked the time he spent here, it was warm and dry, and he felt so safe.

"Do you ever touch yourself, Lucas?" the priest asked, his kindly eyes glinting in the soft light of the room.

"A-aye. Sometimes."

"And do you think about the other boys when you do it?"

"Father?"

"Do you think about other boys when you touch yourself, Lucas? Do other boys excite you?"

Lucas felt the heat in his cheeks and wondered just what it was about him that made it so damn obvious. The other kids picked on him at times for being smaller, for being more feminine, for being "odd" somehow. Lucas felt terrible about it and tried his best to abstain from the solitary sin as much as he could, but he supposed that was what confessions were for.

"Sometimes, Father."

"*Tsk.*" His expression was gentle. He had dark blue eyes, and salt and pepper hair, a little sparse, maybe, but Lucas wondered if he had been good-looking when he was younger.

"You poor child. I was like that, too, when I was your age."

"Really?" Lucas sat up, excited. "How did you make it stop? How did you end up normal?"

"Oh . . . well, my priest had a little game that he liked to play with me. I thought it was very strange at the time, but it led me down the path of righteousness and into the Lord's arms, as you can see." He smiled.

"Can you show me? I want to make it stop."

Father Doyle pet Lucas's soft black hair and let his hand cascade down his pale neck. "Of course, I can show you. Now, you mustn't tell anyone, all right? It's our secret, I don't want anyone to find out what we've been talking about and get you into trouble. Your poor mother would be so sad if she found out about your perversions, and heaven forbid, your father."

Lucas swallowed and nodded. *Obviously, this would have to be kept a secret.*

"That's my boy." He smiled and clapped him on the back. "Now, why don't I get some communion wine and we'll begin. Take off your clothes, Lucas, be as the Lord was in the manger."

Lucas complied, not thinking too much of the request. He stood in the room and cursed himself when his body began to react to the novelty of the situation. Father Doyle handed him a glass of wine and told him to drink it. Wanting to please the priest, Lucas did as he was told as quickly as he could, his nausea swelling as the warm liquid hit his empty stomach.

"Such a good boy," he cooed, coming up behind Lucas and stroking the small of his back. "Now, close your eyes, and think of the Lord."

Lucas's breath hitched a little as he felt foreign hands around his private area, a sudden invasion, and the blinding pain that followed.

"This is the life you're headed toward, Lucas," Father Doyle warned, breathless. "I'm going to cure you. Do you understand? I'm going to make you good."

Lucas gripped the hard wood of the desk and bore the rough penetration, silent tears running down his face. He could endure, he would, then he'd be normal, then his life would be blessed just like Father Doyle's. *Please, please . . .*

The game happened more often after that, until Lucas found himself bent over the father's desk about twice a week. His mother was delighted that the priest had taken such an interest in her son, and never asked Lucas why he was having trouble sleeping, why he occasionally couldn't walk right, or why there was blood on his undergarments. Lucas, of course, said nothing, since he hoped and assumed that this was all a normal part of curing his disease. Time passed, but Lucas never felt cured or better or different. *Oh God. What if all of this was just a trick?* A sick fucking pastime that the pastor liked to play. Perhaps both of them were unclean.

Lucas started making his excuses to see Doyle less often, but duty called, and he attended his private Holy Communions with the priest fairly regularly all the same. And then one day, Lucas found the priest's office empty, his possessions cleared out. Father Doyle had been transferred to another parish, never to be seen again.

His replacement made some excuse about Doyle needing to be with his family, but Lucas had realized his suspicions were correct. He scanned the eyes of the other parishioners, trying to see if there were any other people with whom Kenneth Doyle might have had a *special* relationship. One or two of the boys kept looking at their feet, and Lucas knew for certain that it had been a scam.

The man was a fucking fairy pervert.

Lucas still found his body reacting to beautiful boys at school, still dreamed of men and touched his cock— and he hated that a big part of himself had almost looked forward to his weekly abuses. He must have, right? He'd kept coming back, again and again, even knowing what the priest had in store for him. Father Doyle had treated him like he mattered, like he was someone who was deserving of love, the fucking monster. There was something wrong with Lucas, surely. He couldn't deny that he'd gone there voluntarily, that it had sometimes felt . . . good. He didn't even know if there was a word for what they had done together. Fuck. *Fuck!*

After that, he vowed not to allow sexual contact with anyone again until he was married. But he was a teenaged boy, and it was soon apparent that such a vow might have been a bit premature. Things happened, Mick left them for good, and it didn't take long for money to become a major issue in his family's lives. He lived on fucking Henrietta Street, and he could see that women peddled their wares, and that there was a certain type of man who wanted another type of companionship for a fee. His family was hungry, Lucas was a fairy, it all worked out fucking brilliantly.

Men at the docks would pay good money for his time and expertise. He was small, beautiful, and discreet. They liked the anger in his eyes when they fucked him, they liked the way he didn't make any noise. He didn't particularly enjoy it, but the money was great, and his mother didn't ask questions. He did it as infrequently as possible; it brought back bad memories, and it didn't feel very nice—most of the time, anyway. There was a chap a few months ago— a fucking pig of a man, great big hairy belly and more money than sense. He stank of beer and kept pressing wet little kisses against Lucas's neck. Lucas braced himself against the wall, glad that they weren't face to face so the thick red tongue wouldn't penetrate his mouth. Lucas imagined a slimy film on the man's yellow teeth and stifled a laugh at the chirping and oinking that accompanied his orgasm.

"My boy." The man squeezed his shoulder. "Come to my home next time. I'll show you. I'll show you a good bloody time."

He threw the money to the ground and Lucas collected it with as much dignity as he could muster. As he stood up, the client grabbed Lucas's chin and forced a little tonguey kiss on his mouth. *Fuck. Don't vomit 'til he leaves, bad customer service.*

Lucas jumped in the ocean as soon as the man had departed, scrubbing his skin so hard that it went red and raw. He grabbed some whiskey from his flask and swished it around in his mouth. He couldn't bear to swallow, and he spat the acrid brown liquid onto the pavement. Lovely.

He didn't like peddling his trade. He didn't enjoy getting fucked like this.

Even so, he preferred it to stealing because theft left a much worse taste in his mouth, ironically. He hated the idea that he was taking food off someone else's table; he hated sinking so low as to snatching something he hadn't earned. At least with servicing strangers the money was his, he'd worked for it, he'd been paid.

And so here he was, nearly a man, preparing himself to get some cash and feed his family in the only real way he knew how. No one had bitten at the docks this evening—a big passenger vessel had just left that day, coffers were empty, and maybe he looked as sick as he felt. So, he made his way into the local tavern and resolved to empty someone's wallet. The kids needed to eat, damn it, even if he hated doing this.

He scanned the patrons until he found . . . *perfect.* A big, good-looking idiot was seated at a table at the back, sitting by himself while everyone else in the bar had a nice time. Lucas figured they were about the same age, maybe the other guy was a little older. The guy wasn't from Dublin, his accent was wrong, and he obviously wasn't keeping as close an eye on his possessions as he might have been. Lucas waited until the guy excused himself to the toilet and followed, assuming the man was too drunk to notice someone sliding a hand into his back pocket. He came up behind him, took a deep breath, and made his move.

Lucas slid his hand into the idiot's trousers, his fingers skipping along the leather wallet. As expected, it felt thick and full of cash. What he hadn't been expecting was a sharp sting in his wrist as his hand was wrenched painfully away from his body.

"A thief, huh? My mother warned me about you Dubliners." The stranger sneered, not making any move to let go of Lucas's arm.

"Let go of me! That fucking hurts, you shit!"

"Why should I? You're a common thief, so you are! I should turn you over to the police!"

Lucas panicked. If he went to prison, his family would quite literally starve. "Please don't. I'll work off the debt, I'm sorry. My siblings are starving, and no one will hire me and—"

The other man's expression was soft, and God, he was pretty. This was the kind of guy Lucas wouldn't mind selling himself to.

"You're really thin," the man noted, releasing his grip. "Let me buy you dinner, okay? We can work something out."

"Are you an idiot? I tried to rob you, you shouldn't be feeding me," Lucas protested, backing away. "You probably shouldn't have even let go of my hand! I could stab you!"

"S'pose you could. Bet you won't, though. C'mon, I'll settle my tab and we'll go get some food somewhere. Too crowded here, I reckon, we won't be able to talk properly. I'm new to Dublin, you can show me the good places to eat."

"You're a fucking crackpot," Lucas said, shaking his head. "Honestly, a stupid shit."

"Be that as it may, I'll meet you outside in three minutes." He grinned. "I'm James, by the way. Most people call me Jamie, though. Don't run off, now."

Lucas was glad Jamie had turned away at that point; his entire face had gone red. Jesus Christ, of all the people in all the bars to rob— it couldn't be him, right? It couldn't be. Fate wasn't kind to Lucas; it didn't bring back childhood friends or positive memories for him. That sweet little boy who had held him in the rain. The first human being who had accepted him without being related by blood. He silently cursed his thundering heart, angry at himself for feeling so strongly.

Lucas almost ran off, just to show this asshole what a moron he was. But a little voice at the back of his head told him not to. What if it really was Jamie? *His* Jamie? And besides, he was starving, and the kids were waiting for him. May as well take advantage. Jamie *had* offered, after all. Lucas shoved his hands into his pockets and waited out in front of the pub in the cool drizzling rain.

1916

I t had barely been three months since they'd shipped out to mainland Europe, and Jamie had been coping pretty well right up until Easter. They'd had a night out drinking together, some well-deserved stand-down after a series of horrific battles. Jamie had a massive hangover, and Lucas was giving him a hard time about it. They staggered toward the mess hall, Jamie's arm hooked over Lucas's shoulder. They'd been messing around, laughing about some stupid thing that Lucas, for the life of him, couldn't remember now.

Lucas was glad he'd followed Jamie into the military; he was glad that they could still have moments like this together. He hated to think about how worried he would be if Jamie had come to this place all alone. He was grateful that they'd been put in the same unit, although to be honest, John had probably had something to do with that. Mr. Murray had been in the army as a young man, and apparently was still good friends with one of the Irish Majors who handled these sorts of things.

Lucas hesitated slightly as they approached the food line—the usual cacophony of the soldiers was nearly absent. English soldiers spoke in hushed whispers behind their hands, officers had their weapons at the ready. The Irish cadets were ashen faced and silent— it didn't take long for the news to get around. There had been an uprising in Dublin, the British had violently suppressed it: hundreds of civilians dead, thousands more wounded. Jamie tried laughing it off, it wasn't like he was that much of a patriot at the best of times, but Lucas could see some panic in his eyes. John always worked in Dublin this time of year, there were a lot of big firms that sought his advice. Plus, with all the Irish anger that had been brewing for years, Lucas suspected he'd want to be at the front of the revolution, if there was to be one.

"Jamie . . . " he'd started, putting a hand on his shoulder. "I'm sure he's fine."

"Yeah," Jamie muttered, giving Lucas a brave smile. "What are the odds, right? He always said something like this would happen eventually, that's why he didn't want me to enlist. Those fucking English—"

Lucas clapped a hand over Jamie's mouth. They were in the British Army, they served King George with life and limb. This wasn't the place to get political. It was hard enough being Irish in the army as it was without having some treason bull hanging over Jamie's head.

"Not here," he muttered. "You can curse out those bastards all you want once we get back to our beds, okay? Not bloody here."

Lucas hated the English as much as anyone. He'd seen firsthand how Irish soldiers and officers were treated worse than their British counterparts. The centuries of oppression didn't help much either, to be honest, and trouble had been brewing for a long time now. It was only surprising that it had taken this long to come to a head.

Ireland seemed so far away. Lucas hadn't been giving it much thought recently, although Jamie's father wrote him nearly every week about some new indignity that the unionists had imposed on them. Honestly, Lucas was more interested in keeping both Jamie and himself from getting sent home in a coffin.

There was no letter from John that week. Or the week after that, or the week after that. In time, Jamie was presented with an official notice that his father had been killed during the uprising, and that investigations were being carried out. Those involved on the Irish side of things had been swiftly executed. The majority of deaths had been civilians, and the majority of civilians had been killed by British artillery. Lucas was at a loss.

"Jamie?" he put a hand on Jamie's shoulder. Tried to get their eyes to meet. "Jamie, I'm so sorry."

A stony silence, a hard jaw, tight eyes, dry lips. He'd never seen Jamie like this before.

Lucas wasn't sure what to do. He was great at dealing with anger, violence, or sexual arousal—but grief? Compassion? He was fucking shit at this.

Jamie had had a beautiful, easy life up until now. Nothing bad had ever really happened to him. Everything seemed to go his way; everything always worked out. He had a family who loved him, a fully-funded education with a marvelous future at the end, a steady stream of girlfriends, a cohort of companions who would do anything for him. And now, suddenly, the beast he was fighting for day and night had ripped his world in half.

Lucas had never been close to his own Da', but he'd adored John in the brief time that they'd known one another. He was a kind man, a fair one, and a brilliant father to his only son. He hadn't wanted Jamie to go to war, he hadn't wanted him to face the terrors and the evils of battle, and he certainly hadn't wanted him fighting alongside and for the English. But Jamie's head was full of ideas of glory and valor, he'd read too many books and wanted an adventure. And of course, John had, as always, been supportive and accepting.

"Be safe, little one. I love you and I'll pray for you every day. Save the world and come home to us."

Silently, they made their way back to their bunks in the rest camp and Lucas tried thinking of something to say. They were enlisted, it wasn't like they could just leave whenever they wanted without facing dire consequences. But how could Jamie keep fighting for the English after something like this? The trenches seemed colder and darker than ever, and Lucas felt more suffocated than ever in those narrow dirt tracks. Unfriendly ears were everywhere, it seemed. He wasn't about to leave Jamie's safety to chance.

Once they were alone, Lucas moved closer and wrapped his arms around Jamie's body, trying to convey the love he felt, even if he couldn't bring the words to his mouth. He felt Jamie's arms mirror the motion, felt his heavy chin resting on top of his thick black hair. His fists clenched around Lucas's jacket and Jamie's whole body started to tremble.

"Jamie . . . " Lucas said, stroking his back. *I love you. I love you, and I'll never turn my back on you, I'm here, I'm here and you can count on me,* he thought, but he didn't say that. "Jamie, I'm sorry."

"I should have been there with him, I could have protected him—I could have fought for Ireland, I—" Jamie's breath hitched, and Lucas felt a small patch of wetness where his hair parted. "What the hell am I doing here? He didn't want me here, he—he died thinking I was a fool, fighting for the enemy."

"You're here to protect Ireland, too," Lucas pointed out, trying to be strong, steady. "The enemy is the Germans. You're not fighting for England, you're fighting for Ireland, for your father, for yourself. Your father loved you, Jamie, he was always proud of you. This doesn't change how he felt about you. It shouldn't have happened; he shouldn't have been killed—none of them should have—but you being back in Dublin wouldn't have changed anything. Hell, you might have been the one who was shot. You might have been executed for taking part in the uprising. All he ever wanted was for you to be happy. Look at me."

Jamie released his grip and met Lucas's gaze. His eyes were bloodshot, somehow making the brilliant blue of his irises stand out even more. "I'm fighting for the men who killed him. I should have been there." A bomb went off somewhere in the distance, and Jamie jumped in Lucas's grip.

Lucas held him steady, stroked his broad back with a chilly hand. "You couldn't have known. And you can't change what's happened. All you can do is decide how this affects what you'll do from now on, what his death will mean to you."

Jamie swallowed, looking at the sickly brown fabric of Lucas's uniform.

"Thank you." He drew Lucas back into his embrace. "I don't know what I would do without you."

Lucas pulled away just so their eyes could meet. There was a weighty emotion hanging between them. The air was heavy, and Lucas swallowed.

Jamie licked his lips and averted his eyes, cheeks red, brows furrowed.

" . . . Jamie?"

He took Jamie's hand and squeezed gently. *Change the subject.* "I'm with you no matter what you decide. You want to desert, I'll follow. If you want to keep fighting, I'm at your side. We're in this together, Jamie. You're not alone."

"What would you do?" Jamie looked at him again.

Lucas thought about it. His own father had been a bit of a prick really, but Jamie obviously didn't need to hear about that right now. He tried to imagine what Jamie was feeling, tried to fathom the gut-wrenching loss that he must have felt at that moment. "I guess I'd try and think about what my father would have wanted me to do. Honor his memory through my deeds, and try and make his death mean something, even in just some small way."

Jamie nodded and pulled his hand away from Lucas. "I'll keep fighting. Rise in the ranks, show them all an Irishman can be worth something. And when the war is over, I'll go back and never stop fighting until Ireland is free." He sounded like he was trying to convince himself more than anything else.

"I," never "we." Lucas frowned and looked down at the shiny black of his shoes. He wanted to be the center of Jamie's world, and as close as they were, it wasn't always going to be like that. Hell, his father had just died, why was he even thinking about something as trivial as word choice at a time like this? He felt like he was imposing on Jamie's grief, like he was intruding on his life like he had been for years. Did Jamie need or even want his devotion? It was painful to consider the very real possibility that it was a nuisance, a burden, completely one-sided.

Jamie sniffled a little and smiled down at Lucas, touching his shoulder gently. "I'm so glad you're with me. I don't know what I'd do if I had to go all this alone."

Lucas smiled at that. "You dafty. I told you, you're stuck with me. You and me, we look out for each other." They'd held each other's gaze for a moment.

Kiss him. Kiss him, you idiot, this is fucking romantic as shit.

Except it wasn't, since Jamie was vulnerable and wounded and in no frame of mind to make choices like that. Christ, the timing was all wrong anyway; their first time couldn't bloody have John's goddamn ghost looming over it. God, he wanted to, though.

It took some time for the real impact of Jamie's father's death to become readily apparent to Lucas. It was little things at first, the way Jamie's fists would tremble now when mail call came, how suddenly a man being shot in front of him unnerved him, rattled him.

Lucas caught Jamie a few times not paying attention during an active battle. He was staring off into space, putting himself in danger. It fucking did Lucas's head in, but he did his best to keep Jamie straight.

"Was this how my father died?" he asked Lucas once, shrapnel zipping through the air. "Did he gasp and claw for air like that? Did his bones break the skin? Did his brains get on someone's shoes? Was he alone? He probably—"

Lucas grabbed him sharply and held him down, bodies flush against the dirt walls of the trenches. Jamie would never get his closure, no chance to see his father's body, to say a last goodbye. Hell, he was lucky the corpse had been identified at all. He could visit the grave when they got home . . . *if* they got home.

"Jamie. Jamie, stay with me, now is not the time." He'd meet those beautiful eyes, and for a moment there would be a flash of panic, insanity, and a slight twitch of the skin. Lucas would clasp him on either side of his face and press their foreheads together. "Please, Jamie. Hear me, I'm with you." Sometimes he would listen. Sometimes he seemed to be staring out at nothing at all, Lucas's words not reaching him, his sensibility either turned all the way down or all the way up. Panic or apathy, terror or impassivity, he was dangerous like this. He was a liability.

That had been the start of it. His father's death had been the first little dent in Jamie's mind, and every bomb that went off, every lost limb, and every death, made him become a little worse. Every failure now was a reflection on his father's memory, every little thing that went wrong—*You're not honoring him, you're not making his sacrifice worth it. Why are you here, Jamie, why are you here?*

Lucas would sit with him when these little attacks began, and he stayed beside him every day as they worsened, as his mind became more and more fragile. He'd never seen Jamie like this. Never seen anyone like this, actually. The enormity of his feelings was humbling, and Lucas knew he had a difficult battle ahead of him. He'd keep Jamie sane if it killed him.

1928

Angela was not really one to be deterred, and she insisted that Lucas come to her house for dinner that night. "Come now, you owe me that much at least! To celebrate my engagement! Only one small caveat."

Lucas groaned. "What is it?"

"Tom's friend Ryan is going to be there, and I want you to meet him and possibly even talk to him."

He gave her a quizzical look. "Why the hell would I want to do that?"

"Because he's, well—he's like you, Lucas! And he's handsome, he's nice, he's blond, and goddamn it I'm tired of seeing you mope around the graveyard every single month when you could be out *living*. Jamie wouldn't want you to be hung up on him forever, right? It's not like you and Jamie ever . . ."

Lucas shot her a devastating glare she held up her hands in surrender. "I mean, he would have wanted you to be happy. He'd hate to see you like this—I know he would. He loved you like a brother, Lucas. He wanted you to have a good life."

You don't know what he wanted, Lucas thought. *He wanted to live.* He shut his eyes and took a moment to calm himself. "What do you mean he's 'like me'?" he grumbled, refusing to allow his interest to be piqued on principle.

"I mean he . . . well . . . " She gestured vaguely at Lucas, as though to say, "well, you know, that way you are.' Angela seemed to be aware of Lucas's romantic preferences, somehow, and although she teased him for it now and again, it had never really seemed to bother her. Hell, she probably thought of him as the little sister she'd never had. "He seems to prefer the company of lads. Tom says so anyway, I couldn't possibly comment."

"So, Tom's fucked him, then?" Lucas wanted to get her to blush, but it wasn't easy.

"I doubt he has the energy. I wear him out perfectly well, thank you," she said, without missing a beat. "Please, just meet him. If he's horrible, you don't have to see him again."

"No." He finished his beer and made a move to leave the bar.

"Damn it, Lucas!" She grabbed his wrist. "I never bloody ask you for anything! And this isn't even really for me, this is for you! What's the harm in just talking to the guy? You don't have to blooming marry him, you can throw your drink in his face, for all I care. Come to my home for dinner, please."

Lucas knew he was getting to be on thin ice with Angela, and without her, he really didn't have anybody left in Dublin who cared about him. Jessie and Becky had their own lives, they had no time to be stuck in the past with him. And they had poor Mattie to deal with as well, bless them. There was only so much of Lucas's nonsense Angie would tolerate, really, and she was just trying to do something nice for him. As much as he hated everything on principle, he was willing to make some allowances for Angela every now and again. She meant well, especially with the anniversary coming up. He shut his eyes and sighed. "I don't have to be pleasant, do I?"

"Nah, I'm not expecting a miracle. But be warned, I did talk you up a little bit. Handsome silver-eyed war hero, great in bed, loves his country, that sort of thing." She smiled. "You're a prince, Lucas. Now go home and put on something nice, I want you there for seven." She kissed him on the cheek, and he actually smiled for real. Angela was good like that, good at making him get over himself and his preferences to be miserable and alone. Daft bitch made it hard for him to enjoy his misanthropy like he wanted to.

For all that she drove him mad, he did really love her with all his heart. She was a nutter, and he was glad she was happy with Tom. For a moment, just a moment, he allowed himself to believe that such an end was possible for him as well. But as he was walking home, a man who looked like Jamie threw him for a loop once again. His optimism crashed to the earth as the image of Jamie's lifeless corpse came unbidden back to his mind.

Lucas!

He shut his eyes. It wasn't Jamie, it was *never* Jamie. Jamie was dead and he had been for years. The beautiful lookalike vanished in the crowd, and Lucas realized that people on the street were avoiding him. He was acting erratic again, he needed to pull his shit together. This stupid Ryan guy wasn't going to be able to cope with nonsense like this, no one would. It was hard enough trying to imagine dating as it was: excluding women as well as a good percentage of the remainder for *preferring* women. Plus, it certainly didn't help his dating chances by being fucked in the head.

He went home and pulled on his nicest pair of trousers, a somewhat expensive pair of black slacks that made him feel important. He only had one decent jacket, an old, oversized thing that he kept at the back of his closet. He'd never get rid of it, though. God, when was it? It must've been about fourteen years ago, the war was just getting started, Jamie was thinking about dropping out of school and enlisting in the army . . . nothing serious, just an idea.

Jamie had always been an excellent student, apparently. But there was just something about university that didn't seem to agree with him. He was still in the top five percent of his year, but Lucas could see the tension in his shoulders and how much he was disconnected from the work. Lucas did his best to be supportive, and made time for Jamie at the end of the day to sit with him while he studied.

One night, the two of them made their way to the library, and Lucas quizzed Jamie on some of the simpler topics, terribly impressed by the complexity of the material and how good a handle Jamie seemed to have on it.

"All right." Lucas shifted through Jamie's notes. "Explain what um . . . " He squinted. "Cor . . . corpus delicious means, and why it's important?"

"Corpus delicti, literally the body of the crime. It's an interesting premise. That a crime must be proved to have occurred in order to obtain a conviction."

"Yeah, that's right! Um, Jamie is this helping at all? I feel so . . . " *Stupid next to you.*

Jamie reached over and squeezed his hand. "You have no idea how helpful it is. Honestly Lucas, thank you. I know this must be boring as hell."

"Nah. I like the way you explain things. It's all really clear when you say it."

Jamie made a frustrated noise, and across the room a librarian shushed him. "Lucas I know this sounds so foolish but . . . I'm not sure I want to study law anymore," he whispered.

That was news to Lucas. "Are you sure? You're so good at this shit, and you've worked so hard."

"I know it's just . . . " Jamie ran a hand through his hair. "It's difficult to explain. I'm just starting to see how meaningless this is in the real world. What the hell good is knowing all this pedantic nonsense going to—"

Lucas met his eyes. "You can do a whole lot with a law degree, Jamie. Get through your exams and you can evaluate your life plan afterward, yeah? I'm behind you all the way."

Jamie smiled. "Yeah. You're right, Lucas. I'm just gonna review the cases in this section for a bit. You can head back to the flat if you want."

Lucas smiled and shook his head. "I'll wait. We can go home together." Perhaps Lucas had underestimated how long Jamie could possibly study this material. It seemed like a thousand years, and it wasn't long before Lucas's eyelids became heavy in the stuffy room as rain pelted the windows outside.

He must have fallen asleep. He woke up with Jamie's jacket draped around his shoulders, the garment's owner still studying away across the table from him. Lucas had blinked, snuggled into the fabric, and fallen asleep once again. He was still wearing the jacket the next morning when he and Jamie went out for breakfast. Lucas wondered if maybe he'd imagined the soft, pleased smile that had crossed Jamie's features when he saw it still hugging Lucas's thin frame. He'd tried to give it back, but Jamie wouldn't hear of it. And so, the jacket took up permanent residence in his closet, and he'd been wearing it to formal occasions ever since. He slid Jamie's button into the pocket and fingered it absentmindedly as he approached Angie's house.

Angela rolled her eyes, presumably not impressed by his predictable fashion choice, but welcomed him in anyway. "Lucas! It's been ages!" she said dramatically. "You remember Tom, don't you? My lovely fiancé?"

"Lucas!" He offered a firm handshake and smiled. "How've you been? You're looking alright, you know? Angie won't shut up about you!"

Lucas politely nodded as he shook Tom's hand, giving him a shy smile. He was a good chap; Lucas liked him. "Glad you'll be taking her off my hands, mate," he said pleasantly, and Tom laughed.

"Careful now, I may return her to you if she decides she can't put up with me. You may be stuck with her, boyo." Tom clapped him on the shoulder, and Lucas smiled.

This wasn't going as badly as Lucas thought. For a brief moment, he allowed himself to imagine a happy future. Dinners with Angie, maybe her kids would be there one day, Lucas being normal with a nice man at his side. All he had to do was not be a miserable git for the rest of his life. *Good fucking luck, Connolly.*

"And this is Tom's friend from work, Ryan O'Hare."

Ryan was indeed blond, and handsome; he had bright green eyes, broad shoulders, and a cocky asshole smile that somewhat ruined the resemblance to Jamie . . . but the rest of his features were close enough that it made Lucas's heart leap. Suddenly, he found it terribly difficult to speak, and he extended his hand for Ryan to shake.

"Lucas Connolly," he muttered, feeling like an idiot.

"A pleasure. Tom's told me about you, and Angela's talked you up enough to get my curiosity going."

He certainly was getting something going on Lucas's end as well. Their handshake lingered a little longer than it normally would, and Ryan was doing the subtle flicker of his eyelashes to demonstrate interest. Angela was right, this guy probably was a bit of a fairy himself.

Lucas licked his lips and stumbled through some awkward small talk, mostly content to let Ryan speak about himself. He was charming, he was funny, and he was beautiful. Time had seriously diminished Lucas's memory of what Jamie had looked like, what he'd sounded like, but Ryan was similar enough that Lucas was starting to forget how sad he preferred to be. He didn't register what Angela made for dinner, he didn't react when she started teasing him for how smitten he was acting, but he did smile when Ryan started blushing.

"Christ, if I'd known all I needed to do to get you to shut up was bring a handsome lad in the room I woulda done it ages ago! No offense, Tom."

Angela laughed, squeezing Lucas's shoulder.

"Hello! Lucas!" She waved a hand in front of his face.

He blinked and sipped his tea, trying to play it cool. His plate was still full; he'd been pushing around the same bit of potato for five minutes as he watched Ryan talk.

"Hello, Angela. Sorry." He couldn't think of an excuse that didn't make him feel even more embarrassed. What the hell was wrong with him? He'd never been like this with Jamie . . . and it wasn't like he was completely celibate, either. Maybe it was the distance that time had put between them, how somehow this felt like a second chance. It wasn't gonna just be some fuck in the toilet, he was actually feeling something besides grief for the first time in as long as he could remember.

Ryan offered a quiet smile. "It's all right. My head is always a little in the clouds." He fiddled with his napkin. "Want to join me for some fresh air? I need to clear my head a little."

Lucas nodded dumbly. His mouth was still dry.

"Angela, that was a lovely meal, thank you. And I'll see you at work, Tom," Ryan said pleasantly and put his hand on Lucas's shoulder, gently leading him out into the cool autumn air.

Fuck. This felt right, it felt comfortable and good. He liked this guy, he really did. And shit, he hadn't been enamored to the point of idiotic nausea since Jamie had died.

"Let's go to my place," Lucas said quickly, his heart thrumming away in his chest.

Ryan smiled. "Lead the way, Connolly."

Their fingers brushed against each other as they walked, and Lucas allowed himself to feel something like hope.

1909

"Oi!" Some asshole in his class called out in the miserable communal washroom the boys used to change after sports. "Connolly's got a fuckin' stiffy!"

Lucas's hands moved immediately to cover himself, and he hissed as the sensitive skin of his back came in contact with the icy white tiles.

"He's a fuckin' fairy, so he is! I knew it! You're a cocksuckin' shit whore, you are, Connolly!"

Lucas glowered at his classmates, ready to fight to the death if he had to. Damn it, he hadn't asked to be like this, he didn't want to be like this! What the hell was he supposed to do when he was surrounded by goddamn naked—Jesus Christ.

He staggered home that night, spitting blood and thanking his lucky stars that they hadn't broken any of his teeth. He was a tough son of a bitch, he could hold his own in a fight, but there wasn't a whole lot he could do against his entire bloody class.

It had been this sort of encounter that had motivated him to seek out help from Father Doyle in the first place. How wicked it was that he dreamed of other boys, of kissing boys. How much a brush of a hand on his shoulder excited him. How much he wanted to get pushed up against a wall and kissed until he couldn't breathe.

Lucas had had a rather young introduction to sex, really. His parents fucked loudly and often, their house was small, and his father seemed to take no small amount of pride in letting his children know he'd sown his disgusting seed most nights. Beyond that, Lucas lived in what would not be described as an enviable neighborhood. Step outside his drafty flat and it wasn't hard to find a woman or three peddling her wares to anyone who had the coin.

When he was younger, he'd wondered what the fuss was about hugging girls like that. About hiked up skirts and breathy moans, about what the hell a woman had that was worth spending food money on. Father Doyle had shown him, he supposed. Taken Lucas by force, convinced him that he'd been willing, that it was Lucas's fault for being sick in the damn head. He'd hated it. But he'd kept coming back for more, and it made him nauseous.

Lucas lay awake at night sometimes, staring at the ceiling as he relived those moments. How Father Doyle had touched him, how the priest had made him cum.

"You like that, don't you Lucas? You sick child. You poor, sweet, sick child. Look at you. Look at the way you respond to me." Lips on his neck, teeth followed, Lucas's cries of pain and pleasure stifled by the clergyman's hand.

Lucas must have enjoyed it, then. He must have wanted it, deserved it. He was precocious and perverted, and he got stiffies in the shower, and dreamed of boys who hated him sticking their cocks in his ass. *You deserve every awful thing that happens to you.*

He kept to himself as much as he could from then on, staying away from sports class and situations where the other boys might suddenly take it upon themselves to beat him. It wasn't long before his schoolmates' attention shifted to a new boy in their class— a sweet, gentle thing from the country named Danny Byrne. As far as thirteen-year-old boys went, Danny was absolutely stunning. A bright clear smile, big hazel eyes, silky copper hair, tall, nice shoulders, angelic face. He made Lucas feel like he was about to die of delight whenever they were close, and as such, Lucas avoided him like his father avoided police officers.

The other boys liked Danny at first; he was clever and good at sports. But whatever it was they saw in Lucas, they started seeing in Danny, too. Maybe his eyes lingered too long on one of them, maybe he, too, got erections in the shower. Lucas was heading home from school one afternoon when he spotted the other boys in a circle, taking turns kicking Danny while he lay curled up on the ground.

"Oi!" Lucas called, peeling out of his jacket. "You goddamn cowards back off!"

"Oh ho! Faggot police is here, yeah? You fairies look after each other, don'cha!"

Lucas narrowed his eyes. "You think you're so brave—fucking ten of you beating one kid who's down already." He reached to the ground and grabbed an old bottle, smashing it and brandishing the shardy end. "Maybe we even the odds a bit?"

The other boys looked less certain, and Lucas took a step forward, licking his teeth. "Well? Come at me!"

The ringleader spat at Lucas's feet and shoved his hands in his pockets. "He's crazy." They concluded, shuffling off. "You're a loony, Connolly!"

Lucas knelt down beside Danny, making no show of acknowledging the hiccupping wails emerging from the other boy. "You all right?"

"Yeah." A sniffle, a cough, a sob.

"They're pricks." Lucas patted Danny on the back. "C'mere, lemme get a look at you."

Danny accepted a hand up, and Lucas hid his displeasure at the sight of him. Busted lip, black eye, mud caked in his hair, and clothes all torn to hell. *Jesus.* "They just beat on you?" Lucas wanted to confirm. It wasn't unheard of to teach fairies a lesson using sexual force.

"Yeah." Danny wiped his eyes. "Sorry. Don't mean to trouble you like this."

"It's no trouble." *Better you than me.* "What happened?"

Danny shook his head.

Were they the same? Surely Lucas couldn't be the only poofter in all of Ireland, right? Doyle had been one too, probably. Either that or he just liked *kids*, Christ. "They did the same to me, you know." He licked his lips. How the hell were perverts supposed to find each other? It was so damned dangerous to be honest. "Cause I'm . . . like that."

Danny narrowed his eyes. "Like what?"

" . . . Don't make me say it."

He heard Danny swallow, and watched him stand up to meet Lucas's eyes. His nose was bleeding and snotty, his face was swollen and red, but both of them were bloomin' smiling.

"Let me walk you home." Lucas said, staring at a pebble on the side of the road. "Make sure those boys don't give you more trouble."

Danny seemed delighted with the suggestion, and they walked in a comfortable silence toward a tenement building Lucas wasn't familiar with. It wasn't nice, but it was a hell of a lot more pleasant than Henrietta Street ever was. It was a bit quieter, for one, less crowded, not as much broken glass littering the street.

Lucas looked at Danny and felt his cheeks flush, uncertain what to do or say next. What did normal people do in this sort of situation, anyway? Hold hands or something, maybe find somewhere quiet to mess around. Was it so simple, then? Just finding someone like you and the rest sorts itself out?

"Well. Thank you, Lucas," Danny said, the bruises blossoming prettily on his pale skin. "I . . . um, I hope I can see you around sometime?"

Lucas took that as a good sign and cocked a half smile. "Yeah. That wouldn't be too bad, I think."

Of course, they had to be careful at school, they both had targets on their backs as it was, and if they were suddenly seen together all the time it might make it all the easier to escalate the violence against them.

But Danny was clever, Lucas was eager, and it wasn't hard for the two of them to find little dark corners to hide in, to breath each other in, to touch and kiss and feel away from the watchful eyes of God and their classmates.

An often-vacant supply closet became perfect cloistered haven. Remote, quiet, and stinking of bleach, a sticking door handle provided ample warning of an unwanted intrusion. Somewhere in the darkness they found hands to hold, hair to run fingers through. Father Doyle had never really kissed Lucas on the mouth, so it was probably the only aspect of sex he wasn't especially skilled at. Teeth clacked together, tongues darted, Danny giggled, and Lucas did, too.

"Sorry." Lucas's body was reacting, and he felt like he was flying.

It didn't take long for them to work out a rhythm, soft little pecks turning into something deeper, hands roaming down chests. It felt good. It felt right. Nothing Father Doyle had ever done to him had even come close to this.

The first few times felt like daring trysts—they'd hide and kiss, giggle, taste each other for as long as they could stand before venturing out into the light once more. It was fun, but it was getting a bit old, to be honest. Kissing was all well and good, but Lucas wanted to show Danny the incredible pleasures he'd learned of far too early.

It was after school hours on a Friday, so there was no chance of them being disrupted. Danny was smiling, blushing, and pulling Lucas closer in the closet so their bodies were flush. Danny seemed to like that, the warmth that passed through their clothing as their machinations intensified. Lucas took a step back and started to undress himself, his skin dimpling in the chilly night air. His hands shook as he opened his belt, grabbing Danny's hand, guiding it lower—*please, fuck Danny touch me, come on.*

"What are you doing?"

They were a few feet apart all of a sudden, Lucas tried to catch his breath. "What do you mean?" They were gonna fuck, right? That's how normal people did it, wasn't it?

Danny's eyes were wide. "This. We shouldn't be doing this. It's a sin."

Lucas choked back a laugh. A sin? A goddamn sin? Christ, the whole thing was a scam, right? The church had taught him everything he'd ever needed to know about getting fucked up the ass. Told him he was made wrong, told him they could fix him— he— nothing ever felt right, he did his best and— of course he was going to hell. Of course he was.

"Says who?"

"Says Leviticus! Says the church! Says my pa and those boys who just—" Danny put a ginger hand on Lucas's fingers. "M'sorry, Lucas. We can't."

Lucas shook his head. "Go, then," he said, eyes narrowing as Danny scuttled out of their hideout. Goddamn it. He'd never asked to be like this, he didn't want to ache for other boys, nor enjoy this sort of attention. He just wanted to be normal. Wanted his family to be glad he was there.

Lucas trudged home alone, hands in his pockets. His father was passed out, his mother was tending to Jessie. Lucas curled up on his little cot and tried to sleep. Danny's bruised face came unbidden to his mind, the way his lips had felt, the gentle way he'd nipped at Lucas's neck. He willed himself to ignore the blood rushing between his legs and scrunched his eyes shut.

I'm going to be normal, he decided. *I'm not going to be like this anymore.*

Lucas awoke the next morning with the crotch of his pajama pants wet, sticky, and cold. He rubbed his temples and shut his eyes. Being around boys wasn't helping. He wasn't getting better; he was just getting worse the older he got. No, something needed to change, or Lucas was always going to be broken.

He made his way to the kitchen and found a full bottle of whiskey his father hadn't opened yet, miracle of miracles. He stashed it into his jacket and ran from his home, eyes peeled for someone— anyone— a woman, obviously, who might . . .

He slowed to a stop and approached a woman one of the corners with her hair pulled into a messy bun on top of her head. Her eyes were kind. She cocked her head at Lucas, who was obviously a bit young to be after her services. "What you want, boy?"

Lucas licked his lips, deeply ashamed all of a sudden. No, this was important. He had to do this. He bloody had to. He reached into his coat and pushed the bottle at her. "I want to fuck."

She scoffed. "I don't fuck for a bottle of whiskey, love."

"Can I look, then? Can I touch?"

The woman rolled her eyes, flicking some of her cigarette ash into the street. "Fine. Five minutes."

He followed her into the alley, his anxiety spiking. *C'mon Lucas. You need to do this; this is what normal men do. You wanna get beaten bloody again?*

The hooker hiked up her skirt and Lucas's face crinkled with discomfort. He wasn't sure what he'd been expecting, but a matt of curly hair wasn't it.

"Go on love, get a peek." She was opening her blouse too, her heavy breasts pale in the dim light of the alley. He reached out and gave one of them a squeeze, recoiling when her nipple firmed up beneath his grip. Ugh.

Her smile softened, and Lucas glowered at her. He wasn't bloody here to be adorable.

"You've not been with a girl before, yeah?"

". . . So?" Lucas spat, resisting the urge to run off. "I'm only young."

"So you are." She cupped his cheek, and his skin crawled. It wasn't like this with Danny. It felt so *right* with him.

"Come closer, sweet."

He sank to his knees and moved his face nearer to her genitalia, face crinkling as the stale stench of urine assaulted him.

"You wanted to touch, right?" The hooker moved her hand between her legs and parted her lips for Lucas, a wet little rose of flaps and hair and— Lucas got to his feet and bolted away from her as fast as he could. She was repulsive—she —he couldn't. What the hell did men see in women?

Maybe it was the age difference. Maybe a girl in his class would be better. Cathy, perhaps? She was pretty; the boys liked her. He imagined pushing her up against a wall, imagined cupping her budding breast and . . . there was Danny's stupid lovely face. Lucas slapped himself and tried to think straight.

God fucking damn it.

1914

J amie hadn't really liked living in the university dormitories very much, and his father was the one who floated the idea of buying a flat for his son to use in the city. Of course, Jamie saw it as an opportunity to get Lucas out of his somewhat difficult home life.

John had pulled Lucas aside before the purchase was finalized.

"I wanted to thank you, Lucas. For being such a good pal to Jamie since he moved to Dublin. I think your friendship has really meant a lot to him."

Lucas swallowed. He doubted John would feel that way if he knew the aching desire that lay dormant in his heart. "Of course. Jamie means the world to me, too."

"I think since he left home, he's been struggling a bit. I wonder if law school isn't quite agreeing with him. It's a lot of pressure, surely. He can be a bit of a sensitive sort." A fond smile.

"Sensitive?" That word had never been used about Lucas, rather uglier words encompassing his preferences for men.

"He feels things easily. Passion, excitement, loneliness. I'm not sure what it is, but something's . . . different, somehow. He doesn't seem enthusiastic about school anymore. I worry about him." John took off his glasses and cleaned them. "But you should see him when he talks about you."

Lucas did not let his delight show on his face. "Yeah?"

"He lights up. It's like when he was a wee boy. 'Lucas did this, Lucas did that, you should have seen Lucas give that bloke what was coming to him!'" John smiled. "He loves you. Adores you. I don't know what he'd do without you."

"I don't know what I'd do without him, either." He cleared his throat, blinking. "Thank you, Mr. Murray."

"So. And please feel free to say no, but I was planning on buying Jamie a little flat. Something away from the dorms, where he can relax and focus on his studies. I was wondering if you might want to be his flatmate?"

Lucas was too stunned to speak.

"I just felt it would be good for him to have his own space— or rather, a safe space he could share with someone he loves and trusts. Just think of it— you'd be out of that difficult neighborhood, you could spend every day together, keep his head straight, it'll be grand."

"But Mr. Murray, with all due respect— I don't think I could afford—"

"Hush, lad. I don't want to hear one more word about money. Consider it a gift. Maybe you help out around the house a little, mm? Save me the trouble of hiring a maid for the boy. God knows I don't want to worry about my son getting the help up the duff."

Lucas hoped very much his cheeks didn't go red. *Mm. Suppose maybe he finds another convenient outlet for such urges?* Christ, Lucas could dream.

Initially, Lucas was conflicted about sharing a flat with Jamie. He felt he couldn't leave his family to fend for themselves. But his two surviving brothers were just about old enough to help support their mother and sisters, and both were happy to let Lucas go and live his life a little. He'd done enough for the family. It was time for him to have some peace and happiness.

Lucas couldn't really contribute toward the house's expenses like Jamie could. His salary wasn't high enough, not to mention the fact that he was still sending nearly all of his wages to his family to help keep them fed and clothed. But he contributed in his own way; Lucas was happy to do the chores so that Jamie could spend much of his free time studying. Jamie, of course, had the nicer bedroom, and only his name was on any of the legal documents.

John came to check on them about a week after they'd moved in.

"Boys? You settling in okay?"

Jamie practically bounced down the hall to greet his father. "Brilliant, Papa. I love it here; I only wish we'd thought of it sooner! Thank you so much, honestly. I promise to always be filial and lovely to repay you for your generosity."

John chuckled and fluffed Jamie's hair. "You'd better. Lucas? How are you, son?"

Something warm and deeply pleasant resonated in his soul at the kind words. "I'm great, Mr. Murray. I can't thank you enough." Lucas bowed his head.

"Oh Lucas, come now." John touched his shoulder. "You're doing me a great favor. I can rest a lot easier knowing my boy isn't going to be getting into trouble."

"Pshh! We get into plenty of trouble, don't we Lucas?" Jamie hooked his arm around Lucas's neck and pulled him close.

"Oh yes, we are the midnight stallions of debauchery and truancy," Lucas deadpanned. "Mothers lock their doors when they hear we are out and about."

"Fantastic." John chuckled. "Well, I'd best leave you to it then, eh? I brought you some food from your mother; she's apparently a bit worried you might starve to death. Take care, boys. You know how to reach me if there's trouble."

It was a pretty decent flat, all things considered. Within walking distance to the university, a single master bedroom and a servant's room, a quaint little living room with plush couches and chairs and enough books to keep Jamie busy for years, and a good-sized kitchen with a gas stove. It overlooked a park, which was a tremendous novelty for Lucas. He loved being able to lean out the window and see something green and alive—he even liked the way the air smelled. He went to bed warm and woke up without shivering, his clothes didn't reek of mildew since the house was dry and clean—not to mention that for the first time in his life he could have a wank in relative privacy. It was heaven.

Lucas had a little routine which he enjoyed a great deal: every day, he'd wake up early and go to the nearest local tap to get enough fresh water for them to use in the morning. He'd quickly wash his body, shave, comb his hair, and then move right along into preparing breakfast. Jamie ended up paying for most of the food, which didn't really bother Lucas as much as he'd been expecting. He made up for it by doing most of the cooking and making things that Jamie liked—he'd even gone down to the library a few times to look up different recipes to play around with.

Lucas wasn't used to such a diverse pantry, and it took a few tries before he was a half-decent chef.

"Well?" he asked, plopping some vegetables onto Jamie's plate.

"Perfect. Lovely. As good as mum's, but don't tell her that." Jamie winked and tucked in.

It didn't really matter if he was just putting on a show for Lucas. Jamie's enjoyment of his food had Lucas practically walking on air.

Jamie would often get woken up by the sounds and smells of a fresh breakfast being cooked, and they'd eat together each morning before heading off to school or work.

"Oi! Lazy bones get down here! Some of us have jobs to get to!" Lucas called.

"All right, all right, keep your tits on," Jamie grumbled, wiping the sleep from his eyes.

Lucas resisted the urge to press a kiss to Jamie's forehead as he sat down to eat. "Your hair looks like shit, by the way. You need to brush it, or no one will take you seriously at uni."

"Yes, Mother." Jamie said with a smile. "This is delicious, by the way. What do you call it?"

"Ah yes, a grand recipe passed down by my ilk for generations. We call it: 'toast and butter.' Truly, the food of kings."

They'd head out of the flat together as much as was possible. Lucas's income was unsteady, unpredictable, and his hours were worse still. He'd dropped out of school too young to be picky about what kind of work he did and took any jobs that were available for the most part. It wasn't anything *too* horrific, certainly better than hooking had been, but that didn't mean he liked it at all. Digging ditches, construction work if he was lucky, coal transportation; nothing glamorous, but honorable in its own way.

Lucas had gotten home early one day, having been laid off from his last job after injuring his hand. Some asshole hadn't been paying attention, let his wheelbarrow loose, and it caught Lucas against a wall, crushing his palm. All the money he had in the world was sitting on the table in front of him, and he was straining his eyes trying to imagine how he was going to stretch it out to feed his family this month. Maybe they boys had found some work, maybe he could take up hooking again but—Christ, Christ, what was he going to do?

Jamie came home at the usual time, arms laden with books. The house was dark and the stove was cold. "Mm? Lucas? Where's supper?"

Lucas's eyes snapped up at Jamie, his mouth tight. "I didn't bloody have time today."

"Oh." Jamie seemed taken aback. "What's the matter? What happened to your hand?"

Lucas cradled the appendage to his body. "Work accident."

Jamie sucked a breath past his teeth. "Looks painful." He reached over to touch it, but Lucas snatched his hand away.

"Lucas, we need to get you to a doctor."

"I can't afford a damned doctor. Can't work. Got laid off." He put his head in his good hand.

"Oh, Lucas, that's dreadful. Let me take care of it, pal. You can pay me back if it'd make you feel better."

Lucas hated accepting gifts for nothing, and Jamie knew it. "S'too expensive. Need to look after my family first."

"Lucas . . . " Jamie put a careful arm around his shoulders. "You're always looking after me. I want to help you this time. Please."

As ever, Lucas agreed. After all, he had never been any good at saying no to Jamie.

The doctor was rough and careless as he did his examination. He seemed to be making a point of not making eye contact with his patient, preferring to address all of his concerns to Mr. James Murray who was clearly Lucas's better. Lucas had broken two of the bones in his hand, but nothing seemed displaced; apparently, it'd heal fine. The doctor forbade him from working for eight weeks, which Lucas feared was a death sentence for his mother. Jamie, bless him, sent some money to the wee Connollys during this difficult time. Accepting his help was humiliating, but Lucas had no choice. Jamie's heart was in the right place, and that was all that mattered.

Time passed, Lucas's hand healed, and life settled into something comfortable once again. More often than not, though, Jamie would come to Lucas's workplace of the moment and walk home with him at the end of the day.

"So, we started our unit on criminal law today!" Jamie folded his hands behind his head. "Jesus, Lucas, some of these criminals are masterminds. Some of them, well, not so much. We were reading about this one case where a man was found hiding in a woman's wardrobe, right? He claimed he'd gotten lost in her flat!" He giggled. "How on earth does that happen? He lived across town! The court thought it was ridiculous, of course. Oh, and there was a—it's sort of a strange one, a case where a man confessed to a crime years and years after the fact. Problem was there was no evidence to convict him, you know? Can you really condemn a man just on his word?"

"I'm not sure. Why would he confess all of a sudden?"

"Guilt, maybe? Or he had nothing to do with it and just wanted a sin-free suicide? I don't know. It's a very strange case."

"So, what happened?"

"Dunno yet. The assignment is to read up on relevant law and make our own decision. Personally, I don't know. A murder is a terrible thing to hang over your head. If he really did it, his life must have been so painful."

Lucas nodded. He knew what it felt like to have a secret that ate away at his soul. "Yeah."

Lucas didn't often have a lot to contribute to these conversations as his days were all quite monotonous, but he liked watching Jamie talk, he liked his straight teeth and his easy laugh, he liked his beautiful bright eyes, and he liked the way his golden hair kissed his forehead when he walked. Jamie was nice enough to let them stop at a little stream so Lucas could wash the dirt off from his body before they got home. If he thought anything nasty about Lucas's work, he certainly never said it. He was chipper and cheerful, and it kept Lucas steady.

"So, one of the lads in my year dropped out. Apparently, he got a waitress pregnant, so her parents are making them get married, and he's getting a job," Jamie said as he poured them both some wine to pair with the meal Lucas had cooked.

Lucas's back ached. His new boss had no idea, since Lucas couldn't afford to miss any work. Bastard had stiffed him his pay this week anyway, fucker.

"It's quite a big scandal! I mean he's from a big important family, you know? I'm surprised his parents didn't just pay the woman off or something."

Molly had stopped working. She was getting breathless, she'd fainted once or twice, her feet were swollen to shit.

"Maybe they're religious or something? Christ, I hope I don't get a girl pregnant like that. It'd be so awful to be stuck with someone you didn't love just because of one mistake."

Mattie and Pattie were working as hard as they could to supplement the income Lucas provided, but they were young, and Lucas wanted them to stay in school for as long as they could.

"Lucas? Are you okay?"

"Oh. Yeah, of course. Sorry, I'm just a little tired. Maybe the girl got pregnant on purpose?"

"Maybe! I guess if I were a waitress, it wouldn't be the end of the world to be tied to a barrister's family."

Jamie didn't need to know any of Lucas's problems, he'd only worry and lose sleep over it if he did. So Lucas would smile, listen to Jamie, and keep his worries silent. Luckily, Jamie had some serious difficulties with shutting up, so silence on Lucas's end had never been a problem.

After dinner, Jamie often insisted that Lucas relax "for once." He would clear the table and do all the dishes while Lucas sat on the couch and made his way through the paper. Lucas didn't really pay attention to what he was reading; he just relished the beautiful quiet that filled the flat. Compared to the cacophony from which he'd emerged, their modest little home was Eden to him. He loved living with Jamie, he loved being clean, and he loved being full and warm. Eventually, they'd both tire and go to bed, and Lucas would stare out the window with a little smile on his face. He was happy. It was very strange.

On weekends where Lucas didn't have to work, Jamie would help with the chores, and they'd usually find some activity to do together. Jamie had genuinely surprised Lucas in the last two years and had actually wanted to engage and spend time with Lucas's family. The siblings adored Jamie and would clamber over each other to sit beside him whenever he came for a visit.

"Ah, ah, one at a time! I'm not getting any younger, kiddos, if all of you sit on me at once I'm liable to break a bone and then Lucas'll have to take revenge."

"Mm hm. You are not going to cripple my flatmate. It'd be a terrible faff to replace him."

Becky rolled her eyes. "*Jamie*, can't you get Lucas to stop being a grumpy shit?"

Jamie laughed. "I can try, Little Miss, but there are some things even my benevolent spirit cannot salvage. On a brighter note, I brought three different types of curry from the new restaurant that's opened near us. What do you think?"

The children gasped and relieved Jamie of the food and began rationing it out. Jamie smiled and placed a box of fresh pastries on the table as well, a gesture met with squeals and frenzied chomping.

Lucas simply watched them all together, his own smile warm and enamored. What had he done to deserve such a man in his life?

"Jamie?" he said one night as they left his mother's home.

"Yeah?"

"I . . . I'm really glad I tried to rob you." *Why was this so hard?*

Jamie's heavy arm clunked down over his shoulders, his smile was broad and warm. "Me too, Lucas. You're a part of my heart."

Lucas had never really been in love before. It was all bull, as far as he could tell but . . . Christ, Jamie. He wondered if what he was feeling could be anything else than love, and he thanked a God he barely believed in every night for bringing the two of them together.

1928

Lucas and Ryan were barely past the threshold of Lucas's flat before they started kissing. Lucas pressed him hard against the wall and slid a leg between his thighs, letting out a soft moan as his lips found Ryan's neck. Ryan didn't seem to mind, and made an appreciative noise as he ran his hands through Lucas's hair.

These trysts tended to be short and sweet. It was dangerous to linger, and partners were so few and far between that most of the men didn't like faffing around and playing at romance. It was a nice novelty, therefore, that they had the privacy of Lucas's home to mess about in. They could have taken it slow if they wanted to, but Lucas wasn't in the mood.

It had been a while; Lucas didn't often give himself to other people anymore. He had dabbled occasionally with strangers now and again when Jamie was alive, but it was all very empty and abrupt. And equally, since Jamie had died, he hadn't really allowed himself the pleasure of another man's company very often, preferring to linger with his grief. Each time he had coupled off he found himself making comparisons, agonizing over what might have been . . . it was just release, an ephemeral connection to another human being for about ten minutes at a time and nothing more. This was different. Ryan gave him goosebumps. Ryan's hands sent little sparks running down the small of his back and up his neck.

Maybe Angie was right, maybe it was time to move forward with his life and try to find happiness. Ryan was nice, he was attractive, and he was interested in Lucas in a physical way. Objectively, there was nothing wrong with acting out on his instincts and trying to achieve some level of normalcy with his social life. Still, somehow it felt like a huge betrayal of Jamie.

This wasn't like his last few flings, quick little fucks in a back alley, faces in shadow and no names given. No, this wasn't disgusting. He was actually aroused, excited, invested. It was warm, it was comfortable—it wasn't like it had been with Jamie but . . . It had been a very long time since he'd felt anything like this. Lucas knew it was stupid; he knew that Jamie had never thought of him that way, and he knew that nothing would have ever happened between them. Ryan kissed him then, nipped at his lips and forced his mouth open with his tongue. *All right, all right Ryan, I get it. Focus on the moment. Feisty little bugger, aren't you?*

Angie had said Jamie would have wanted Lucas to be happy. Maybe it *was* time to let go, start living for him in a positive way rather than forever wading through the black tar of his grief. He could see himself waking up in the morning, his head draped lazily over Ryan's thigh. "Did I ever tell you about how me and Jamie first met?" Ryan would chuckle and pet his hair. "You mean when you tried to rob him?" And Lucas would smile and kiss his palm. "No, it was before that. I was a little boy in the rain and . . . "

Ryan was able to shake him out of this temporary paralysis of conscience as his hands skimmed down Lucas's chest. "Your mind's elsewhere," he noted, kissing his neck and flicking open the first button of his shirt. "Let me get you back in this room." He smiled and cupped Lucas's face, bringing their lips together again.

Was this what kissing Jamie would have been like? Soft, plump lips, a subtle cologne, his breath hot, his straight teeth grazing against Lucas's mouth?

Jamie, he thought. *Jamie, yes, just like that.*

Ryan was young and attractive; he was confident and experienced. He took the lead from Lucas and tried to rein his mind back into their little foray, and was doing a damn good job of it at that. Nimble fingers began working at the buttons on his shirt again, and a stray hand went to push the jacket off Lucas's shoulders.

Normally, Lucas wouldn't have let anyone touch that jacket. Normally, he would have flipped his lid if someone let it crumple to the floor like Ryan just had, but his mind was with Jamie, fucking Jamie, right here in his living room. Lucas started undressing Ryan as well, silencing the little catty thoughts that invaded his consciousness. Ryan's body wasn't as lovely as Jamie's had been; he was slender and not as muscular; his chest was a little hairier. It didn't matter, it didn't matter, Jamie was dead, and this was as close as he was going to get.

Lucas pulled him in close and kissed him hungrily once more, pressing their hips together with a soft growl so Ryan could see just how much he wanted this, how much he needed it.

Ryan smirked and kissed his neck. "Eager, are we?"

"Yes." Lucas tugged on his wrist and dragged him to his kitchen, pointing at his small wooden table. "Fuck me here," he instructed, bending over with his hands against the hard wood.

"As you wish," Ryan purred, working open Lucas's belt and pulling down his trousers. His hands were strong, and his delicate fingers skimmed along the pale flesh of his backside.

It was better this way; Lucas didn't have to see Ryan's face. He could imagine it was Jamie with him, Jamie in him, Jamie pretending that this meant anything, that they weren't just strangers rutting.

Lucas grabbed some cooking oil off his kitchen counter and shoved it into Ryan's hand. "Use that, it's fine," he muttered, ever the romantic. His eyes slid shut and he tried to focus on the sound of Ryan getting himself ready, slicking himself up. It had been a long time since anyone wanted him like this, longer still since he'd accepted. It was nice. He was enjoying himself.

And with that brief realization, the guilt came crashing back: he was happy, and Jamie was dead. His mind kept flashing to the image of Jamie's face as the life drained out of it, of the mud that caked his hair when he slid to the ground . . .

The memory hit him with a physical pain that he had never forgotten, the moment he understood that Jamie was gone and was never coming back. Lucas falling to his knees beside the lifeless Lieutenant. Lucas screaming and screaming and screaming, no one hearing him over the endless din of the bombs falling. Why the hell was he messing around with some guy when Jamie was dead and couldn't experience anything anymore? It wasn't Jamie behind him; it wasn't Jamie inside him, kissing his neck.

"*Lucas?*"

Jamie's voice. He was hearing things now.

"*Lucas.*"

The guilt was making him crazy.

"*Lucas!*"

Jamie's pale face, the blood dripping out of his mouth, his last word echoing in his ears again and again. *Lucas . . . Lucas . . . Lucas . . .* the moment his hand went slack, his body hit the ground with a squelch. His face was so pale, his eyes so lifeless and dull. Lucas made a guttural sound and gripped his head. No. This was wrong, it was all wrong.

"Get the hell off me!" Lucas snarled, snapping his neck around at Ryan who looked, if nothing else, extremely perplexed.

Ryan obeyed Lucas's wishes, backing off, covering his shame with his hands. Apparently, he wasn't the type of man who would continue sex in circumstances like this. "What—did I do something wrong?"

"No. You have to leave." Lucas offered no further explanation.

Ryan looked hurt. Confused. "What's the matter? You look like you've seen a ghost."

Lucas could imagine he looked in a right state; his face was pale, he was sweating, his eyes hollow and sunken. He felt physically sick, and every time he shut his eyes, Jamie's sweet dead face came into his mind. He was a fool to have tried this, a fool to think he was worthy of normal love, happiness, or understanding from another human being.

"Please. Just go. I'm sorry." He was. "Tell Angie I'm sorry, too."

Ryan shook his head, taking a few steps back. He picked up his clothes, not turning his back to Lucas for even a second.

Lucas swallowed and followed him back into the living room. They didn't say anything else to each other. Lucas knew Ryan wouldn't want to see him again, and he wasn't sure he'd be able to face him even if he did. He opened the door, let Ryan out, and quietly locked it behind him.

He made his way to the center of the room and picked up Jamie's jacket, silently smoothing it out before he clutched it to his chest.

1912

Lucas waited patiently for Jamie outside the pub, his hands shoved in his pockets. Eventually Jamie joined him and seemed pleasantly surprised to see that Lucas hadn't run off. He pulled on his cap and smiled. "I didn't catch your name."

"Lucas. Lucas Connolly. Do you care where we go for food or what? I mean you're buying, so . . . "

Jamie smiled and thought about it. "I don't mind, really. Something warm, it's bloody freezing out!" He nudged Lucas's shoulder, presumably to show there were no hard feelings.

Lucas thought about taking him to some ridiculously expensive restaurant and taking full advantage of his generous offer. But Lucas didn't actually know any nice restaurants, so he led Jamie down Great Brunswick Street to his favorite fish and chip shop instead. He felt a bit uncultured, but the food was cheap, delicious, and hot. The shop had been there for years; a nice man with a mustache owned the joint and sometimes gave Lucas leftover fish at the end of the day. It was a little run down, sure, but Lucas liked the way the place smelled, the gentle warmth inside, and the way the windows fogged up in the winter.

"Ah, good choice. My granny told me about it, it's supposed to be really nice," Jamie said, although Lucas very much doubted it was true.

"What'll you have?"

Lucas glanced at Jamie, unsure how far his generosity would go.

"Can I have two orders of the one and one please?" He'd be able to bring more back to his siblings that way.

"You *are* hungry," Jamie laughed, placing the order. "So, do you rob people often?"

"I suppose. I try not to do it unless I have to, but no one was biting at the docks today." He shrugged, finding the question a fair one.

"Oh, you're a fisherman, then?"

Lucas laughed. "Of a sort. I think everyone's a bit hard-up these days, no one wanted what I was selling."

"Well, everyone has an off day, I guess. Maybe those little buggers will bite better next time."

The cook handed them their food. Lucas tucked the carefully wrapped package into his jacket, not minding the grease or the heat of it.

"You're not eating? It'll go cold and horrible!" Jamie pointed out, popping a steamy chip in his mouth and smiling.

"I have to bring it home for my family, they're probably starving by now," Lucas said softly, avoiding Jamie's eyes. He hadn't been lying about his motivations. He wouldn't steal if he didn't have to support a family of five.

"Oh." Jamie's expression was hard to read. "Have half of mine, then," he decided, leading them to a small table at the back of the shop where they could sit. "Come now, I insist, you owe me one since I didn't hand you over to the coppers." He had a tender smile, and Jesus Christ, he was pretty.

Lucas wondered if Jamie was flirting, wondered if he even knew that two men could flirt. He very seldom approached other men socially when money wasn't involved, so this was all very new to Lucas as well. What was the correct thing to do here? If he read Jamie wrong, he could end up in rather serious trouble like that Wilde fellow. Maybe just . . . drop a hint. "Do you trade?" he asked softly, carefully nudging his foot against Jamie's.

"Trade what?" Jamie asked, popping a bit of the fish fillet into his mouth. "This food is pretty good, actually! Makes me think of home. I just moved to Dublin recently—I think I already told you that. I'm just starting university soon, so hopefully I can get settled in."

Jamie didn't seem to be too bothered by the whole foot contact thing, but he also didn't seem to have noticed. He certainly hadn't picked up on the polari slang either. Well, that answered that. In contrast, every single touch he afforded Lucas, every nudge of their shoulders, every time their hands brushed together among the warm, battered fish gave Lucas goosebumps and nearly robbed him of the ability to speak.

Lucas was getting the impression that Jamie wasn't thinking about sex at all. His mind was in the clouds and there was a dumb smile on his face. He was probably seeing himself in his university gown, graduating with honors, making his whole stupid family so bloody proud of him. *Must be nice*, Lucas supposed, *to have dreams beyond going to bed with a full stomach.*

"So, tell me about your wee family," Jamie said, cheerfully tearing a fish fillet in half and offering Lucas the larger portion.

"It's not really so wee." Lucas was eating more quickly than he should have, a bad habit he'd developed over the course of his short life. Then again, he never knew when he was going to be fed, really. "There's me, I'm the oldest. I live with me mum and four of my siblings." He ran his tongue over his lips. "Some of 'em died when they were little so . . . I guess it's not as many to feed as it could be."

"Where's your father?"

"Dunno, he ran off a few years ago. It's just as well he did, he and I didn't get along. He was a scary son of a bitch most of the time."

Except when he wasn't. Lucas's heart clenched sometimes even now when he remembered that once, a long time ago, his father had loved him a little. "And at least now I know my money's not going to the drink." His eyes darted up to Jamie, wondering if he remembered their encounter as children.

It seemed he didn't. "Right. What are your siblings like?"

"It doesn't really matter, does it? They're little and hungry and they're going to grow up poor and wind up with a house full of little hungry kids of their own one day." He looked away from Jamie's beautiful face. Lucas squeezed his eyes shut and pinched the bridge of his nose. "Christ. I'm sorry, I shouldn't snap at you. It's just hard. You should be snapping at me, if anything."

"Nah." Jamie patted his forearm. "You're not a bad person, you're just trying to survive." He playfully nudged the largest bit of fish fillet toward Lucas and smiled when he popped it in his mouth.

"What about you? What's your family like?"

"Aye, just normal. My parents and my baby sister Fiona. She's just at that age where she needs to decide what to do next with her life . . . I hope she becomes a nun, then I won't have to worry about the lads going after her." He laughed. "She's a pretty wee thing! My father's a barrister, he keeps us all comfortable—that's what I'm going to university for as well. I want to help people. And my mum is a normal mother, I guess. She's warm, she's gentle, she wants me to get married as quick as I can, but I told her I needed to finish my studies first." He laughed and Lucas couldn't take his eyes off his perfect face as he did. Jamie put a chip into his mouth and chewed thoughtfully, perhaps considering Lucas's predicament.

"How old are you? You might be able to join the military, steady income that way at least."

"I've thought about it, but I'm a bit too young. Plus, I have a criminal record. I don't know if they'll be too happy to have me." Lucas took a small sip of water. "Besides, I don't really want to put myself in harm's way, my family relies on me too much."

"Oh, come now Lucas, I'll have you know they provide an excellent pension for family members of dead soldiers! That way everyone's happy!"

Lucas blinked and burst out laughing. "You're a bit odd, you know that?"

"So they say. I'm sure some people find it endearing. Anyway, the military might be worth a shot when you're older, you never know."

"Mm." This *was* Jamie. There was no doubt in his mind that this Jamie was the same one who had sheltered him from the rain when he was a boy. He looked the same, acted the same. Hell, he even sounded the same. Did Jamie remember too, though? Lucas tried to think of how to phrase his query.

"This might be a bit of an odd question but . . . is it possible that we've met before?"

Jamie considered it. "I . . . I'm not sure. I haven't been to Dublin since I was little, so maybe not." Jamie was silent for a moment, his mouth closed as he chewed. "Have you ever been to Waterford before?"

"I've never left Dublin," Lucas confessed.

"Let me think. Well, I went to Dublin with my father when I was a kid. We were staying with my granny, and it was raining . . . and . . . " His eyes widened, a delighted grin sweeping over his face. "You're not—? Lucas? *My* Lucas? Shit! I never would have recognized you!" He shook his head. "I can't believe this! You look great!"

Oh, thank God, he remembered, he remembered! And better still,

Jamie didn't seem to fear him or resent him. In fact, his memories seemed positive! Lucas's heart felt like it was singing. "You do too, Jamie. Christ. Small world."

Jamie's hand fell heavy on Lucas's shoulder. "You're not kidding. Holy hell, my mum always said I was charmed but— running into an old friend on my first night in Dublin? I should sell locks of my hair for good luck! I'm so happy to see you, Lucas."

They were both silent for a bit before Lucas spoke once more. "Jamie . . . I'm sorry. For trying to steal your wallet." He was a worm. The boy who had sheltered him from the rain, had hugged him and fed him. Goddamn it.

"Lucas, it's all right." Jamie had such a kind face. "I remember your father. I know life can't have been as easy for you as it has been for me. I understand." A pause. "I wish I'd been able to contact you. I've thought about you a lot."

"Me too." *You have no fucking idea.*

A comfortable silence followed. "Well, I shouldn't keep you any longer. Go see your family and give them those chips before they get too cold." Jamie fiddled with his tie. "Do you want to exchange addresses? I'd love to meet up again, if you want."

Lucas. You stupid shit, don't you dare blush like a schoolgirl.

"Ah, maybe. I work a lot when I'm not . . . " *You know, robbing people.* "Where're you staying? You're new in Dublin and I don't want you to get lost. I'll walk you there."

"Christ, there's a question. The hotel lost my booking, my dormitory doesn't open for students until next week, and my granny is out of town for a funeral."

"Are you joking? You're a complete and total idiot!" Lucas couldn't believe this guy was going to university. "I'm worried if I leave you outside, you'll look up at the rain clouds and drown!"

Jamie couldn't stop laughing; Lucas's insults seemed only to make his circumstances funnier. Jamie probably had a long history of things working out for him.

"All right, you daft bastard, you can stay with me tonight, seeing as how I owe you one. I must warn you: the house is tiny and disgusting, but I keep it as clean as I can. But just for one night, just because you didn't rat me out and you got me dinner and you're so unbelievably stupid."

Jamie smiled, squeezing his shoulder. "I don't want to impose, but I certainly can't turn down an invitation like that! Lead the way, Mister Connolly."

They finished their food and Lucas's stomach filled with dread. He really did live in one of the worst parts of Dublin, and he hoped Jamie wouldn't think less of him because of it. He wondered why the hell he should care so much about the opinions of a fool like James Murray, but he did.

Jamie's broad shoulders bumped against Lucas's as they walked, and he found himself smiling. Lucas had never brought anyone to his home before, partially because he didn't really have any friends, partially because it was mortifying to live in such conditions. He resided on Henrietta Street, for heaven's sake, and he didn't particularly want this stupid idiot to see how he lived, but . . . Jamie hadn't called the police on him; he'd bought him fish and chips. Lucas decided he might as well be forthright.

"Now I'm warning you, you've never stayed somewhere as shit as my home," he said. "My house is full of loud children and the whole place stinks of piss, and I wouldn't be surprised if you woke up with crabs."

Jamie laughed at that, presumably not realizing Lucas wasn't kidding. "Well, I'm sure it'll be an experience, anyway. Beggars can't be choosers, right? So, who am I going to meet?"

"My mother, Molly. She's kind, she'll probably offer to feed you, even though we don't have a lot. Please keep that in mind if she does. There's Becky, she's fourteen. She's going to think you're quite fit, please ignore her. Then we've got the twins, Matthew and Patrick, they're thirteen and they think they know everything, but they're good kids. Then there's Jessie, she's nine, and been a bit poorly recently." He squeezed the small package in his jacket close to his chest. It was gonna be the best part of his night when she saw how much food he was bringing home.

"My Da' walked out on us a few years ago, as I said. So you don't have to worry about him." Obviously, Jamie would remember Mick-Fucking-Connolly. "It's been quite peaceful since then, actually, but money's tight. I'm so sorry I tried to rob you," he added quietly.

Jamie's face was soft in the dim light of the streetlamps; there was a small smile tugging at the corner of his lips. He let his arm drop heavily on Lucas's shoulders and left it there. "You're making it up to me by letting me stay here tonight," he decided. "We'll call us even."

"Well then, I still owe you for dinner, since you're a twit and felt the need to do *two* nice things for me in one day. Plus, I owe you for when we were kids." *Shit, he was gonna be indebted to this asshole forever.*

"Eh, I'll think of something. Nothing too nefarious, I assure you."

Jamie's countenance did change a little when they got into the tenement street that the Connollys called home, and Lucas felt Jamie shift closer to him in the darkness. His eyes were wide and darting; Jamie was obviously experiencing some level of regret. Lucas's own eyes stung from the ammonia in the air. There were people in the gutters, broken glass and rats everywhere. Thousands lived in these tiny buildings; men, women and children crowded into drafty stone coffins. A severely underweight man was emptying the contents of his stomach onto the street, and a number of drunks leered at the two of them. The ground squelched as they walked, the lighting was poor, and the whole place reeked of piss and blood and fear.

"I've got you," Lucas said. "No one will touch us." Probably. He put a hand on Jamie's shoulder. As they walked, a haggard looking young man approached them with a bottle of beer in his hand.

"Aye, Connolly, who's the pretty fellow? You got anything for me, boyo?"

Ugh, he hated Bert. He was drunk all the time, and Jessie was terrified of him.

"What about you, Blondie?" Bert grabbed at Jamie's jacket.

"No. Get out of the way, I'm in no mood for this." Lucas smacked Bert's hand away from Jamie's chest, eyes cold and distant. "Don't you touch him."

"What's that, Connolly? You get a rich friend and you're too good for us now? Eh? Eh?" He lunged forward slowly, swinging his fist.

Lucas sighed and blocked him easily, bringing his elbow down on Bert's greasy head, sending him to the ground. Bert groaned but made no move to get up.

"Guess I *am* too good for you." Lucas decided not to spit on the ground in case Jamie thought that was uncouth.

Jamie shook a little, standing behind Lucas. "Ah—that was brilliant. Well done." He looked impressed, if petrified. "Friend of yours?"

"No. He's some creep who lives in our building. He never gives the girls peace. I hope he dies."

Jamie chuckled at that, hooking his arm around Lucas's shoulders and bonking their heads together gently. He was apparently quite grateful for his rescue and feeling affectionate now. Lucas didn't stop him.

Was Jamie flirting with him? He wasn't giving him bedroom eyes or making any overtly sexual movements but . . . Christ, this was confusing. Lucas didn't get a homosexual air from Jamie, exactly, but . . .

Gradually, he came up to his tenement block and led him up the dark, narrow stairs, letting Jamie stay close. He unlocked the door, and Mattie and Pattie barreled into him.

"Lucas! What've you got, what've you got?" Patrick bounced on his heels.

Lucas smiled and opened his jacket, showing the two full orders of fish and chips that were still warm to the touch. The boys' eyes widened, and they snatched the parcel away, running to the corner of the house that functioned as a dining area. The girls sat down beside their brothers and all of them ate until they were stuffed. It was at this point that they noticed the large, handsome stranger who'd accompanied their brother and dinner through the door.

"Um, who is this?" Becky asked nervously, curling some of her soft black hair around her finger. Her face was red.

"Jamie Murray, at your service." He bowed politely and gave her a wink.

Lucas rolled his eyes. Great, now Becky was going to be in love with him for the rest of her life. Nice one.

"He's some idiot I met at a pub," Lucas explained quickly. "He paid for dinner and didn't have anywhere to stay tonight, so I invited him over. I hope that's all right, Ma."

"Of course! And don't call him an idiot, Lucas, it's rude. Mr. Murray, thank you for buying the children dinner, it means so much to me. Please, come in, make yourself at home! Let me get you something to drink."

"Ah, no, Mrs. Connolly, that's fine." Jamie was peering around the flat, no doubt noticing all the dirty laundry and the lack of privacy. He was probably wondering where the bathroom was.

"Oh, I insist! Sit, sit! Children, make room." Molly started fussing around the kitchen, putting the kettle on for tea.

Matthew and Patrick approached the handsome stranger and gawked at him. "So, are you homeless? Why'd you want to stay here, of all places?"

"I'm temporarily homeless. I'm starting university soon and the lodgings weren't ready for me yet. Your brother was kind enough to offer his hospitality."

"I think you'd be better off homeless," Jessie suggested, licking her fingers. "'Cause then you could sleep in the park or something and it might be quieter."

Jamie laughed. "But then I never would have met you lot! Come, shall we play a game? I've got cards."

The five of them sat in the middle of the flat and played happily for a good hour while Lucas watched. Molly eventually decided they all needed to get to sleep and bopped each of her children on the head with a rolled-up bit of paper.

Jamie had made the whole house seem warmer, somehow. His smile was so tender, his laugh so rich and genuine that Lucas almost forgot how cold it was. The children seemed happier, too.

They were all smiles, warm cheeks and full tummies. Lucas was grateful for what Jamie had done for them. He would never know just how much his small actions meant. At the mention of bedtime, Jamie nodded and stood up, not really sure what "bed" meant exactly in the context of this nearly furniture-less house.

Lucas guided him to his corner of the flat, which he kept as neat as possible. "I know it's not much, but you're welcome to whatever I have." He met Jamie's eyes and was shocked once more by how lovely they were. "I really appreciate everything you did for me and my family today, even if you are an idiot." Lucas had a small cot he used, and Jamie could have it. He'd made it up as nicely as he could, giving Jamie all of the spare blankets and pillows he could find.

"I'm not taking your bed while you sleep on the floor, Lucas," Jamie said firmly.

"I'm not making you sleep on the floor after I tried to rob you," Lucas replied, not budging.

"We appear to be at a standstill," Jamie decided, his smile returning.

"Okay. Wanna share? It'll be close but it'll be warm."

Lucas raised an eyebrow. He scanned Jamie for sexual intent, a quirk of an eyebrow, a slip of his tongue over his lips, a stiffening bulge in his trousers . . . nothing. Platonic as a duckling eating a damned breadcrumb. Adorable, if anything. Jamie obviously didn't mean anything untoward; he was genuinely just being nice. It was odd. It was very, *very* odd. "Okay, but I must warn you, I'm apparently a supreme blanket hog."

Jamie laughed and nudged him with his elbow. "Well, I'll just yank it back if you do end up taking it. Fair?"

"Fair."

Lucas kept as much a distance from Jamie's warm body as was possible on such a small bit of furniture. All in all, it was a horrible night's sleep. It wasn't quite like when they were children, no. There had been no sexual energy then, all gentle, cozy safety. But now . . . good lord, Lucas wasn't sure if there was any blood going to his brain at this point. He fell asleep with a smile on his face, Jamie's broad back against his.

1909

One thing that had become abundantly clear from Lucas's sessions with Father Doyle was that his tendencies toward homosexuality were only getting stronger, despite all of the priest's intervention. It wasn't something people talked about openly, really. Lucas's exposure to what it meant to be homosexual was limited to jokes at school, offhand remarks from his father, and the church decrying the dangers of unconsecrated sex.

There was no one for Lucas to talk to about it. His friends thought being so afflicted was the worst thing in the world, and his parents were out of the question. It was just such a shameful, awful thing. He couldn't even imagine getting the words out—

Ma'... I... I like... I want...

Why were love and sex such a big part of life? Most stupid books had love as a central theme, had marriage as an end goal— either that or the books had no women at all, just an unhealthy attachment to plot and action. Lucas liked that sort of story more, liked to imagine a world without women where no one would give him any bother about whom he fucked in his dreams.

He kept to himself, wondering if maybe he could take the cloth one day. No one expected priests to get married. Maybe that was the best way. Christ, maybe he could step in and show them how to have a good time and stop them from touching children. Honestly, how many of them took up the priesthood to hide their preferences?

Danny had learned a valuable lesson too, it seemed, and figured out what he needed to do and not do to avoid getting beaten by the rest of his class. They kept away from each other for the most part, but Lucas caught Danny staring at him from time to time, which secretly made him terribly pleased.

Weeks passed, final exams were looming, and Lucas couldn't help but notice Danny fidgeting with his fingers and glancing at him just as the school bell rang to dismiss them.

"Lucas!" he called.

Lucas cocked an eyebrow.

"I, um, I was wondering if you wanted to study together? My mum's visiting her parents, so . . . "

So, it wasn't a sin anymore? Hah. But Lucas smiled. "Yeah, sure."

They didn't have very much in common, as far as Lucas could tell. It was just as well that Danny seemed too nervous to maintain conversation as they made the short journey to his home. Lucas wasn't really interested in talking.

The house was much nicer than Lucas's. It felt warm as soon as they walked in; he could smell food and not piss. He tried to find it in himself to be bitter, but his curiosity got the better of him. Through the hallway, past the sitting room . . . right into the young boy's bedroom. *My, Danny, how forward.*

Danny sat down on the bed and licked his lips, his hands trembling a little as he looked up at Lucas.

"Um . . . "

"What did you want to study, Daniel?"

Lucas took a small amount of pleasure in the way Danny's cheeks reddened. " . . . don't make me say it."

Damn it. He didn't want to feel pity and empathy for this kid, but he sat down next to Danny and took his hand. "I thought it was a sin."

"I know. It *is* a sin, and I keep telling myself how wrong it is but . . . Lucas, before, when we . . . "

"Yeah?"

"I really liked it. I really liked you. It felt *so* good."

"Oh come on," Lucas scoffed. "You don't even know me." He was under no delusions himself, really. They were attracted to each other, they liked kissing, but this wasn't love. It wasn't even close.

"I know, I know. I just— I keep trying to stop thinking about you and I just . . . "

"Just can't." Lucas swallowed. "I had a priest once who said he could fix me."

"You did?" Danny's eyes were wide. "What did he do?"

Christ, it was too easy, almost. Let me fuck you and you'll be cured. God, why had he been such a fool?

"He lied to me. He made it worse."

"Oh." The other boy wilted a little and Lucas sighed.

"But he also made me wonder if it's something that *can* be fixed. Maybe we're just like this because God made us this way."

"Why would God do something like that? Why the hell would he want anyone to be like—"

Lucas interrupted him with a kiss and held him steady for a moment, pulling away with a coy little smile. "Let me show you."

Lucas pulled his shirt off and gently pressed Danny down onto his mattress, eagerly perching on his hips. Lucas wasn't accustomed to taking the lead sexually, but there had to be some benefit to getting abused by an adult for close to a year, right? Something at the back of his mind wondered if Danny was maybe too young for this shit, but Lucas had always been a bit precocious. Maybe that was the problem.

Danny's shirt came off, too, and they kissed and kissed and kissed. It was probably a bit early for sex, but . . . clothes kept coming off, and Lucas's smile just kept getting bigger. It's what people did, right? They kissed; they fucked; they died. He was getting acquainted with Danny's belt when the door burst open, and a middle-aged man descended on them. Lucas felt a large hand around his throat and could do nothing as he was grabbed and slammed into the wall.

He saw white for a moment, then the room came back into focus. Danny was in hysterics, trying to pull his clothes back on, pointing at Lucas, screaming and crying words he could barely even hear.

"Da'! I never—it was Lucas— he made me—"

Danny's father turned on Lucas once more, grabbing him by his hair and forcing him to his feet. "Connolly's boy," he growled. "Of fucking course."

Lucas was all fingernails and teeth as he tried to free himself, but Mr. Byrne just gripped harder, slapping Lucas across the face as hard as he could. Jesus.

"Get off me! I'll kill you!"

"You little cocksucking piece of shit," the man seethed. "You ruined my son."

"I didn't!"

"You'll be sorry, boyo."

Jesus. Lucas wondered if he could be any sorrier if he tried. Mr. Byrne didn't let Lucas get his clothes as he dragged the boy out of the house and down the street. Lucas called for help, he screamed and cried, but no one paid him any mind. Mick Connolly's boy getting dragged through the streets was no surprise to anyone. He looked like a gypsy, and he'd obviously been stealing or doing something reprehensible. People looked down their noses at him and Lucas wanted to die.

"Please," he begged. "I didn't."

Mr. Byrne was ignoring him now, dragging him by his hair, his ears, the back of his neck, to the pub where his father spent all of their money.

"Connolly!" Danny's father called out. "Connolly, get out here!"

Mick made an appearance, swaying and red-cheeked as the warm light of the pub lit him up from behind. "The fuck you doing with my boy?"

A little speck of hope surged up in Lucas's chest— maybe his father would actually help him. Yes. His eldest son was in danger after all, so it was possible that Mick would . . .

"Tell him, boy," Byrne spat, shoving Lucas to the ground. "Tell him what you did."

Lucas looked up at Danny's father, eyes wide with terror. "Please. Please Mr. Byrne don't, I'll make it up to you, I won't do it again, I'll do whatever you want, please, please, please, please don't make me— don't tell him, please!"

Lucas's father looked down at him. "What did you do, lad?"

"This . . . *child* was—" Mr. Byrne was struggling to speak. "He was trying to bugger my son!"

"Liar!"

Lucas's eyes widened as his father came to his defense.

"I caught him, Connolly, I caught *them*—I caught your boy on top of mine, they were kissi—caught this little shit with his hand in my son's trousers! On my mother's grave, I saw him!"

Mick was silent, his hands trembling as he crouched down toward his son. "Is this true, Lucas?"

Lucas opened his mouth to deny it. Goddamn it, no. It wasn't his fault, and he wasn't going to lie about it any more. He licked his lips and avoided his father's eyes.

Mick yanked Lucas to his feet, twisting his arm. "We're going home, boy."

"Please." Lucas begged anyone who would listen. "He's going to kill me. He's going to kill me. Please."

Mick apparently had enough sense not to murder his child in public. He dragged Lucas to their little flat and threw him against the wall as soon as they passed the threshold. "You." He punched his son in the face, and Lucas could hear something in his nose crack. "You disgusting buggering trash."

Lucas went to his knees, coughing and spluttering as blood ran down his throat. Mick kicked him in the ribs and looked down at him.

"I always told you, Lucas. You're the reason we're starving. You're the reason we're miserable. I always wondered why that was, well—" Mick shook his head. "You sick cocksucking shite fucker. It's not me, Lucas, it's not your poor mother—it's you. Something in you is broken, boy, something in you is cracked and Godless and wrong. You're the reason your siblings died, you're the reason I drink. Everything you touch breaks, Lucas. The world is a worse place for having you in it."

It hurt when Lucas's tears ran through the cuts on his face. It hurt when he inhaled to sob.

"I tried to make it work, boy. I tried to provide for this family. I can't. Not with you like this. You make me sick, boy. You're rubbish, and you're no son of mine."

Lucas shut his eyes and waited for his father to finish it, cut his throat, free him from this stupid miserable world, but he didn't. Damn it, why not?

He looked up and watched as Mick threw some things in a sack and hoisted it over his shoulder. "Your mother gave it up too easily too, you know. You lot are made for each other."

"Please." Lucas crawled toward his father. "We'll starve."

"You shoulda thought of that before you did this to us, Lucas." Mick's face twisted violently with anger and hurt. "This is your fault. Stop your bloody whinging. You did this to yourself."

"What'll I tell Ma'?"

"You shoulda thought of that, boy. Tell her the truth, yeah? You fucked a boy and killed your family." Mick spat on the ground. "See if she still loves you, Lucas. See if anyone could."

He stormed out into the cold, letting a bitter draft in as he departed.

Mick didn't come back that night, or the one after that, or the one after that. Molly went to the police station and the morgue and was perhaps a little relieved to find that neither of them had any idea of what had become of Mick Connolly. She didn't ask Lucas what happened, though she must have seen the blood on the floor and made some assumptions.

Lucas quit school the next morning and went looking for a job to support his family. He found that it wasn't so easy to find employment with his father's name and reputation chasing him. His father was right-- it was his fault, after all, and he didn't ever want to see Danny again. He didn't love or even like his father, but the sudden lack of his income hit the family quite hard. His siblings barely made it through the winter.

Lucas found himself on the docks at night, looking for men with coins in their pocket. He didn't kiss, he didn't smile, he tried not to enjoy it. He was sick and he wasn't getting better . . . might as well make some damned money out of it.

You're broken. You're ruined. You destroy everyone you love.

The curse of the Connollys ran through his veins, and after a while he stopped fighting his nature. He was going to hell anyway, so what did it matter?

Lucas could turn his curse into an asset, use vice and weakness to separate fools from their money and keep his family afloat. His father's words echoed in his chest, and he tried to stand tall, stand proud. He couldn't change his nature, no. But he could embrace it.

1928

Lucas had been waiting to hear from Angela. Surely by now she would have found out about the debacle that was his evening with Ryan. And surely, sooner or later he'd be getting an earful for it. He was dreading it, he was embarrassed and confused enough by his outburst without having her stick her big fat nose into everything. An altercation was inevitable. As predicted, she came to find him during one of his lonely vigils at the graveyard.

"Lucas!" she called, and he narrowed his eyes at her.

She got close. Put her hand on Jamie's tombstone. In all the years he'd known her, Angela had never come this close to the grave. This was sacred ground; this was not her space to invade. "What do you want?"

"I wanted to talk. I figured I'd find you here."

Lucas felt bad as he saw the worry on her face, the way she was looking at her cuticles as she always did before she started biting at them. He'd been acting more and more crazy lately, surlier and more hostile. Maybe it was just that the anniversary of Jamie's death was coming up. Maybe he was truly losing his sanity. He was certain that thought had crossed her mind. Surely she'd seen such a thing happen before in her tenure as a nurse.

Ech, the thing with Ryan hadn't made it any easier, really. For one evening, he'd let himself believe that he could have a normal, happy life. Christ. It wasn't Ryan's fault and Lucas knew it. No, it was the moment when the hope of a normal future curled up and died in his kitchen. That anniversary, his mind playing goddamn tricks on him. He was getting worse and not better, and every day was harder than the one before it. It hadn't been this bad since Jamie had died, actually. He'd never let himself believe in a better future before. Losing that had devastated him.

Angela hugged her jacket close. "I just want to talk, Lucas. Please?" She was clearly distressed, her eyes annoyingly compassionate. It wasn't a pleasant day to be at Grangegorman Military Cemetery, and Lucas watched her discomfort mount as the temperature dropped. If she were anyone else, he would have suspected she was in love with him.

"I don't know what to say."

"Tell me what happened, Lucas. I want to help, this isn't like you— I mean, you're never—"

"Angie, it's fine. Stop bloody coddling me, I'm not a child. I can handle being alone, I prefer it, even. And I don't want you trying to set me up again, either!"

"Tom is worried about you too, Lucas, and the old guys from the unit, they don't know what to think. And Ryan, he . . . They're scared of you; they think you're losing your mind. I don't want you to be alone any more, it's not good for you! I mean—Jesus, Lucas! You just ruined a good thing with a nice guy, and where do I find you? In the same damn spot you were ten years ago, fighting the same battles and mourning the same losses. This is not normal, Lucas!"

She looked like she regretted it as soon as the words left her mouth. "I'm sorry. It's just, you're behaving so erratically. Ryan said you were like a crazy person, Lucas. He said he was terrified of you, scared of being alone with you. You need help. Don't you wish Jamie had gotten help before . . . ?"

He saw red and ripped his arm away from her. "Don't you bring him into this, don't you fucking dare!" he spat. "How can you ask me that? You, of all people, how can you ask me something like that?" His voice cracked a little and he cursed the hot little tears that were pricking the corners of his eyes.

Angie moved closer, trying to calm him down.

"Stay away from me."

She stepped back, clearly frightened by whatever she was seeing in his eyes. There was a twinge of remorse in his face as he pushed past her, storming back toward his flat. Angela didn't know what she was talking about; she was a harebrained busybody.

It was Dublin, for Christ's sake, there were too many people around for anyone to notice any unusual behavior from Lucas. Maybe he'd had a few outbursts in public, maybe he'd been talking to himself at the graveyard more than normal, dreaming about Jamie and hearing his voice a lot more than normal. Maybe he'd ruined a chance with a nice bloke because he'd hallucinated that a dead person was screaming at him, but that didn't mean he was losing his mind, did it?

Strangers avoided Lucas on the street as he marched home, but he didn't think much of it. People had been avoiding him in the street since he was a child, out of pity, fear, disgust . . . it didn't matter. A man resembling Jamie moved through his periphery and Lucas averted his gaze. Lucas fiddled with the button in his pocket as he walked, turning it over and over in his hand. He stormed into his tiny flat and slammed the door, still fuming. Angie could go screw herself; she'd probably enjoy it, too. *Daft bitch.* He covered his face in his hands and breathed in and out of his nose. He never wanted to see her again, he decided, never ever, unless she apologized for using Jamie as a weapon. For taking his greatest strength, his greatest weakness, and turning it on him.

The somewhat rational part of his mind chided him, telling him that Angela was right, but surely even someone as poorly educated as Lucas would be able to tell he was losing his mind, right?

"Then again, if you're aware of having lost your mind, you probably won't have lost it." Jamie might have said. He would have smiled, with those perfect pink lips and the little dimples that creased his face when he was happy. Still, it was hard enough staying sane these days without the stress of one's dead best friend's memory haunting every action one took. He was seeing Jamie everywhere these days, maybe because it was getting close to the anniversary of his death. He was seeing him in crowds, hearing his voice in his dreams . . . Angela could hardly blame him for going a bit barmy with all that spinning around in the back of his mind.

"Lucas?"

He sat up straight and looked around his disheveled and empty flat. Nothing, no one there— nowhere for them to hide, either. His eyes darted wildly from one end of the living room to the other as he tried not to panic. Slowly, he moved one hand to his pocket and grasped the small knife he always carried with him. *Fuck, fuck, it's not possible. Jamie's voice . . . there was no doubt, it was Jamie's voice again.* Just as he remembered, just the way he'd imagined in the cemetery. He could almost hear him smiling.

"Lucas? What's wrong with you?"

He scanned the room, still nothing, still nothing, he wasn't mad, he couldn't be. He shut his eyes and covered his ears. Had he been hearing Jamie's voice for real, then, and not just imagining it? Oh Christ, Angie was right, he belonged in a loony bin.

"Fuck off! You're not real!"

"I'm not?"

Lucas supposed the real Jamie might be patting himself up and down his uniform, trying to figure out if he had mass. The real Jamie would be confused by the accusation, affronted but amused by the whole thing.

"I feel pretty real." He sounded like he was smiling. "Come now, Lucas, you're being rude."

Lucas peeked out of one eye and gasped when he saw a somewhat transparent version of his dead best friend sitting on the box he used as a chair.

"You're not real," Lucas repeated. "I'm sleeping. I'm losing my mind. I've been visiting you at the cemetery too often and it's messing with my head. Angie is right, I need to spend more time with real people."

Jamie looked a little hurt. "Does it matter if I'm real? I'm real to you."

"You're a hallucination, there's no such thing as ghosts," Lucas insisted. But good God, it was nice to fucking see him. He moved closer; his hand extended out cautiously. Jamie had believed in this sort of nonsense, but Lucas had seen enough of the church to know that any mystical wonders were a fabrication pulled out of some old prune's ass to con idiots into giving ten percent of their wages away for nothing.

"Okay, how about I prove it? You ask me something only the real Jamie would know."

"The problem with that, Jamie, is that if you are a hallucination then you and I know exactly the same things, so any answer you give will be directly from me. And if you're not a hallucination, and you say something I don't know, there's no way for me to know if it's true. Therefore, there's no way for me to prove if you're real or not. Idiot."

"Clever!" Jamie—or the spirit or hallucination or whatever the hell it was—clapped his hands. "Unless we find a way to verify my claim independently somehow."

"Which is a problem considering it's been years and I've got no way of digging up your past without bothering your relatives."

"Which is a possibility, you know."

"You're such an ass," Lucas muttered affectionately.

Jamie was in his old army uniform, his Lieutenant's stripes embroidered proudly on his shoulders, brass buttons shining. Just like Lucas remembered him, forever twenty-four, as beautiful as he'd been the day he died. More so, maybe, since his face was adorned with his brilliant smile instead of cracking with panic and cries of terror.

Lucas suddenly realized he was too old for Jamie now; they probably wouldn't even be friends like this. Jamie would probably think he was an old fogey, they'd have nothing in common anymore. Lucas glanced down at his body. He'd never been self-conscious about his appearance before; he'd been a reasonably good-looking man when he was younger. But time had taken its toll, and all at once he was agonizing over how much he'd aged. Flecks of gray peppered his silky black hair, there were small lines developing by his eyes and mouth, his body was no longer the sleek muscular machine it had been during the war. He'd stopped looking after himself after Jamie had died. What was the point of trying to be beautiful when the light of his life was gone? He must have looked haggard, overly thin, wizened and grizzled, and *fuuuuck*, he would have looked after himself better if he'd known there was a chance Jamie would come back from the dead to judge him, prick.

"You look good." Jamie smiled, and the fact that his words seemed designed directly to placate Lucas in that moment made the whole 'hallucination of a madman' thing seem more likely. "I wonder if I can hug you like this."

"I have a brain tumor," Lucas said mildly. "This is probably what it feels like to have a brain tumor. I suppose there are worse ways to go."

The apparition—Jamie—laughed and stepped nearer to Lucas, putting a glowing, effervescent hand on his shoulder. There was no weight to it, no heat, but Lucas leaned into the touch all the same. "I hope you don't, I'd hate for you to have a brain tumor. What've you been up to while I've been away?"

"While you've been dead, you mean? Not much." That was true.

Jamie was just smiling. "Christ, I missed you," he whispered, wrapping his transparent arms around Lucas's thin frame. There was something like love in his eyes, desire almost. That was more than enough to tell Lucas that none of this was real.

At the back of his mind, Lucas wondered if maybe this was a second chance for him. For them. *Don't be an idiot, Lucas. He's not like you.* Jamie had never felt that way for him, never had, never would.

1917

P art of the problem was that Jamie was so clever, and so driven; it was quite likely that he was hiding the severity of his impairment, even from Lucas. He was irritable for a start, not sleeping, barely eating, his hands shaking violently whenever he was alone.

They'd been in a shelter together, waiting out a bombing when Jamie's facade started to crack—he squealed like a child and sobbed, clutching at Lucas, rocking back and forth, eyes staring at nothing as he rode out the worst of it. Even as the noises outside subsided, Jamie couldn't get control of himself; he hiccupped rather than breathed, his whole body convulsing with fear.

"Jamie," Lucas soothed, stroking his hair, trying to get him to respond, to hear. "Jamie, I've got you."

But he was miles away, trapped in his nightmarish dungeon of fear. It was hours before he was lucid, before he could even see that Lucas was with him. His whimpers quieted, his heart slowed, and he looked up at Lucas as though seeing him for the first time. Jamie remembered nothing, thought nothing was wrong. All he wanted was to go back out to the men, to support them as best he could through this battle, through the next.

"Jamie, we need to talk to someone. You need some time away from the front lines. You can't keep going on like this."

Jamie wasn't listening; Jamie wouldn't hear any of it. He couldn't accept his mental deterioration. His men needed him after all, he'd given up a lot to be here. It had to mean something, right?

So, Lucas did the only kind thing he could think to do, which was to go above Jamie's head.

It wasn't an easy thing for him. He'd never gone behind Jamie's back before, never defied him, but Lucas was going to lose him at this rate. He knocked on the Colonel's door and bowed his head as he entered.

"Private Connolly." Lucas was surprised the man knew his name. "What is it?"

"I . . . I'm a little concerned about Lieutenant Murray." He pulled off his hat and fiddled with it. "He's a good man. A great man actually— he's smart and he's careful and—"

"Private. Get to the point please, there's a war on."

Lucas swallowed. "I think he has shell shock, sir. He's not himself. He's not thinking clearly; I'm worried he's gonna get hurt." *Or—or hurt someone else.*

"Oh?"

"Yeah, he—he keeps forgetting things— he's panicking a lot more than he used to. I can't get talk sense into him. It's like I'm not there sometimes and it's not . . . it's not like him." Lucas licked his lips. "I was thinking maybe he could go to a casualty clearing station to get checked out. Maybe get some help. He's a good officer, Colonel. He's just not at his best right now."

"I see. I'll look into it. Thank you for your concern, Private."

Lucas watched as the Colonel observed James Murray. The way his brows creased when Jamie crumpled to his knees with a scream, the way he locked himself in his quarters during the worst parts of the shelling, emerging with red eyes and white skin, shaking, his back ramrod straight, his gait unnatural. The examination of his behavior was brief, but apparently it was enough.

Jamie was informed the next morning he was being sent to the Casualty Clearing Station for assessment, and with wild eyes he backed himself up against a wall. "I don't need to go to medical!" he barked.

"It's all right Lieutenant. There have been some concerns about you. We're going to look you over, nothing serious, no disciplinary actions in the works or anything like that. Come along, now."

"No! I'm fine! Who? Who told you I wasn't!?"

"Relax, Lieutenant." The man put his hands on Jamie and gripped him tightly. "It's just for a check. Relax."

Jamie's eyes went wide, he thrashed his body to free himself. "Get off me! I'm fine! Fucking—get off me!"

Lucas couldn't watch this. "Let him go. Please." He touched Jamie's arm. "It was me, Jamie. I told them. Please, please let them help you."

Lieutenant Murray stopped struggling, and he looked down at Lucas with cold, distant eyes. Without a word, he let himself be loaded into a vehicle.

Lucas's heart ached as he watched him leave. He briefly considered shooting himself in the foot so he could be with Jamie while he recovered, but realized such a plan could spectacularly backfire. Angie would see right through such a stupid wound.

Instead, he waited and prayed that Jamie would come back, his mind whole again. Jamie was temporarily replaced with some young upstart who lacked the experience and the character to lead anyone into anything, and morale had plummeted.

"Nice work, ass! Getting Murray carted off, yeah? The hell you thinking?"

"New guy's a piece of work. Gonna get us all killed cause Connolly's a rat."

"Murray was doing his best! Alright, he's a bit of a princess sometimes, but . . . Christ, rich boys are just . . . fragile. No shame in it, no need to ship 'em up to casualty clearing just for that."

Lucas kept his head down and bore the fallout. These men didn't know Jamie like he did, they didn't know how much he'd changed in Belgium.

Even so, he too was suffering terribly with Jamie's absence. He ate alone, he slept alone; he just bided his time until Jamie came back. Christ, something funny would happen and his first damned instinct was to run over and tell Jamie about it. Obviously, that wasn't possible. Now, more than ever, he did his best to survive, knowing how badly Jamie would take it if Lucas were killed in his absence.

God, he missed him. War was no fun without Jamie; nothing felt like it had a purpose anymore. Whenever he had a free moment, he fretted about him—how he was, if he was getting better, if he was angry at Lucas for doing this. Shit.

It took a few weeks, but soon enough Jamie was declared once again fit for service and returned to his old squad. Lucas's heart leaped when he saw him.

"Heya, how—"

Jamie wasn't smiling at him; he gave Lucas a distasteful look.

"What is it, Private?" he asked coolly. Jamie had never called him private before. Hell, he'd never called him anything other than his name or some equally friendly pet name. Oh fuck. Oh fuck, Jamie hated him.

"I . . . I wanted to see if you were feeling better," Lucas stammered.

"It would appear I am, otherwise, they wouldn't have let me come back. Is that all?"

"Yes, Lieutenant." It hurt. Getting beaten by his father never hurt like this. He felt like the hole in his stomach would kill him. He traipsed back to his cot and sat down, head in his hands. He'd known this was a risk; he'd known that undermining Jamie was a great way of pissing him off. But he'd made a judgment call that Jamie needed help, no matter what it cost. Still, after so many years of friendship, it cut Lucas to the core to see Jamie treating him like a stranger. He took a deep breath and tried calming himself. At least he knew where Jamie was now; at least he could protect him again. *Had he been wrong? Could Jamie have managed on his own? Perhaps he coddled Jamie a little too much, worried a little too much. Jamie was a grown man, right? He could handle these things, surely.*

A new round of shelling had just begun. Lucas raced to his station and prepared himself for battle. He had his rifle cocked and ready, but his heart wasn't really in it. He peered through the muddy trench at Jamie, seeing how he reacted to the descending chaos. The Lieutenant kept a level head. He barked out orders, and people seemed to be listening to him. Good. Good.

Just beside Jamie, a soldier took a bullet in the face and went down silently, blood and brains gushing from his skull onto the Lieutenant's boots. Jamie's eye twitched and he stepped away, taking a deep breath but maintaining his demeanor. It went on like this for what seemed like hours, until gradually the sun began to set. Lieutenant Murray assigned a night watch and retired to his small room, which Lucas had kept spotless for him in his absence.

Lucas retired to his own little cot once more.

"Good to have the Lieutenant back, eh?" Seamus Kelly was yammering on again. Lucas tried to tune him out. He was about Jamie's age and seemed well suited for combat. He never shut up about his blasted girlfriend, though, which had Lucas convinced that he was going to die any second now because that was a very common theme in literature as far as he could tell. He had an enviable mustache and a prominent jaw, and for some reason he'd made it his mission in life to befriend Lucas by any means necessary. Maybe he just wanted to get close to the Lieutenant.

"Aye. Have you talked to him?" Lucas replied dully, glad to harvest any little tidbits on Jamie he could get.

"Not really, idiot, we had a bloomin' battle to get through. Not much time for gabbing, really. Why? Christ, look at the state of you, you're more of a mess now that he's back than when he was gone!"

"Go fuck yourself."

"Would if I could, boyo, it's been a hell of a long time, true enough. But I just mean, you've been pining for your pal all this time, he's sour at ya for sending him up the loony way, go bloomin' talk to him 'fore I smash your head in. The more time you allow to come in between ye', worse it'll be, I reckon, so get your melancholy ass in that pretty boy's bunker and leave me to my thoughts. I've got to write to Winnie anyway, she'll be wondering how I am, so she will."

Lucas acquiesced and made his way through the rotten trenches to the Lieutenant's room. The ground squelched under his feet, and he tried to ignore the idea that there were rats and worms burrowing through their belongings every night. The whole place reeked of piss, blood, sweat, and death. He hated being here. It reminded him too much of the cesspool he'd crawled out of in Dublin, and it had been so much worse when Jamie had been away.

He let himself in; he never usually knocked.

"Private, this is an officer's quarters. You do not come in without knocking, and you need to get back to your bunk," Jamie said, not even looking at him.

"Like hell I do." Lucas moved behind him and put a hand on his shoulder. "Jamie. I'm sorry I went behind your back. I'm sorry I got you sent to medical, I was just really, really scared for you, and I didn't know what else to do. I thought I was going to lose you . . . and maybe I already have." He shut his eyes. "Tell me to go. Tell me to leave again, and I will."

He felt Jamie's warm hand envelop his own and he let himself relax.

"You shouldn't have gone behind my back. You should have told me you were worried."

"I *did* tell you, you dafty. You didn't listen, you didn't believe me. I didn't know what else to do." He spun Jamie's chair around and knelt down in front of him, taking his hand. "What would you have done, if it were me having the shell shock? If I was having memory lapses, night terrors, panicking while on duty, and I said it was fine. If you thought I was gonna get shot, that you were gonna lose me . . . What would you have done, Jamie? What would you have done to protect me?"

Jamie nodded and gave Lucas's fingers a squeeze. "I know you're right. It was just humiliating. To be treated like a mental patient, kid gloves on and all . . . I worry the men don't think as much of me anymore, but I know you're right. I might have shot someone, I might have gotten us killed otherwise. I needed the time off; I can see that now. Thanks for looking out for me, pal. I'm sorry I was an ass to you."

"You're often an ass. I still choose to be with you, though, which I suppose makes me the idiot of the pair of us," Lucas teased, pulling up a chair and sitting beside him. "So how was it? Tell me everything. I was so worried about you I was thinking about getting shot so I could make sure you were doing okay."

Lucas, stop. He knew he sounded like a damned fool.

"It was all right. Quieter, for one. I think they were glad to see the back of me, though, I ended up bedding two of the nurses." He laughed. "It's not my fault, what do they expect to happen if they keep us away from women for months at a time! And besides, I'm hardly even maimed at all, the wee girls all found me quite smart, I think. Christ—I hope I didn't catch anything."

"You dafty," Lucas repeated fondly. For a moment he imagined himself in Jamie's lap, running his fingers through that golden hair. God, if only. "Just need some loose women to keep you sane, is that it?" Normally Jamie's promiscuity bothered him, but . . . God, it was so damn nice to have him home.

"Seems like. Maybe we can have some sent to the front lines. Keep me straight. Although to be honest, I doubt they'd much care for trench life. Plus, women seem to get sick of me after a while; one of 'em slapped my sweet little face!"

Lucas laughed. "Why? What did you do?"

"Well, Shelby found out I was messing about with Abbie, and I suppose she found out somewhat directly as she walked in on the two of us, um . . . " He blushed and shrugged. "'I think you're as well as you're gonna get, Murray!' Shelby said, and she slapped me, and then Abbie must have realized *why* she was so cross and slapped me on the other side, didn't even let me finish. It's a shame, but to be sure I looked quite rosy."

"You ever thought of monogamy, Jamie? I hear some people find that very attractive." Christ, he was so lovely. He had missed this; his life had had no joy in it when Jamie was away.

"I'm not normally such a Casanova, you know! It's extenuating circumstances! It's not often I'm around women these days as it is, let alone when I'm apparently 'suffering from mental duress.'" He shrugged, smiling at Lucas. "She didn't even give me her surname. Guess she didn't want me to write."

"Is it possible you're crap in bed?" he teased.

"I suppose you might be right, Lucas!" Jamie laughed, shaking his head. "I'll have to ask the next one to critique my performance."

Or you could sleep with me. I'll give you a full report. But of course, Lucas didn't say that.

"And how have you been, pal?" Jamie said pleasantly, slipping out of his chair and taking a seat on the floor beside Lucas. "Taking care of yourself?"

Obviously not. Lucas had bags under his eyes; his hair was a mess; he'd probably lost five pounds since the last time they saw each other.

Jamie *tsked.* "Have you been checking your feet, at least? Lucas, what am I going to do with you?" Jamie's smile was warm and radiant as he nudged himself closer to his friend.

Lucas's mouth went dry as he watched Jamie's strong fingers work the knots of his bootlaces open, pulled back the tongue, slid the leather down and over his ankles. "Jamie— you don't have to—"

"Nonsense." Those blue eyes flicked up, encased as ever by the thick reeds of golden lashes. "We're meant to check each other, no? Make sure we don't get the dreaded trench foot?"

Jamie's fingers slid up Lucas's calf and hooked under the rim of his sock, slowly drawing it away from the pale flesh of Lucas's distal appendage.

"Sod off!" Lucas almost kicked him, not wanting Jamie to get a whiff of his sweaty toes. "Jamie—!"

But Jamie only silenced him, a long finger to his soft lips, the edges nipped up in a smile. "Hush now. What are you worried about?"

"It— I haven't had a chance to clean off and— I don't—" He could feel his blush deepening, Christ, how embarrassing.

"Lucas." Jamie's hands skimmed down Lucas's calf, to his ankle, up and over the arch of his foot, stopping at his toes. "There is no part of you that repulses me."

Lucas wasn't breathing. He wasn't sure if his heart was beating or if he'd died while Jamie had been away. Was this heaven? Did heaven involve feet?

"Jamie," he whispered.

"Lucas." His beautiful eyes were dilated, his fingers fanned out over Lucas's sickeningly pale leg. He licked his lips and moved his hands over to the other boot, starting the process once more.

Lucas could hear his heart in his ears. His blood was draining from his head in some unproductive direction; he could barely think straight. The knot flicked open, those hands, *those hands . . .* !

"Jesus, knock it off." He stood abruptly, though his words lacked their usual bite. "Check your own damn feet, idiot."

The spell was broken, and Jamie just smiled. "My feet are dainty and lovely, thanks."

What the fuck had that been? Lucas didn't want to know exactly what Jamie thought about him, if he knew deep down what he was. Jesus, he didn't even want to think about it. It'd be like Danny all over again. He'd lose everything, everything that mattered. No, it was better to leave it unspoken. It wasn't perfect, but they were together and that was all that counted.

As much as Lucas trusted Jamie, as much as he adored him, he knew better than to arm him with a secret like that. To encourage him when his mind wasn't sound— to take advantage of him— Jamie would hate him, think him disgusting. He'd get him kicked out of the army, thrown out of the flat; he'd never want to see him again. It wasn't worth the risk. Lucas didn't want to jeopardize the only relationship in his life that mattered to him over something as trivial as love.

1912

Lucas awoke the next morning still tangled up in Jamie's arms, hard as he'd ever been. Damn it. He dislodged himself and wished for the millionth time that he had some modicum of privacy; how was a man supposed to masturbate like this? He didn't need much time, so he went into the communal hallway and wanked ferociously. Christ, lucky Jamie was a deep sleeper; that could have been problematic otherwise.

He went back into the house and realized they had almost nothing for breakfast; couple of eggs, bit of bread for seven people. Damn it. Maybe he could make some tea instead, since that would be better than nothing at least. Hell, he should have robbed Jamie after all, saved himself the humiliation of being a bad host.

Jamie stirred a little in his bed, grumbling softly. "Mm . . . Lucas?" he croaked, sitting up on the cot. His beautiful hair was all mussed up, his eyes half-lidded with sleep.

"*Shhh*, you smarmy fuck. The wee ones are sleeping." God, how much he wanted to trail his fingers through that silken gold, brush it away from his face, press a kiss to his temple. "C'mon, lemme get you back to civilized society before you get stabbed."

Jamie yawned and nodded, rubbing his eyes. "I haven't slept that well in a long time, if you can believe it." He smiled and straightened his shirt. "You're really comfortable, Lucas."

Well yeah, that was why strange men paid him for sex. He rolled his eyes but smiled, his cheeks flushed. "All right, you dafty. Is your granny back today?"

"Mm. I'll soon be out of your hair, don't worry." Jamie collected his things and kept nice and quiet until they were out of the apartment. He couldn't contain his excitement for long, though, and as soon as there was no danger of waking the kids up, he began chattering again.

"Lucas, that was amazing when you kicked that drunk fellow's ass last night!" He punched the air, taking up a boxer's stance. "You must teach me to fight sometime!"

"You're very odd, you know that?" Lucas smiled, putting his hands in his pockets. "Does your granny still live in the same place?"

"Oh, do you want to visit her? I'm sure she'd be delighted to see you again."

"Ah, no that's all right, I've got work soon." He was ashamed of his background, still; he wasn't sure he could stomach seeing that sweet woman right now.

Lucas walked him to her home and deposited Jamie on the front steps, glad to be rid of him once and for all.

"Okay. I kept you from getting killed all night and ensured you got home safely. We're even. Bye."

"Not by my count we're not."

"How do you figure?"

Jamie grinned. "Didn't turn you into the police, sheltered you as a child, got you dinner. That's three things."

Lucas crossed his arms, clenching his jaw to stop his smile from getting out. "Technically, your father sheltered me as a child, not you."

"And technically my father is unavailable, and I, as his sole male heir, inherit his boons. So, I don't think we're quite done yet, Connolly."

Lucas sighed melodramatically. "What do you want, Murray?"

"Lemme come visit tomorrow. Show me around Dublin. I get the feeling we could be great pals."

"And I get the feeling you're an idiot."

But Jamie wasn't to be deterred by Lucas's standoffishness. Sure enough, he met Lucas on the cusp of the tenement village the next day, and the day after that, and the day after that. Initially, Lucas was horrified to see the golden-haired fool putting himself in such danger just for the sake of his company, but little by little Lucas warmed up to his companionship.

Jamie would meet Lucas early in the morning, walk him to work . . . hell, he'd even do the odd construction shift with him sometimes. He'd meet him in the evenings too. They'd go to a pub together, ending up so drunk that they broke out in songs.

One night they got kicked out of the bar and Jamie thought it was so funny he couldn't stop giggling.

"It—it's just—" He was gasping. "We're so—we're so bad at—we sound like—"

The laughter was contagious, and Lucas was having a hard time pretending to be grumpy. "Cats fucking."

"Exactly!" Jamie hooked an arm around Lucas's neck and meowed. "I never—I've never been asked to leave a pub before!"

"Why exactly are you enjoying this?"

"Because we're alive, Lucas! This is living!"

Lucas assumed the visits and the friendship would stop after Jamie started university, but they didn't. After a while, Lucas made the effort to see Jamie, too, meeting him after his classes and doing whatever inane thing Jamie had in mind that day. He taught him to box, he taught him how to gamble, and Jamie returned the favor by teaching Lucas how to do complicated math and lending him books.

The friendship developed little by little over the coming weeks, and for the first time in his life, Lucas felt like he mattered, like there was some good in him after all. If someone like Jamie wanted to spend time with him then maybe . . . Jamie was brilliant with Lucas's siblings, too, and Molly adored him. He was a decent sort.

It was difficult, however, to keep Lucas's attraction to Jamie under wraps. Jamie was so damned physical, and as much as Lucas relished the contact, it was a nightmare to pretend that he didn't.

An arm draped over his shoulder, bonking their heads together affectionately, falling asleep together. Jesus, it was torture to be so close and keep such a distance.

There were a few instances in which Lucas almost, *almost* instigated something physical. Once, when Lucas had stayed the night at Jamie's house, they had fallen asleep together in the large bed in Jamie's room. Lucas had offered to sleep on the sofa, but Jamie wouldn't hear of it. Damn thing was uncomfortable. They only had one bed. Nothing weird about two friends being close, yeah?

Lucas loved sleeping here; the sheets smelled like Jamie, and he was addicted to the feeling of being wrapped up in him. Jamie occasionally upped the ante by being something of a chronic sleep-cuddler, which Lucas simultaneously adored and loathed for similar reasons. He awoke tangled in Jamie's arms and watched him for a while. Christ, he was beautiful. The way his little puffs of breath made his silky fringe waft over his forehead, his lovely thick eyelashes. Lucas found himself staring, mesmerized. *Kiss him. Start with his forehead, play it off for laughs if he thinks it's weird. Maybe he likes it, maybe you kiss his cheek next, then his ear, then his lips . . . Arch your neck for him, Lucas, feel his teeth on your throat.*

Jamie's eyes fluttered open, and he smiled. "Good morning sunshine. Sleep okay?"

Jamie never seemed to be bothered by waking up like this, which Lucas assumed meant the situation was so far from sexual that the thought had never even occurred to him. "No. You're a blanket hog, you snore, and you stink up the room."

Jamie wore a devilish smile as he grabbed Lucas's wrists and pinned him to the bed.

Oh hello.

"I'll show you who stinks up the room!" Jamie let loose a mighty wind and did not let up until Lucas cried for Granny Murray to come rescue him. It was not his most dignified moment.

Despite the difficulties, Lucas was quite content to enjoy their time together without making it about love or sex or any of that nonsense.

Winter was harder for the Connollys; there was less work to be had for Lucas, and it was nearly impossible to stay warm. Right around Christmastime, Molly received a letter from the local authorities saying that Mick Connolly had been found dead in a derelict hovel a few hours north. They queried how she planned to pay off the debts of her deceased spouse. Molly's health wasn't the best anymore, and she didn't know what to do.

The whole thing sent Lucas to a terribly dark place. He stopped going out to meet Jamie, stopped responding when he came to call. Jamie was never one to be put off by a little friendly resistance, though. He made his way into the Connolly's flat when Lucas wasn't there, surely aware that Molly wouldn't be able to say no to him. Lucas came home to find his friend pleasantly sitting with his mother at the table, a tepid cup of weak tea in his hands.

"Lucas . . .!" Jamie's face lit up when he saw him. "I've been worried—Molly told me about your father . . . Lucas I'm so sorr—"

"What the hell are you doing here?" Lucas growled. "I don't want any damned company." He didn't need Jamie's pity, or his charity, or his friendship right now. Lucas was a Connolly through and through: a mean old bastard who would destroy everything good in the world and leave a trail of broken promises and misery in his wake. To hell with Jamie. To hell with Mick! He didn't need anyone.

"Lucas!" Molly's face flushed pink. She struggled to her feet and took a few moments to catch her breath. "Don't speak to him like that! Jamie's been nice enough to come visit. He's even brought sweet buns for the children!"

Lucas's face contorted with anger as he grabbed Jamie by the wrist and dragged him outside. He needed to get this off his fucking chest; he didn't want to be censored by his own goddamn mother. "What the hell is wrong with you?" Lucas snarled, once they were out in the alley. "You can't take a bloody hint, can you?"

Gray slush lined the streets, and Jamie's beautiful hair was being evenly dusted with snow. "I thought we were friends, you prick! I wanted to see you because I was worried about you!"

"Why, Jamie? What a fucking joke—who the hell do you think you are?" Lucas threw his hands in the air. "Some rich golden pretty boy with a stick up his ass, oh yes, I love coming to the worst part of Dublin, I love staying in a house that smells like piss and failure, I love watching Lucas bloody Connolly try to scrounge together enough money to feed his family while I can afford to shower the whole dirty lot of them in sweet rolls! What the devil's wrong with you, Jamie? I tried to rob you, I could have killed you, and you want to see me? Want to spend time with me? You got a death wish?"

Jamie watched him with an obvious fear in his eyes.

Say something, you coward!

Lucas stepped forward, his eyes wild with anger. "Oh, and of course my stupid mother tells you my father died. Christ. Christ! He was a drunk wife-beating piece of shit who crippled us with debt and—and—I'm no bloody better than he is."

Lucas's voice cracked and his head fell forward. It was true. It was all true. *He'd* been the reason his parents got married. If not for him, none of his siblings would have been born either, none of them would have starved and died. His father had always told him he was broken, he was wicked . . . hell, he'd left because Lucas was. . . shit. It was *all* his fault.

"He always said it, Jamie. People like you don't like people like me. I'm poison, I'm a cancer. I'm a dirty thief, I'm a *sinner*. I'm the reason my family is starving, I'm the reason we're all miserable. Who I am—*what* I am has spoiled everything. I'll break everyone I love."

"Oh . . . Lucas . . . ," Jamie whispered. "That's awful, I never . . . what a terrible thing to say to your own son."

"Yeah, well, not all of us have filthy rich fathers who love us and pay for us to go to university, mothers who don't have to keep working until they get ill, a bunch of siblings rotting in the ground already!" Lucas shoved Jamie, knowing full well his anger was misdirected. But all of this venom had been festering in him for so damned long, it was hard to stop himself now that he had the chance to vent. "I'll ruin you if you let me. I'll kill you, Jamie. I'll destroy everything you are." *Something inside of me is broken.*

His ears were burning red; his lip was quivering ever so slightly. Oh no, he was getting emotional. He tried to feel angry again, he needed this to get Jamie off his back once and for all—push him away. Push Jamie away, protect him, protect him. "And I don't need your damn charity! I never want to fucking see you again!"

"You asshole!" Jamie stepped forward and put his hands on Lucas's arms. "Where the hell is this coming from? You're not wicked, you're not broken! You're worth knowing and you're worth loving! You're not your bloody father and you never will be! You think he ever gave one second's thought to what his choices were doing to his family? No! He was wrong about you then and you're wrong about yourself now! I see good in you, Lucas Connolly, and I want you in my life. I care about you. I worry about you when you're struggling, stupid." Jamie pulled Lucas into a tight embrace, and Lucas found himself clinging right back.

"Jamie . . . " he sniffled, burying his face in Jamie's jacket. "He beat me, and he disappeared one day, and I was so glad, because I prayed that he'd never come back. We didn't have enough food. Jessie nearly died that winter— he always said it was my fault, Jamie, if I wasn't like . . . if only I was born different, he—"

"Fuck him," Jamie whispered. "Look at me." He met Lucas's eyes and smiled at him, the dim light of the streetlamp illuminating the sheen of gold in his hair. "I admire your strength, Lucas, your honesty—you're the type of man I want to be. Someone whom his family can rely on, someone who always puts others first. I look like a coddled little twat next to you—you make me want to be a better person. On top of that, you're funny, you're clever, and you're cranky and bitter . . . but deep down you've got the sweetest heart in the world. I can't get enough of you, Lucas. I want to be with you, and you make me so damned happy." He gripped Lucas's shoulders and met his eyes.

"Look at me."

"You're worth knowing, you're worth loving. You are not broken, there is nothing wrong with who you are or what you are. Stand with pride, Lucas; love the man you are. I wish I could make you see yourself the way that I see you. Please," Jamie whispered, "don't tell me to leave."

The halo of light danced around Jamie's hair, and for the second time in his life, Lucas thought he was seeing an angel.

"Never, Jamie, never."

In the dark of the alley, on a snowy night in December, in one of the worst parts of Dublin, Lucas Connolly found his reason for living.

1928

Lucas simply gawked at the . . . the thing, Jamie, whatever it was. He so often imagined what he'd do or say if he ever saw Jamie again. Would he confess his love? Tell him how much Jamie had meant to him, how awful it had been since they'd last seen each other? How sometimes—no, most times—Lucas envied Jamie for being dead, for not having to carry on in the mortal coil alone?

"I'm so sorry, Jamie," he said finally, tears pricking his eyes. "I'm so sorry, it's all my fault, I just . . . "

Jamie looked a bit confused and patted Lucas's shoulder, not that he could feel it. "That I died, you mean? Lucas, you can't possibly blame yourself for that, can you? It was a war, right? People die in wars all the time."

Lucas stopped and stared at Jamie, watching his face for any clue or sign that he wasn't being truthful. "You don't remember what happened, do you?" He wanted to be sure.

"I remember we were together; I remember I was panicking; I remember they were trying to take my gun off me. You stopped them, you kept them away so I could be alone for a second . . . then . . . then I got shot. It was in Belgium. Right?"

Lucas was well and truly horrified, and suddenly Jamie seemed unsure of himself.

"I don't remember everything from my life, I remember my father. I remember you." He paused, seemingly collecting his thoughts. "Is that not how it happened?"

Lucas shook his head slowly. "Yeah. Yeah Jamie, that's how it happened. But it was my fault that you died. I couldn't protect you; I couldn't help you."

"Lucas . . . " He hugged him around the chest and huffed as his hands passed through the smaller man's body. "Damn it! I hate being ethereal! Absence of physical matter is a bit shit, honestly. I want to hold you. I want to make you feel better. I missed you."

"It's okay," Lucas said softly. "I'm starting to believe in God, Jamie, just seeing you here like this. It's a bloody miracle." He'd ached for this. He'd prayed for this. A life, or a limbo, maybe, with Jamie. A second chance, a clean slate, a shot at redemption. Yes, definitely a brain tumor. He smiled, and found his facial muscles were so unfamiliar with the expression as of late that it actually hurt his face.

"Jamie?"

"Yes, pal?"

"What's your middle name?"

Jamie seemed a bit surprised at the question. "Why?"

"What do you mean 'why?'"

"Because I can't remember what it was, and if you can't either, it means you're in my head. It means you're not real. It means I lost my mind and none of this means anything."

"Could also mean I don't remember everything from my life. I've been dead for years, that'll wreak havoc with anyone's memories, no?"

"You don't know your middle name."

"Lucas . . . " Jamie looked a little worried about that fact himself. "Alan. My middle name is Alan."

Jamie might have been making it up to make him feel better, his mind playing tricks, knowing that he vaguely remembered a funny acronym but it didn't matter, it didn't. If Jamie wasn't real, then so be it. Being completely insane was better than living without Jamie for one more second.

"Alan. Good strong name," he said softly, but he wanted to change the subject. It felt better to imagine he was real, and he didn't want any evidence mounting to the contrary. "So. Um." He had never been good at small talk, and his abilities had only declined over the last decade. Jamie being dead wasn't helping much, either.

"How's the afterlife? Death? God? That sort of thing?" Jamie offered, sitting down on Lucas's couch and letting himself relax.

"It was abrupt and terrifying. Everything went white, then I didn't feel anything. It was like before I was born. It was like just *not* being. I didn't see God, I didn't see heaven, there was no light at the end of the tunnel. There was nothing, and then there was you." Jamie smiled. "Perhaps you and I have some unfinished business? Some debt I need to repay before I can get to heaven, that sort of thing. A task I need to complete. What do you think?"

He had such an energy about him; it was so perplexing. Lucas felt a little disheartened, actually. He hadn't seen Jamie this vibrant and alive since . . . since before the war—since way before he'd died. Lucas had almost forgotten how sweet and lovely he'd been before . . . everything. He'd lost so much of himself; England's war had stolen it from him.

"Dunno, mate," Lucas shrugged, sitting on the couch and putting his hands behind his head. "S'pose we could see if anyone else can see you, then we can sell tickets and make a fortune," he teased, sneaking a glance up at Jamie's sweet face. Christ, how could this be real? He was almost afraid to accept it, afraid of his heart shattering if the illusion fell apart. But there was no version of Jamie that Lucas wouldn't accept, and even if he ended up being a devil or symptom of his brain deteriorating, Lucas was glad to have him back.

"S'pose we could." He bit his lip. "Lucas . . . how long has it been? I don't know anything about your life right now."

"Oh . . . Jamie . . . " He swallowed. "After you died, I lost myself. I was completely inconsolable, they almost had me shot for cowardice. I was sent to medical— I don't remember anything from those weeks. Angie found me eventually— the war was already over by then. Ended about a month after you . . . " His eyes darted up; he wasn't sure how Jamie would take the news that if he'd only survived a little longer, they all could have gone home.

"I couldn't hold down a job," he continued. "Patrick was killed, I don't know if you remember, and Mattie's hurt, hurt bad. The girls moved to the countryside, and they asked me to come with them. But I couldn't leave Dublin. I couldn't leave . . . " *You. The memories we built here, the only happy moments in my life.* "I figured there might be another uprising, I thought maybe I could help, but . . . no, I'm full of shit. I wanted to help Ireland, I thought that would be what you wanted.

"I couldn't hold a gun anymore, I couldn't be in a military setting, it was too painful. I . . . " His voice cracked a little. "I put up a grave for you. I thought that would make up for it in a small way." He looked up at Jamie, his beautiful, perfect face just the way it always had been. "My life ended when yours did, Jamie. I couldn't go on without you," he whispered, putting his face in his hands. *I'm sorry I'm so pathetic.*

Lucas looked up. "It's been ten years. Ten years today." Jesus. No wonder he'd been feeling so strange lately, seeing Jamie, hearing Jamie . . . maybe heaven had some arbitrary time frame for getting expelled as an adorable ghost.

Jamie said nothing for a while, and Lucas couldn't bear to look at him. "You're not pathetic. I'm sorry it's been so hard on you." He touched Lucas's knee and their eyes met. "I was worried you weren't going to tell me the truth just now. I'm glad you did."

"Jamie . . . ? Did you know?" he asked, his voice barely audible. *How I have felt about you all this time? How I've obsessed and agonized over you for the better part of two decades?*

"Yeah," he said softly, not looking away. "I think I did."

" . . . And you still wanted to let me be a part of your life?"

"Yeah. You're my best friend, and I love you with all my heart." He smiled sadly. "Maybe that was cruel of me, eh? I'm sorry, Lucas."

That he couldn't give Lucas what he needed, what he wanted. That he didn't crush his hopes once and for all when there was still time.

"'S'not your fault. I didn't choose to be this way. I never needed that from you. Being near you was enough . . . your friendship was enough."

"I should have let you go. I should have pushed you away, I shouldn't have let you hurt like this."

Lucas felt cold all the way down to his bones, his eyes wide and his jaw clenched. "No," he whispered. "No, Jamie, no. Please don't say that."

The sound of Lucas's own voice was unfamiliar in his ears, the shrill tendrils of panic. He hated how vulnerable he was in this moment. He'd spoken so seldom in this room, had company so infrequently. Jamie could take his heart and crush it into dust. Jesus. This is why he'd never expressed himself in the first place. These emotions were foreign, old forgotten relics of his time before he lost Jamie. Life was much easier when he only felt misery and grief, damn it.

"You made my life beautiful. You made me want to live for the first time, you made me think I mattered. Please." He was trying in vain to stop the tears running down his face. "Please, Jamie, don't leave me again. I can't handle it. I can't."

Jamie tried to brush a tear off Lucas's cheek and sighed. "Right, no physical matter. Okay, Lucas. I'm not going anywhere. I'm with you. And I won't leave unless the Lord himself pulls me out of here. Fair?"

"Not to you. I don't want to keep you trapped here for the rest of my life. Then again, if I have a brain tumor it probably won't be that much longer, so . . . "

Jamie laughed. "You always see the bright side of things, don't you, boyo?"

His laugh was like bells, he was so dear, and Lucas found himself stupefied with the immeasurable love that was swelling in his chest for this man. It didn't matter if he was real, if he was a ghost or a devil, or nothing but a fraction of Lucas's steadily deepening madness . . . he was here, he was here, and Lucas was never going to let him go again.

1918

Lucas didn't care about the details of the battle, the mission, or any-thing that they were doing, really. They were in Belgium; Britain was finally getting the upper hand after four terrible years. By then, the Irish divisions had been largely split up due to poor recruitment, and the war was coming to a close. Lucas and Jamie had been kept together, thank Christ, and were due some leave any minute now. It couldn't be much longer now, right? How long could a war go on?

Jamie had been holding steady, as far as anyone could tell. He had his lapses of fear and panic, but Lucas had been able to shake him out of them relatively promptly . . . most of the time, at least. The weather was getting colder, and Lucas could only pray that the end of the war was in sight.

Jamie had been going over battle details with the men, his hair just brushing over his eyebrows in a way Lucas found charming.

"We'll flank them on the left." He pointed on the map. "Their sup-plies have been dwindling, I doubt we'll have much resistance. If we can break that port of communication, we're in very good shape for the next few week—"

A bullet came out of nowhere, ricocheting off one of the metal containers they had lying about. It struck Jamie in the shoulder from behind, sending him to his knees with a gasp.

Lucas saw red. He pushed the other men out of the way and began pawing at Jamie's clothes, trying to see the wound. *His lungs— oh Jesus what if it hit him in the lungs, I can't lose him, not now, not bloody now.* "Someone get a fucking medic!"

Jamie laughed and caught Lucas's wrists. "It's all right, pal. Doesn't even hurt much."

Still, there was a lot of blood on his coat, on Lucas's hands, and he helped Jamie strip down to his undershirt so he could see the damage. He'd never really imagined his first time disrobing Jamie would be like this, it was *substantially* less romantic than he had been hoping for but . . . Jamie's skin was so white and unblemished, free from the horrific scars that told the story of Lucas's life all too clearly. This gaping, bleeding wound was an affront to him, and Lucas tore his own sleeve off to put pressure on it.

The medic Lucas summoned determined that most likely Jamie's life wasn't in danger. Still, it would probably be for the best to send him to get the bullet pulled out and have some disinfectant applied.

"I'll be fine," Jamie assured Lucas. "You're really sweet to worry, you know that?"

Lucas felt himself blushing and cursed himself. "Shut up. Go get better before *I* shoot you."

Looking back, Lucas realized, that was the first time he'd heard Jamie's laugh in a very, very long time. Jamie's eyes had been worn and hollow for as long as he could remember, his voice was dry and mechanical. The bullet had barely fractured his shoulder blade and missed all of his vital organs . . . he'd been lucky. And luckier still to have a nice long chunk of time away from the shell-torn fields of Belgium while he recovered. Lucas thought it would be a really good change for him. Hell, it might even give them a chance to have some leisure time together. Lucas was well overdue some leave anyway. He could hardly get the full eight weeks Jamie would have for his convalescence, but he took about a week just at the end of Jamie's recovery period. Luckily, they'd been able to send some letters back and forth, but Jamie didn't sound like himself.

> *How is it? Boring, I bet. Captain Miller thought he got shot in the cock and went into a right flap. Apparently, it still works. He's bragging to the point where I thought he'd show it to me, and I'd have to shoot him in the jewels for real. You'd have laughed. Thinking of you, LC.*

> *Dear Lucas, It's fine here. Quieter. My shoulder feels better, they're thinking I'll be back in a week or two. James Murray*

> *We still on for meeting up in Ypres? You need to show me around.*

No reply.

> *Looking forward to seeing you. I miss you.*

No reply. It wasn't like Jamie, and Lucas had an awful feeling about all this. He was officially granted leave and took the train to Ypres, his leather bag heavy in his hands. He had been pining for Jamie and was looking forward to spending some time off with him. Those letters hadn't been very encouraging, but Lucas didn't want to assume the worst. *He hates you. He's going mad. You're going to lose him, he's breaking, he's broken.* He shook his head and imagined a world before the war. Where they could go back to the way things had been in Dublin, before John had been killed, before . . . before Jamie had started to crack.

Lucas was still wearing his uniform when he went to find Jamie. He watched civilians from under the bridge of his cap as he wandered the streets. The weight of the war was felt everywhere in the nation, to some degree, but it always surprised Lucas to see how normal life was even twenty miles away. Girls going to school, bakers selling bread; but for the headlines in the newspapers, it might have seemed a perfectly normal little piece of paradise. As if there weren't men a little over a hundred miles away spilling their blood, brains, and guts all over the earth.

Jamie was expecting him and waved erratically as he saw Lucas approach. Lucas trotted up and they exchanged a warm hug, a handshake that turned into a second hug, and a doe-eyed smile from Lucas before heading away from the barracks, hoping to forget everything for a little while.

"So, tell me everything!" Lucas's enthusiasm felt forced. There was something a bit off about Jamie, and he wanted to help however he could. "Screw any good nurses, Romeo?"

"What?" Jamie pinched the bridge of his nose. "No."

"Too ugly?" *Please smile. Please.*

"No."

"Jamie?"

Weary eyes looked down at him. "Yes?"

"I'm here for you. Whatever you need."

Jamie nodded and shoved trembling hands into his pockets.

The leave went by in a blur, the wound was healing well, but Jamie was still different. Lucas couldn't help but feel that he was a little more reckless than he normally was, a little more withdrawn. Jamie was smiling less, drinking more. . . He never went home with girls anymore, he never even tried. The little twitch beside his eye had returned, and as they slept side by side in the barracks, Lucas could see that his nightmares were coming back. Jamie lashed out in his sleep, whimpering and sometimes shouting at imagined enemies that hounded him relentlessly. Lucas did what he could, up to and including climbing into bed with Jamie to hold him and keep him steady while his panic ripped through him. Lieutenant Murray clung to him like an infant, fingers tearing at his clothes, his whole body trembling as he burrowed his way under Lucas's chin.

"Jamie . . . " he said gently into the darkness, shaking his shoulder, "Jamie, come on, we're not even in the battlefield right now, there's nothing to be afraid of."

Jamie's breaths were coming in steady gasps. His eyes were wide, and more than once Lucas had to cover his mouth to stop him from screaming. He made Jamie meet his eyes, as this sometimes helped to ground him, but there were whole days that passed where Jamie wasn't himself. Where he couldn't be calmed, couldn't be reached, where even Lucas couldn't soothe him. Jamie was getting further and further away with each passing day, and Lucas could feel his own heart crumbling to dust.

"Jamie . . . tell me what happened. Did they do something to you at the recovery center? Talk to me, I'm here."

"No . . . no, they didn't," Jamie replied, his voice low and soft. "But it wasn't like the first time. It wasn't just minor injuries being sent here, Lucas, it's so horrible. I saw a man with no face, no eyes, just an open, gawping mouth . . . and he screamed, Lucas, he never stopped screaming 'til they held him down and sedated him until he was silent . . .

"Christ, Lucas, Jesus Christ . . . some of them were from our unit, for heaven's sake. Ole Ken's got no legs now, he'll be pissing into a bag for the rest of his life—and Mack, you know Mack? His lungs, Lucas, they bruised so badly, he just— he was fine, and then little by little he choked to death on his own blood . . . he knew it was happening, Lucas, he knew, he knew, he knew."

Jamie trembled and licked his lips. "He begged me to help him, and I couldn't. They never stop screaming, Lucas, they're dying and it's all my fault, I can't help anyone, I can't—" His breaths came in little hiccupping gasps, his whole body shaking as they lay side by side. "Why do I keep surviving? Why does everyone else get hurt and I keep scraping by?"

"It's not your fault, Jamie, I swear to you it's not." Lucas had been saying this more often recently, with diminishing returns. It was dawning on him, and it had been for a long time . . . that Jamie was getting further and further away from him. He was going to lose him at this rate. "Jamie . . . I'm with you, I'm always with you, I'll always stand beside you and remind you that you're only human . . . You're not a monster, Jamie, you're . . . "—*the light of my life, my sin and my soul, everything, everything*—"you're so dear to me and it kills me to see you like this." His voice was soft and weak, he couldn't quite commit to saying the words.

Jamie's trembling lessened a little, yet he couldn't meet Lucas's gaze. "Jamie?"

Nothing. No light in his eyes, the man was a puppet.

"Jamie, look at me."

His beautiful face moved mechanically to Lucas, the muscles of his cheek and mouth twitching uncontrollably. His mouth opened, then shut, and he turned away once more.

It was like talking to a dead fish at the market.

They returned to the battlefield together after that, and despite everything, Jamie managed to keep his head together well enough to lead the men into battle for a few days. Maybe he wasn't completely mad, and Lucas didn't want to have him shipped off to CCS again for his shell shock. It had done more harm than good, last time. As Lucas feared, however, it wasn't long before the cracks in Jamie's mind began to widen.

It'd been a relatively calm day, actually— only two rounds of shelling, bit of rain, nothing out of the ordinary. They had been huddled up next to each other for warmth after they'd had their evening rations. Jamie was a mess. His uniform wasn't tidy, his hair wasn't combed, his stubble was coming up in uneven patches on his cheeks. Lucas had coaxed him into the officer's area and sat down beside him on his cot.

"It's all in my head, isn't it?" Jamie's eyes were dull and hollow, his voice was croaky. "The idea of being a hero, of saving the world, making it up to my father, none of it is real. I gave up my education for this, I gave up the chance to die beside my father, I . . . I dragged *you* into this mess, too."

"Jamie, no." Lucas had hugged him tight, releasing him only so he could look into his eyes. "I'd follow you into hell and back. There's nowhere you could have gone that I wouldn't stand beside you."

"That's what I mean, Lucas! *I* brought you here! *I* cost you your job and your home and your health and—and Mattie and Pattie never would have joined if you hadn't—Pat would still be— and Matt . . . "

It was true. But it had been Lucas's choice to follow Jamie, and he didn't blame him for it. They were both grown men, they both had to follow their hearts. Jamie had followed his heart to heroism, and Lucas had followed his to Jamie. "I don't care. You didn't start this war, you didn't gas my brothers, you didn't want any of this to happen. You're a good person, Jamie, a great man, and I wouldn't be here with you if I didn't think so."

"I'm so sorry, Lucas," Jamie whispered, and buried his head in Lucas's shoulder. "I'm gonna get us both killed, I know I am— I'm gonna cock up when it matters most and let you down—I let everyone down—I . . . I just . . . I just wanted to—"

"You won't let me down. You've never let anyone down. I know this isn't what you wanted, what you imagined, but we've survived this long and I'm gonna keep your head straight until we get home together. I'll protect you 'til the end of this, Jamie. I'll help you; I won't let anything happen to you. Just a little longer, okay? I promise you, Jamie—I'll help get you better, I'll keep you right. We'll go home, get back to our flat, I'll make us dinner, and we can drink beer and sit by the fire and just . . . be normal."

"I don't think I can ever be normal again." Jamie trembled against Lucas's skin and Lucas didn't know what to do or say. "I messed up, Lucas. I had this stupid dream of honor and glory and saving the world and what the hell good has it done me? All I wanted to do was make the world a better place, leave a mark on the earth that said James Murray did something and it mattered. It— it was so selfish, wasn't it? I didn't give a shit about Germany, about Ireland, about anything, did I? This war has destroyed me. I threw everything away, everything that mattered, my father, my career, my *mind* . . . I put you in danger, and for what?"

Lucas didn't know what to say to that. It was true. Neither of them would be in this mess if not for Jamie, but Lucas had never resented him for it. After all, it had been his choice to follow.

"Jamie . . . "

"I feel like a ghost, Lucas. Every moment, it's like my mind is broken. I can't. I can't do this anymore. I don't want to. I never feel safe. I never feel good. Every fucking second, it's like I'm dying, and I can't— I can't!"

Lucas held him in silence. What could he possibly say that would make this any better? He couldn't bear to watch him like this. He could scarcely remember the last time Jamie had been calm, had been happy.

It all culminated at the Battle of Courtrai. The bombs began falling, and Jamie ordered his men into action. Lucas stood at his side, watching over him as he always did. A shell exploded beside them, and a bit of shrapnel ripped through Lucas's arm, causing him to cry out as blood dripped down his sleeve. Two other privates closed in immediately to help.

"Lucas!" Jamie cried out, pulling out his pistol and pointing it at the nearest cadet. "Get away from him, you British cunt bastards!"

It was hard to hear what was happening, bombs were falling all around them after all. The two men looked confused and hesitated. Jamie's eyes were wild and erratic. He cocked his revolver and steadied his hand, the shot lined up perfectly with the young private's heart.

Lucas grabbed Jamie's wrist, pulling the gun away from him and meeting far more resistance than he was expecting. He didn't know what was happening, and in that moment, Lucas was genuinely afraid of what Lieutenant Murray was capable of doing. Jamie got a shot off before Lucas wrenched his gun away. The bullet missed the target, but the other men started to advance all the same. Shit, he was gonna get a court martial over this.

The gunshot in their close vicinity hadn't done much to help his mental state, and Jamie was flush against the wall of the trench, grasping at Lucas's sleeve like a child. Still, the other soldiers closed in on him.

"Back off," Lucas warned, and his eyes made it quite clear he would finish what Jamie started if he needed to. "Give him some space, I can handle this."

Jamie was whimpering, hyperventilating, his eyes were darting around in his head, and he seemed wholly unaware of where he was. A bomb went off close enough to send dirt scattering in their direction. Jamie screamed, clinging to Lucas. The two soldiers looked at him, a mix of pity and disgust creeping over their features. *He hates it here. He hates it here more than anything. Shit.*

"Quit your fucking gawking, give us some goddamn space!" Lucas barked a second time, his voice cracking. "He's not a coward!"

They backed away, presumably to go get some help because Jamie was going off the damned deep end. Lucas barely heard them muttering—"No bloomin' time for this, in the middle of a war for Christ's sake. Murray's fuckin' lost it."

Lucas didn't care, he was glad to be rid of them. It was hard enough to calm Jamie down with all the explosions still going off. Jamie screamed wildly, his hands were over his eyes, and his weapon had fallen into the mud. Lucas pulled Jamie into his arms and moved him against the wall of the trench. "Jamie. Jamie, come on, look at me." *Come on. Come on Jamie, please.*

He wouldn't, he wasn't there. His blond head lolling on his shoulders, his eyes wide, his white teeth a stark contrast with the mud on his face. He'd never been this bad before, and he was only getting worse.

"Jamie! Goddamn it! I'm going to protect you; I'm going to help you! I *promised* you!" Lucas tried again, his voice wavering as his fear and frustration began to surge forward. He shook his friend sharply by the shoulders, trying to knock the real Jamie loose from his terror and despair. How much more of this could he take? How much more of himself was it possible to lose?

"Jamie, for heaven's sake."

He couldn't see him like this. He was barely even Jamie anymore, he was just . . . a broken, beautiful thing.

"Lucas?" he whispered, as if seeing him suddenly. "Jesus Christ, Lucas . . . help me."

Oh, thank God. Lucas swallowed, wrapping his arms around Jamie's broad shoulders. "Jamie, I've got you," he said softly, cradling him. "I've got you." There were tears in his eyes, but his resolve was steady. "Look at me."

"Lucas . . . thank you." Jamie grabbed Lucas's hand and squeezed tight— he looked so damn peaceful. Even with the chaos that was descending around him, in this one small moment, Jamie was okay. It was him. Jamie was here, he was whole, he was lucid.

Thank God. Thank fucking God, it's him.

Their eyes met and Jamie smiled. Lucas smiled back.

With his other hand, Lucas slowly pulled out his revolver and pointed it at Jamie's heart. "I love you, Jamie. I love you."

Lucas squeezed the trigger and kept his hand as steady as he could as Jamie's blood sprayed all over his face. There was a moment of confusion or betrayal that crossed over Jamie's features, his smile still playing on his lips, his eyes trying to register what had just happened.

"Lucas . . . ?"

The steady thrum of his heart slowed quite suddenly, his hand went slack, and the life drained from his eyes. All around them, the war seemed to go quiet.

"Jamie?" Lucas whispered, his voice wavering, his head shaking with disbelief . . . The gravity of his action began to sink in. What had he done? What had he done!?

"Jamie!"

He shook his body, Jamie's blood still hot and slick on his hand. His blond head flopped over to the side, his mouth ajar. Jamie's beautiful eyes were still open, and Lucas let him drop to the soft wet ground, unable to support his weight any longer.

Jamie's body squelched in the mud, and Lucas fell to his knees and screamed.

1928

Lucas was almost afraid to sleep now that he had Jamie back. He was afraid of waking up, finding that Jamie had vanished, and realizing that it had all been a beautiful dream. He stayed up as long as he could, just talking to Jamie about this and that for hours at a time . . . just like they used to. Jamie seemed so young, still, he seemed so alive. Gradually, though, Lucas found sleep, and he awoke with a start, gasping Jamie's name.

"Heya! Don't worry, Lucas, I'm not going anywhere, apparently," Jamie said cheerfully. He wasn't wearing his military uniform anymore, rather one of the outfits he used to have as a student.

Oh, thank God he's still here. Thank Christ. Lucas smiled at him, rubbing his eyes. "Do you sleep? What have you been doing all this time?"

"I guess not! I watched you for a while, but I felt well creepy, so I nosed around the flat. Lucas, what the hell do you eat? I found an onion." He laughed. "So, you and I are going to the market and we're getting you some damn vitamins before you end up dead, too. I have to say, Lucas, not having a physical form is a bit shitty." He tried to hug Lucas and passed right through him.

"You never know, if we were both spirits, we might be able to touch each other. Cancel out the masslessness, maybe?" Lucas felt like he was weightless anyway, he felt like he could float off the ground.

Jamie pondered the matter. "Let's try and avoid it anyway; took me ten years to show up here again and I don't know how to locate other ghosts. Lucas? What do we do if other people can see me?"

"I already told you, I'll sell you to the circus." He grinned. "So, you'd better hope you're all in my head."

Jamie laughed and put on a transparent hat. "You're a cold son of a bitch, Connolly."

Lucas could see Jamie wanted to hug him, wanted to put his arm around his shoulders like he used to do when he was alive. Jamie had always been such a physical man . . . this must have been torture for him. "And you're still an idiot," he said affectionately. "Shall we?"

They went to the market together and sure enough, there was no widespread panic in Jamie's wake, no one fell to their knees and started to worship him . . . okay, the brain tumor theory was panning out well. Jamie didn't seem to be too bothered by his invisibility, though, and he cheerfully pointed at various produce items he wanted Lucas to buy.

"Oh! You have to get the carrots! Look how nice they are, Lucas! Oh, those sweets are new! Lucas, do you like them? Get some, tell me what they taste like!" He was like a little boy, and Lucas found it terribly adorable. He did as he was told and made himself the first nutritious meal in ages. The house smelled lovely, and Jamie settled in at the other end of the kitchen table while Lucas ate.

"I've been thinking about why I'm here and all that. You're the only one who can see me, right? So, I must be here to help you with something. Do you think I'm supposed to get your life back together? Show you it's okay to live?"

Without being a weird depressive obsessive mental patient.

"Jamie . . . " Lucas started, a slight edge to his voice. *Did he want to leave? Did he want to leave already?*

"Or maybe you have something specific you need to work out." Jamie thought about it. "Something related to me?"

The fact that I murdered you, probably. Lucas thought, swallowing. "Jamie? Is this whole ghostly existence painful for you?" His voice was small. As much as having Jamie's ghost floating around his head was a wonderful gift, he would gladly give it back if it meant granting Jamie peace.

"It's not that, I'm just really confused and lost. Lucas, I love you so much, I really do, but there are whole parts of my memories that are missing. I can't touch you, no one else can see me. What kind of life is this?"

"What kind of life is death? Christ, Jamie, that's a question." He laughed sadly.

"And then why did I come now? Why not five years ago, ten years ago? Who's to say I'll even be here in a month? God put me here for a reason, and I want to help you before it's too late. What the hell was the point of my life? I didn't do anything for anyone, I didn't even finish my studies." He looked at his hands and sighed. "You're my chance at redemption, too. Otherwise, I was just a coward who lost his mind in Belgium. I never did my father proud; I never gave my mother any grandchildren, I never helped anyone. And look what I did to you, Lucas. I ruined you."

Lucas shook his head, tears threatening to fall from his eyes. "No, Jamie, no. Your life had meaning. You meant everything to me, you were my sunlight, you were my angel. You still are. I've never forgotten you, even after all this time. Not a single day goes by without you in my thoughts. You were the best thing to ever happen to me. Never think that of yourself, never."

He'd robbed his friend of his chance at life, his chance to be redeemed in his own eyes. All Jamie saw were his failures, his inability to avenge John, to carve out meaning for himself, the happy simplicity of a wife and children who adored him. If Lucas had waited another three weeks . . . they would have gone home together. Jamie might have healed. He could have moved on.

"I was a damn liability to the army and . . . and they probably should have shot me for cowardice." Jamie swallowed, trembling a little. "Guess it's lucky the Germans got me first . . . "

He covered his eyes with his hand and let out a long, shuddering breath.

"Okay, Jamie," Lucas said softly. "Let's figure out what the hell is my problem and get you to heaven." He offered him a weak smile. "I'll be all right." He'd find Jamie peace, and once he was happy that Jamie was happy, he'd shoot himself in the head. His penance would be repaid if he aided Jamie in this matter, and . . . God. He couldn't face life without Jamie again, he couldn't do it. An eternity in hell would be preferable to losing this man once more.

"Really, Lucas?" Jamie asked. "You think we can? Brilliant!"

He put on Jamie's old jacket and met his eyes. "Of course, you dafty."

Jamie followed Lucas out the tiny flat and through the busy streets of Dublin, keeping his thoughts to himself. It wasn't like Jamie when he was a young man, an exuberant little chatterbox who saw the whole world as an adventure. This was more like Jamie in the war; a hollow, broken thing with pain etched in his eyes. Lucas hated to see him like this, to know Jamie was suffering again and it was all his fault. He took a deep breath as he approached his destination.

Jamie peered at the name on the door and gasped. "Angela! You're still friends with her? Lucas, that's great, how's she been? Did you two ever . . . ?" He had a sly little smile on his lips, and Lucas wondered sadly if Jamie had ever truly understood him, his nature. Well, he was about to.

"No, dummy. Now hush up, I've managed to trick her into believing in my sanity for this long." Lucas steadied himself and knocked on the door.

Angela answered and was seemingly quite defensive when she saw who her little houseguest was. "Lucas? What do you want?"

He deserved that. "To apologize, for a start. Can I come in, please?"

Jamie hovered in his periphery, cocking an eyebrow. "For what? Lucas, what did you do?"

Lucas shot him a look, then met Angie's eyes again.

" . . . all right, Lucas. But this better be good."

Angela took his coat and made some tea, seemingly incapable of being anything but an adequate hostess. "So apologize, ass."

"Ange, I'm sorry. I was rude and cruel to you, and you didn't deserve it. All you've ever done is try to help me, and I took you for granted. I've been having a hell of a rough time lately, much worse than usual, and I shouldn't have taken it out on you . . . or Ryan."

"Lucas? Who's Ryan?" Jamie paused, frowned, and silenced himself. Poor thing. This whole being dead thing must have been torture for him; he was such an inquisitive, personable man.

"That's a start," Angela acknowledged. "Forgiveness pending." She smiled a little, taking him in. "Christ though, Connolly, what the hell is going on with you now? You're . . . chipper? It's dead unsettling boyo— Oh my lord, did you patch things up with Ryan? Lucas, you sly dog! Man's a saint then, Christ! I never thought . . . "

"I didn't," he said, curbing the sharpness that normally would have been in his voice. "Angie, I don't know how to say this . . . "

She handed him a cup of tea and met his eyes. "Spit it out."

"You're going to think I'm completely mad. Off my nut. You're going to ship me off to the loony bin."

"I haven't yet, Lucas. And I've certainly had grounds." She touched his hand. "This is a good first step, talking to me about it. I'm really glad you're here, I'm really proud that you're trying. There's nothing you can say that will make me give up on you now. I've already invested a decade into this friendship, you know."

"You say that, but . . . " He sighed. "You know the last few months I've been a lot worse— my mind's been darker. I've been hearing Jamie's voice, seeing him places where I know he couldn't be." Lucas watched her reaction, but her features didn't change. Jamie was listening intently, too, his expression pained.

"It's been making me on edge, making me act erratically, I can see that now. I had Ryan back at my flat, we were gonna . . . " He looked at Jamie and swallowed. "And I heard Jamie's voice, clear as day. It was just like when he died, Angie, I closed my eyes and I could see his face losing its color, his eyes losing their light, I lashed out, and Ryan ran for it. I thought that was the end of it— I hoped it was the end of it. My guilty conscience stopping me from being happy, fair enough. Right?"

Angela nodded, clearly unsure where this was going.

"I came home after you and I had that argument, and as soon as I was alone, I could hear him again, I knew I was losing my mind. I shouted, I cried, I said it wasn't real. And then . . . there he was." He smiled a little, despite himself. "Jamie's spirit, clear as day."

Her eyes widened a little bit, and she took a little step back from him. "Are you serious, Lucas? Jesus. Jesus Christ. You need help."

"I know it sounds preposterous. I know I've probably lost my mind; I know you're probably wondering why the hell I'm telling you this, but . . . Angie, I think he's trapped here. He needs to help me finish some unresolved bull or he's gonna be stuck here, and I didn't know where else to turn."

Her expression softened a little, though she still looked a little disturbed. "Is . . . he here now?"

"Yeah. He's sitting on the couch." Lucas gestured over toward Jamie, who waved politely.

But of course, she couldn't see him. "Can you prove it?"

"That's the problem, he's either real or I have a brain tumor. I'm not even sure myself which one it is. Jamie? Can you think of a way to prove that I'm not *that* insane to Angela?"

Jamie thought about it. "It'd be something I know about her that you don't, right?"

He racked his brains, and Lucas watched him with wide, terrified eyes. He didn't know anything about Angela, he wasn't real, none of this was real, Jamie was dead and there was nothing he could do, he was insane, he was out of his mind, Angela was gonna have him shipped off and—

"Lucas! Lucas, stop, it's fine." Angela hugged him. "I believe you. Sort of."

Lucas trembled in her embrace. She couldn't have known the gravity her kindness carried. He himself wasn't convinced that Jamie was real. If they could prove conclusively he wasn't, if he failed to know a single thing about Angela that Lucas himself didn't know . . . then this was all in his head. Jamie was dead as he'd ever been, and Lucas was truly alone. If that were the case, his world would fall apart. "Thank you," he whispered, clutching her close.

"Shut it, you daft bastard," she said. "I'll help you, okay? We'll solve the mystery of your chronic assholishness and set Jamie free. Then maybe all three of us can move on with our lives and you can buy me a pint. Deal?"

"Yes." He stopped hugging her and took her hands. "You're a little bonkers yourself, you know that?"

"Aye. Makes life more interesting, doesn't it?" She grinned at him and sat down beside Jamie on the couch. "So. Where do we start?"

1918

Lucas didn't remember anything after watching Jamie fall to the earth, but the story came out little by little in what he could hear the nurses whispering through his drugged-up stupor. Apparently, he had gone berserk, would not stop screaming, and shoved his gun in his mouth. It was coming back to him, little by little. Jamie's blood still hot on the muzzle. It was salty in his mouth, but he didn't dare to spit it out. The metal clacked against his teeth as his hands shook in desperation, but Lucas had no bullets left. That was the only thing that had saved him. At the back of his mind, he could remember the maddening clicking of the trigger as he pulled it again and again to no avail.

"I have to be with Jamie! I can't let him go alone! I have to fucking be with Jamie!" His voice cracked.

The others didn't know what to do, and their eyes darted around like the flies that were coming for Jamie's corpse.

Tears were running down Lucas's face, and he scrambled to get Jamie's pistol from where he'd thrown it earlier. He crawled along the ground like an insect, Jamie's blood sticky and warm on his hand. Lucas just managed to grab it, pull it toward his face again . . . *I'll be there soon Jamie, wait for me, wait for me.* But two other soldiers found their mettle and tried to wrestle the gun off him, and he'd lashed out so violently with it that he cracked the eye socket of one of the poor sods.

Eventually help came, and they were able to overpower him, perhaps his grief made him weaker. In retrospect, Lucas was lucky they hadn't shot him right then and there. He woke up in the casualty clearing station with a sore head and an empty heart, awaiting medical and psychological evaluation. As soon as he was awake, he began thrashing around, striking out at the nurses and physicians who were trying to assess him.

"Jamie! Jesus Christ, I have to go back for him, we can't leave him there, we can't fucking leave him—he hated it here, he hated it so much! I promised him I'd protect him. I swore to him—I—!"

They had to sedate him and tie him down to the bed with restraints. He cried out in frustration, tears running down his face.

"Fuck you! Fuck all of you fucking cocksucking piece of shit motherfucking assholes! Let me out of here, I have to get to Jamie, I have to get him back . . . please . . . I promised him! I promised him!"

His mind was a blur. Jamie was breaking, Jamie was losing himself, No, Lucas was losing Jamie. But in that last moment Jamie had come back. He was himself; he was whole— was it a mercy? God damn it! He had to get him back. What had he done? What had—

He went limp as the sedatives took hold of his muscles. In his dreams, Jamie died over and over and over again. There were always screams in the night here, and Lucas couldn't tell which were his. Time passed, he didn't know how long he was there . . . the days were slipping together as there was nothing but grief to punctuate them.

He awoke with a start and found Angie sitting next to him, patting his hand.

"They told me you were here, Lucas." He couldn't bear to see the pity on her face as she stroked his palm with her thumb. "What happened?"

No one had been able to get a clear version of events, apparently, and certainly not from Lucas. At the moment, the official version was Murray had become violent and erratic, and Connolly had taken him aside to calm him down as he'd done a hundred times before. Murray was shot; Connolly lost it. The idea that Lucas had killed Jamie on purpose had never crossed anyone's mind, it seemed. After all, why the hell would he do that? They were always together, they loved each other. It was no wonder that Lucas had snapped when the Lieutenant died.

"I . . . " Lucas wanted to cover his face with his hand but couldn't, as his wrists were both tied to the bed. He groaned in frustration, a small little noise that died in his throat. "Ange . . . Jamie's dead," he whispered, tears pricking the corners of his eyes.

"Jesus. Lucas . . . " Angela whispered, her hand covering her mouth. "I'm so sorry. What happened?"

"You can't tell anyone," he started, struggling against his restraints again as he tried to sit up. Angela undid the leather cuff and let him do as he wished. "You can't say anything."

"Okay, Lucas, I won't." Her voice was gentle, but he wasn't sure he believed her.

"It's like I told you before, he wasn't all there, Angie, he was so scared, he was panicking, I thought he was going to shoot one of the men—" Lucas took a long, shuddering breath. "They'd hang him for cowardice if—if he . . . so I took his gun off him and . . . "

And he was himself, and he was whole, and he knew peace. I had him. I had him fucking back and I couldn't lose him again.

" . . . and he couldn't defend himself and he got hit."

I shot him. I shot Jamie. I shot Jamie and his blood got on my face and I watched the life drain from his eyes and he's dead and I should be dead with him. The words hammered at the back of his teeth, but he couldn't say them. He felt like he needed to throw up.

"He went quick, he didn't suffer. But I don't want people to know his last seconds were like that. I don't want anyone to think he was a coward— he wasn't, just— he couldn't take it anymore. I couldn't protect him from his mind anymore." Lucas lifted his hand from his eyes. "Little by little, he was losing himself." *And I was losing him, too.*

Angela was quiet for a few moments. She cleaned her glasses as she considered what Lucas said.

"Are they going to shoot me?" he asked, his throat dry. "For treason? For disobeying a commanding officer? For . . . any of this?"

"No, Lucas. They're not going to shoot you."

His disappointment was probably obvious. He shut his eyes and felt the hot tears running down the sides of his face. "They won't let me get his body. I'll fight for them; I'll do whatever they need I just— I need to get him back. He hated it there, Angie. He won't be able to rest there."

She took his hand in hers and stroked it. "The war is over, Lucas."

"What? How is that possible? Who won? How long have I been here?"

"We won," she informed him, as gently as she could. "You've been here less than a month."

No. He covered his eyes, disappointment and rage crushing his heart into dust. Never in his life had he felt pain like this. Less than a month? If they'd just held on just a little longer, Jamie would have been— "No, no, no, no." The muscles in his neck tightened, he banged his fist against the mattress. "Jamie . . . Jamie, I should have . . . "

Angela climbed into the bed with him and cuddled up close, trying to ease the pain he was in, if only a little. "I know how hard it is. It felt so awful when Euan was killed. Grieve. It's okay to grieve, it's okay to feel like the world is ending."

Lucas was not an overly affectionate person, but he curled into her embrace and let himself weep. Less than a month. If they'd just held out another few weeks, if Jamie had gone back for medical evaluation, if he'd been signed off— if Lucas had just been patient . . .

The war was over. The war was over, and Jamie was never ever coming back.

Lucas shut his eyes and Jamie's face conjured itself up at the back of his eyelids, that confused little smile stuck on his lips, blood dribbling out of his mouth, his eyes glassy and unfocused. Every second since he'd woken up in the hospital had been haunted by his sin. Jamie was still alive and thriving in Lucas's mind. And then just . . . dying over and over and over again.

Help me, Lucas. Jesus Christ, help me.

Lucas tried at times to figure out just what it was that had driven him to murder the only man he had ever loved. He didn't consider himself very intelligent, and certainly had no business trying to dissect the psychology of his singular lapse in sanity. Was he trying to spare Jamie a court martial? Was it so black and white that he was guilty of the crime of cowardice? A death with dignity, a death in the arms of a loved one— was that the gift he had imparted? No. He knew for certain his ambitions could not have been as noble as that. As he moved into the darkest parts of his mind, the bile began to rise up in his throat and his head pounded. He couldn't face this demon yet; his mind would fall apart if he tried.

Lucas cuddled into Angie's breast, and she kissed the top of his head. His whole body was trembling, and he felt absolutely pathetic.

"It's not your fault, Lucas. You spent the last two years protecting that man with everything you had. You couldn't protect him forever; you couldn't protect him from himself."

Jesus Christ, Lucas. Help me. Blood running out of his eyes, his body heavy and cold, covered in mud, the skin rotting away, ribs poking through the hole where his heart used to be, he's dead he's dead and you killed him, you murderer.

"Ange. I can't live like this. Get me a gun. Please help me die."

Her body stiffened. "Lucas, I can't do that," she said, still stroking his hair. "You're so young, Lucas. You've got so much to live for."

He looked at her bitterly. "What? What the *hell* do I have?"

She met his gaze, her own eyes hard. "Your sisters, you asshole. And Matthew—he's got it a heck of a lot worse than you do."

Lucas was mortified. Of course, he had Angela, too. Christ, he *was* an asshole. He nodded and glanced away from her dark brown eyes.

"And your friends, the other boys in your squad who love you and would lay their lives down for you. Then there's me, of course, the stupid bitch who can't tell a lost cause when she sees one." She smiled at him and brushed his tears away. "And . . . there's Jamie."

Lucas stiffened. "Watch it."

"No one on earth loved him as much as you do. He's alive in your memories, Lucas. The way he laughed, the color of his eyes, how he made you feel . . . it's all there in you. If you kill yourself, he dies all over again with you."

His suicidal resolve began to waver. Angela was right. Lucas's whole face was dull and disinterested, but he nodded and threaded his fingers together with Angela's. He didn't deserve to be happy; he didn't deserve to rest with Jamie. He deserved to live the rest of his life suffering— that was the price of his sin.

He'd live another fifty loveless, empty years if he had to. For Jamie's sake, he'd endure.

1914

Lucas slumped home one night after work, his face swollen and a patch of dried blood dusting his lip. One of the other laborers had sucker-punched him in the nose over a misplaced hammer, of all things, and Lucas didn't want to dwell on it too much. He plopped himself down on the couch and pretended to read the paper, not quite up for facing his flatmate. Jamie had of course been horrified to see the state of Lucas's poor visage and wouldn't stop badgering him about it all throughout dinner. Jamie cleared the table and moved to study, but Lucas caught him glancing at him again and again to the point of being annoying.

Lucas ignored him and tried relaxing. He shut his eyes and listened to the sounds of Jamie breathing, of his teacup hitting the table when he set it down, and of the soft sound the pages made when Jamie turned them. That would have been a perfect evening for him, really. Quiet, calm, safe. But it wasn't meant to be, Jamie wasn't going to let him have peace.

"Lucas, I've been thinking . . . " Jamie paused and bit his lip as he always did when he was trying to make something a little less awkward. "Have you ever considered maybe going into a different line of work?"

Lucas shot him a glare. "No, Jamie. I *love* putting bricks in a line, I love working with a bunch of smelly drunks, I love getting hit in the face for saying the wrong thing to some jackass who reminds me of my father. Why do you ask?" He regretted his tone the second the words had left his mouth. Jamie hadn't meant any damned harm. "I'm sorry. You know I can't be picky."

Jamie squeezed his shoulder and looked into his eyes tenderly. "I know. But listen, I was talking to the head of school today, they're looking for someone to be the new custodian. I put in a good word for you. It's a bit of a pay rise, the work is steady, safe— it's mostly just keeping the grounds and classrooms clean, and you're so good at that anyway. And we could walk to school together every day, I wouldn't need to worry about you while you're at work . . ."

Lucas had had a few close calls, not just with other coworkers but with unsteady working equipment, freezing temperatures, frequent injuries to his hands and back. He knew Jamie fretted.

"I just thought it would be a nice change," Jamie concluded.

For heaven's sake, Jamie. It was such a sweet, kind thing to offer but . . .

"Wouldn't you be embarrassed?" Lucas asked, setting his own teacup down on the table. "For all your friends to see that you live with a caretaker?"

That was what mattered most to him. He'd work digging ditches or laying bricks for the rest of his life if he thought it would make Jamie happy.

"Of course not. You're my best pal, I'm not ashamed of you. All my friends already know about you anyway; it's not like you're some big secret." Jamie had finally managed to make a few decent friends since he'd started his studies. Lucas really, really didn't want to create any difficulties for him.

He frowned. "They know you live with a working-class gutter rat who tried to rob you?"

"They know I live with my best friend, Lucas Connolly, who saved my ass when I moved to Dublin and has been nothing but a brilliant companion and asset to me ever since. They know that you can't go to university, but that I think you're a good person who deserves happiness. And they know that if any of them have a problem with you, I'm not going to spend time with them anymore."

Lucas's face must have looked quite touched, or moved, or confused, because Jamie moved across the couch and hugged him for a good long while. Lucas squeezed his eyes shut and enjoyed the embrace, silently hoping that Jamie couldn't feel the way his heart had sped up.

Jamie pulled away and met Lucas's gaze. Christ, Jamie's eyes were so beautiful, they were like a bright summer sky, they were like the ocean on a clear day. *Kiss me. You fucking asshole, kiss me.* He wanted to touch his face, he wanted to cup his cheek in his hand and bring their lips together. He wanted to get fucked on this couch.

"So, what do you say? Shall I tell the head of school you're interested?"

Damn him, damn everything about him! His bloody perfect easy smile, his stupid beautiful golden hair, his stupid gorgeous face.

"Yeah. If you're sure you won't feel weird about it, I'd really enjoy that. You're right, it would be a nice change."

Lucas never knew how Jamie managed to work little miracles like that, but he always could. Within a week's time, his nose was more or less healing, and he had started his new job at Trinity College. His mother was delighted for him and saw it as quite a step up from his previous work. Lucas tried keeping away from Jamie for the most part, he really didn't want to embarrass him, but Jamie wouldn't hear of it.

His friends still kept an offensive distance from the surly newcomer, but Jamie didn't really seem to care. They ended up eating lunch together nearly every day, and Lucas had never been happier.

The work was easy, but he enjoyed it. He liked bringing order to chaos. He could take his time and focus as he gradually made the world more beautiful.

Still, Lucas worried that the cost to Jamie was too high. Jamie was supposed to be making friends and connections for his future career. Spending most of his time with a custodian was not going to help him one bit. So, when Jamie approached him with a novel social idea, he felt he could hardly turn him down.

"I'm meeting some of my school pals at a pub tonight, you should come! Andrew's getting his girlfriend to invite some of her mates from the nursing school, so there'll be loads of girls to choose from! Please? You're gonna have to lose that cherry eventually anyway," he said with a smirk.

Oh Jamie, if only you knew. Lucas sighed and nodded. "Do they know you're inviting me?"

"Yup! I want them to get to know you better, I thought this would be perfect. I'll lend you a nice jacket, we can head out together."

Lucas was a little tense on the way to the pub. He wasn't really sure how this was going to go. He'd do it for Jamie, but he wasn't happy about it. They arrived and Jamie's friends flagged them down, and Jamie treated Lucas to a beer.

Jamie introduced everyone, they awkwardly acknowledged one another, and Lucas watched the doors for a while, knowing the girls would be a welcome distraction.

"So, this is the famous Lucas, eh?" One of the lads broke the ice. "I've heard loads about you. Jamie tells me you guys met as kids. What was he like?"

Lucas glanced at Jamie, who gave him an encouraging nod. "Christ, he was just as stupid as he is now. About a thousand times cuter too, dunno what the hell happened to him. Time is cruel."

That garnered a laugh, and three rounds of drinks later, they were all the best of pals.

He was quite enjoying himself by the time the women arrived in a pack and descended on the men. Jamie of course was the favorite, and the whole lot of them gathered around him first.

"Andrew, you didn't tell us about this one!" a lovely buxom brunette protested, batting her eyelashes at him. "I'm Maggie, hi." She had pert tits and a nice ass, her eyes were a charming blue, and she was petite and adorable. She was exactly Jamie's type and Lucas hated her for it.

"Hi, Maggie," Jamie purred easily. "You know, there's a very good reason why Andrew didn't tell anyone about me . . . you see, I have a terrible secret." He paused for effect; the girls were eating it up. "I'm actually a vampire. I have a terrible propensity to consume the innocent, and I have an irresistible attraction to necks."

Lucas hated to watch this and was glad at least that his mates all seemed equally put off by his display.

"Really?" Maggie giggled. "I've never met a vampire before." She tilted her head a little so her creamy white neck was more exposed.

"James Murray, at your service." He pressed a soft kiss to the perfect skin and smiled. "You should be more careful, my sweet, vampires are very dangerous, you know."

Lucas turned away and focused on his drink; he didn't want to see any more. The other girls admitted defeat and gradually made the acquaintance of the remaining law students, gradually pairing off and canoodling at various parts of the pub. None of them wanted to speak to Lucas, which was all the same to him. Jamie and Maggie had long since disappeared, and Lucas decided maybe he should just go home. This wasn't exactly Lucas's idea of a fun night out. Stumbling back to the flat alone, the man he loved wrapped up with some idiot floozy— he shook his head. He didn't want to think about them together.

"That's always the way, isn't it?" one of Jamie's friends said quietly, smiling at him with warm eyes. "Not enough girls to go around. Guess us losers will have to stick together, eh? Dillon, cheers." He clinked their glasses together and finished his beer.

"I was thinking about leaving, actually," Lucas replied. Crap, there was something about the way Dillon was looking at him . . .

"What's the rush? We could get to know each other a little better. I was just thinking of going cottaging this weekend," Dillon said softly, a tiny smile playing on his face. The guy knew polari . . . he was interested. They made eye contact, and Dillon licked his lips a little.

"Mm. Are you so? You're into rough trade, Dillon?" He had to confirm, it wasn't safe otherwise.

The other man nodded.

"I'm flattered but . . . you're Jamie's classmate; it's not a good idea." If Jamie ever found out, Lucas wasn't sure what he would do. "I'm going to go. It was nice meeting you."

He made his way to the cloakroom to get Jamie's jacket and paused once he was past the threshold. He could hear Jamie, just barely, groaning softly in the corner. Maggie's thin fingers were tangled up in his golden hair, she was pressed up against the wall. Jamie was holding one of her legs up while she used the other to support herself.

"Oh, James!" she crooned delicately, as Jamie's hips rolled upward. He silenced her with a kiss and his beautiful body moved effortlessly with hers.

Goddamn it, Goddamn it Jamie. Have some decency, you fucking prick. Lucas doubted he even knew this woman's surname. At least he didn't tell her to call him Jamie, at least he'd denied her that one little intimacy . . . it hurt all the same. He grabbed his jacket and found Dillon by the bar, looking pleasantly surprised to see Lucas approaching him again.

"Come on. I don't have all fucking day," Lucas muttered, taking Dillon by the wrist and dragging him toward the toilets for a proper cottaging. It was Jamie's lips he imagined against the back of his neck, Jamie's hands working his belt open, pushing him up against the wall. Lucas shut his eyes and his stomach lurched pleasantly as he recalled the strong, confident movement of Jamie's narrow hips. That whore's name on his lips, her hands in his hair, his soft little moans as he—

Fuck it. Fuck everything. He felt disgusting when they were finished; he didn't even make eye contact. He didn't want to speak. It had been a long time since he'd had sex with anyone, longer still that it hadn't been for money.

"I'll see you," Dillon offered lamely. "Right?"

"I work at the university, stupid. It'll be hard to avoid you," Lucas snapped. "Don't talk to me there, I don't want Jamie to know. I suspect you don't either," he said, a slight threat in his voice. Dillon had a lot more to lose, after all. "This was a mistake. I'm leaving."

He wrapped Jamie's jacket around himself and went home without another word. He washed himself off and went to bed as soon as his hair was dry. He didn't want to see Jamie right now; he didn't want to smell Maggie on his skin. It wasn't the first time Jamie had had a girlfriend or female companion, not even close, but it was the first time Lucas had seen his fornication firsthand. He felt sick with envy, absolutely disgusted with himself. Jamie was the first person to make him feel like he mattered, that he was worth something, that he could have self-respect and make a positive contribution to the world.

There was a light around everything Jamie did, a beautiful glow that gave Lucas peace . . . and for the first time since they'd met, that halo was diminishing.

1928

Lucas wasn't really sure where to begin. His psychosis with Jamie had been decades in the making, and he seriously doubted there was an easy fix to his problem. "Uhh . . ." He cast an uneasy glance at Jamie, suddenly regretting his decision to ask for Angela's help while Jamie could watch and hear everything he was going to say.

"Well, start at the beginning. You loved Jamie for years, right? Was he the first man you ever fell in love with?"

His eyes widened a little bit and he looked at Jamie in a panic. He hadn't been ready for that, to have his feelings broadcast so abruptly and bluntly.

"Angela!" he said sharply, watching Jamie's expression. It was sad, confused, troubled. If anyone was going to tell Jamie about how Lucas felt, it should have been Lucas. Could have softened the blow a little that way, given him some warning. But to be fair, he'd been sitting on his feelings for nearly two decades. Maybe Angela had been right to give him that last little push.

Angela looked at the empty spot on the sofa beside her and shook her head. "Ah. Right. Lucas, are we going to be able to have a productive conversation about this if —uh—Jamie is here? Is there a way to make him, say, sit in another room?"

"I'm not sure," he admitted. "To both questions."

Jamie looked really hurt, and he started to get up to move away. Could he leave? Was it physically possible? Lucas didn't really want to find out. "Jamie, stop," he called out. He couldn't watch Jamie walk away from him again.

"I'm sorry, Angela. I think this is a conversation Jamie and I need to have privately."

"Can you, though? Part of the problem was your fear of losing him, your fear that revealing your true nature would make Jamie stop loving you. And now you finally have him back." She reached over and touched Lucas's hand. "And no offense, but you're not the most open person in the world, especially about your feelings, *especially* when it comes to Jamie."

"I know you're right," he admitted, trying his best not to look at Jamie's sweet, familiar face. "But he needs me to do this. If there's even a chance that I can help him . . . well, suffice it to say I'd endure much worse for him."

Angela smiled. "Okay, Connolly. You came for my advice, and so I'll give it to you. If Jamie is real, he probably has some unfinished tasks he needs to help you with. Since you're the one who can see him, we can assume that it has something to do with you. I'd dig deep and try and find the parts of your time together with him that have left you with the most regrets. Might also be that Jamie has some unfinished crap of his own he needs to sort out, and he might need you to act as a vessel to enable his freedom."

Lucas nodded and tented his hands. "Yeah. Hell, if he can get my head sorted out, he'd more than earned his way into heaven. I guess if he's not real, maybe my mind is trying to work some bull out. I guess part of my worry is that if I solve my problem, and he leaves, I don't know what I'll be left with." A chance for a fresh start, maybe. Did he deserve one, even now? Would Jamie want him to be happy if he knew the truth? "The other possibility is that he's real and I need to help him. . . or he really needs to help me. Or I really have a brain tumor, in which case he's here forever and I'd best make him pay some damn rent. I have no clue which one it is."

Angela licked her lips. "He's here, right? Right now?"

Lucas frowned. "Yes. He's beside me."

"Can . . . I touch him?" She'd always been a scientific sort, deep down.

Jamie nodded, and it struck Lucas all at once that his silence was out of place and unwelcome. He was suffering, he was struggling, and it was Lucas's fault *again*. " . . . Jamie? I—" God, he must have looked so stupid. "I'm sorry all of this is so hard. I just want to help you because I care about you. Please try and remember that."

Jamie managed a tiny smile and Lucas attempted to rest a hand on his knee, coming into contact instead with the sofa cushion.

"Jamie said it's fine," Lucas permitted, and Angela groped the air where Jamie was seated. Her hands went through his form. It didn't seem painful; his shape stayed the same.

"Can you feel him, Lucas?" she asked, fingers fluttering through Jamie's face. Jamie moved aside a little, not thrilled with this development.

"No. He can't touch anything, either. It's not easy for him. Ange, knock it off, you're probably tickling his brain." He took her wrist gently. "Here, put your palm up straight." She did as she was instructed, and Jamie did the same, bringing their fingers together. "He's touching your hand."

She treated the moment with a reverence that surprised Lucas, considering she very obviously thought the whole thing was a load of shit. "Thank you, Jamie," she whispered. "I'm rooting for you both. Please come see me if you need anything at all, okay? I love you, you miserable bastard." She gave him a quick hug and kissed his temple.

Jamie floated beside him in silence as they made their way back to Lucas's flat. He wondered what in particular had set Jamie off . . . what had turned his mood so sour so suddenly. Lucas locked the door behind them and looked up at Jamie, his cheeks a little red and embarrassed.

"Jamie? Please say something."

Jamie's expression was often difficult to read, and ten years of being apart hadn't made it any easier.

"Was Angela right? Were you in love with me?"

"I . . ." Lucas hadn't known fear like this since the war. It wouldn't look great if he threw up all over the pavement; it certainly wasn't a good start to this whole new honest open communication thing. Not great for the sex appeal angle either, to be honest.

"Yes."

His hollow companion said nothing.

Lucas tried meeting Jamie's gaze, but it was killing him to see those cerulean eyes so completely devoid of warmth. "I . . . I thought you knew— earlier—earlier I asked you and . . . you said . . . "

"Christ." Jamie shook his head. He looked hurt; he looked disgusted. "I thought you were asking if I knew how it was my fault that your life had fallen to pieces. I never— Jesus, Lucas."

Lucas had never felt so awful about his nature before. He'd never wished he weren't a perverted abomination so much in his entire life.

"Jamie . . ." What could he say? How could he apologize for a piece of his soul?

"So, we were never friends, then?" Jamie shook his head. "It was all just a lie? All this time you lived with me and—and what, you had some designs on me?"

"What? No!" Lucas stood up, starting to get angry as well. "How can you say that? After everything we've been through together, after everything I've done for you, how can you ask me something like that? Yes, I was in love with you, but more than that, I *loved* you. Time and time again, I pushed away those feelings of sexual love—of romantic love, even, because being with you meant more to me than anything.

"I know you never saw me that way, I know it never even crossed your mind. But when I was sixteen, I decided that just being with you was enough for me. That I'd never fall in love again, that I'd never get married or settle down, that I'd stand by you and be your right hand until you told me to fuck off. That you meant more to me than sex or love or— that you meant more to me than anything. I'd kill for you, Jamie. I'd die for you. And for the last ten years, I've lived only for you."

Lucas stared at him with bloodshot eyes, daring him to question his motives again.

"Say something!"

Jamie looked chastened, remorseful. "Lucas . . . I'm so sorry."

"All your bloody girlfriends, I supported you and I prayed for your happiness. All those times you got so drunk you couldn't see straight, I held you and I cleaned you up and made sure you got home okay. When your father died, when you needed me in the trenches . . . I was there for you, you prick! I never asked questions, I never judged you, I never walked away from you. How— how could you even . . . ?"

Jamie tried to embrace him, forgetting once more that it was impossible. "Lucas. Look at me."

Lucas glared at him. Unbelievable. This absolute fucking bastard. Lucas had always made a point to keep his feelings so, so well hidden but . . . maybe deep down he'd assumed Jamie had noticed, had known, had even reciprocated a little. Lucas had just been too much of a coward to make anything happen.

"You're right. I shouldn't have spoken to you that way. It . . . was just a shock, is all. I'm sorry, Lucas."

"Tch," Lucas scoffed, refusing to meet his eyes once more.

Jamie swallowed. "From the bottom of my heart, I'm sorry that I questioned our friendship for even a second. I can't even imagine how hard this all must have been for you . . . to hide your feelings for so long, to have me react like that when you finally told me the truth. Please, please forgive me."

Lucas looked up, seeing real fear and remorse in Jamie's eyes. He softened a little, nodding at his friend. "I never said anything because I knew you didn't— I mean . . . I think once or twice I hinted but . . . I knew you weren't a homosexual." He swallowed. He didn't like using that word. "And I didn't want to spoil what we had just because of my stupid feelings. Beyond romantic love, I loved you like a friend, a brother, a partner. I didn't need to get fucked to be happy, I just needed to be with you. I still feel that way."

Jamie's smile was cautious and reserved. "Can I ask you more about it?"

Lucas was still feeling a bit prickly, but he nodded all the same. This was exactly the sort of closure that Angela thought he needed, after all.

"Were you always —was it just me or—? Are you attracted to women at all?"

Jamie's curiosity was fair enough. He'd probably never had a conversation like this before. Never met a real live homosexual in all his naive days. Not knowingly, anyway.

"Yeah, from when I was quite young, I was always a little different . . . I was always more drawn to boys than I was to girls. It wasn't just you, no. But you were the only man I ever loved, and . . . after I met you, I didn't want to be with anyone else. And to your last question, no. I've never been attracted to a woman."

"But we met when you were so young, Lucas. Surely you weren't— you haven't been celibate that whole time, have you?"

"No, I haven't. Even when we were living together, I had the odd tumble with a stranger. But I respected myself a lot more after I met you, I was a lot more discerning. And it wasn't often, mind you. Sleeping with other people was always quite hollow and empty—I'd compare them to you, and they'd always fall short. I still do that, even now. I don't like how I feel afterward, I always feel dirty and drained. Heh. I don't think I ever had a healthy relationship with sex. I don't think I ever had sex with anyone where it felt right." Christ, what was he doing?

"What do you mean? Does—I mean how does it even work?"

Lucas laughed so hard he started coughing. "Jamie, do you really need me to explain the mechanics of two men having sex? Now?"

"You could draw a diagram."

Lucas threw a pencil at Jamie, which went right through him. "You're such a tit. What I mean is— I guess it's hard to find someone to have sex with when you prefer men. It's hard to know who's interested; it's hard to know who's safe. You proposition the wrong man, and you end up in a labor camp for years. So, I kinda took what I could get. Never thought I deserved better. Some of 'em were violent, some of 'em were disgusting, some of 'em were pedophiles."

"Jesus, Lucas. I'm so sorry."

"I used to wonder if—" He shook his head. Surely Jamie didn't need to hear about this.

"Tell me, please."

"If getting raped as a kid made me this way. I doubt it, to be honest.

I kinda decided maybe I was born like this. I always thought it was a punishment, or a curse." He licked his lips. "But then I met you." *And the world didn't seem so dark anymore.*

Jamie's brows were pinched together. "That must have been dreadful."

Lucas's curiosity got the better of him. "What would you have done? If I told you I wanted you like that? Be honest."

"Lucas . . . I don't know. Honestly, it probably would have made me rather uncomfortable around you. It probably would have changed everything between us. I might have avoided you, assumed the worst about you, maybe. I don't think we could have stayed as flatmates, but . . . "

Jamie's spirit turned pink.

"To be even more honest, I *had* thought about it. How much I liked touching you, being with you, how beautiful you were to me. Christ. I never— I mean in a million years I never would have labeled that *lust*, I guess. I just . . . liked it when I could feel you. I had a dream we kissed."

"A nightmare then?" Lucas stuck his tongue out.

"No, no it was a good dream, I woke up really . . . confused. Conflicted. Thought about it a lot afterward. Felt dead weird about it, actually."

Lucas's eyes were saucers. "Jamie, I hate to break it to you, but I think you might be a bit of a fairy yourself, boyo. Just a little." Good. Deflect. Try not to get caught up in how awful it is that they could have—*would* have been lovers. Doesn't hurt at all.

"Does that even happen?"

"You dafty. Yes. People just don't talk about it."

"I wonder what my father would have thought."

Lucas didn't even want to think about it. John Murray was a very sweet but religious and traditional man. He probably would have kicked Lucas out, blamed him, and made sure that he and Jamie never saw one another again. Just like with Danny. No, there was a very good reason Lucas kept his dick to himself. "Your father loved you." Lucas decided. "Even when you were being an idiot."

Jamie smiled. "So, do you have anyone special now or . . . ?"

Lucas took a deep breath. "No. There was someone, but I just couldn't get it together. I don't care about sex anymore, really, but I am a man, still. Sometimes you just need to be close to someone to feel alive." His eyes flicked up to Jamie, dead Jamie. "To feel human."

"Wasn't it painful for you? To be so close to me and not say anything? I was always so touchy-feely with you."

"I made my choice," Lucas affirmed, managing a little smile for him. "You were my sunlight, my angel, my reason to get up in the morning. Any pain was more than worth it for the joy and fulfillment I got from being with you."

"God, Lucas. I wish I'd known. I'm sorry."

"Jamie, can we leave this topic for now? I just need a little time to process everything. Please." He doubted he could take much more emotion at the moment; he was liable to explode.

"Okay. One last thing, though. Is the fact that you were in love with me"—Jamie's cheeks flushed scarlet—"Is that why you haven't been able to move on?"

"I think it's a big part of it. But more than that, I feel like I should have been able to save you. I feel like I let you down. How can I be happy when you're gone? How can I live and thrive and make something of myself when you can't? We were so young, Jamie. I should have gotten you out of there. I wanted to protect you from all the awful things in the world."

"Lucas, don't be silly. It's not your fault that I died." Jamie smiled warmly at him and put his slightly glowing hand on top of Lucas's. "I would have died a lot sooner if it wasn't for you, probably. You protected me, you stood by me, and you kept me sane for two miserable years in those trenches. How can you blame yourself for that? People die in war zones, Lucas. I know you would have taken that bullet for me if you could have. You would have gone to hell and back for me. It's not your fault I died, please stop blaming yourself for that."

Oh, Jamie. No. Lucas's hands trembled; he could actually feel his breakfast starting to creep up his throat. He couldn't— Jamie trusted him so implicitly, believed the best in him even now, even now. Jesus. Jesus Christ, Jamie no, no, no, no.

"Lucas? What's wrong?" Jamie's smile was warm and tender, his eyebrows knitted together with concern.

Lucas, in contrast, felt like a ghost. "Jamie—you don't understand—I—"

"Lucas . . . *shhh*," Jamie coaxed, sitting closer to him. "It's not your fault I'm dead, it's not your fault I'm trapped in limbo, there was nothing you could have done to stop that bullet from killing me." He smiled and put a weightless hand on his friend's shoulder.

"I absolve you of your guilt."

Lucas put his head in his hands and breathed in and out. Idly, he wondered how hell could feel so tepid and gentle.

1904

Thunder crashed outside Jamie's home and Lucas awoke with a start. Annoyingly, he had to piss, and he somehow managed to dislodge his tiny body from Jamie's possessive grip. He carefully tiptoed through the halls, looking for the washroom. In his house they had a communal toilet that the whole block shared, but he strongly suspected Jamie probably had something a little nicer. *All right, toilet. Where the hell do rich people shit?* He bit his lip and resolved to see if John was awake. The alternative was to go outside and pee on a bush or something. He heard voices and peeked his head around the corner, not wanting to interrupt.

"He's only small, but . . . " John said. "Poor little thing, he was half-frozen when Jamie found him. I just couldn't bear to leave him out there, not with the rain as it was."

"John . . . you don't know who he is, he could be a gypsy boy or he may have bad people who'll want him back. Or they might have left him there on purpose, hoping someone would take him in so he can ransack the place." The grandmother shook her head. "He's very sweet though, isn't he? And the Bible says, 'but when you give a feast, invite the poor, the crippled, the lame, the blind, and you will be blessed, because they cannot repay you.' I suppose the real problem is how hard it'll be when you and Jamie have to go back to Anna and wee

Fiona. You can't take him with you, can you? He'll just be back on the streets."

John just shook his head. "I don't know. I have to pray on it."

Lucas tiptoed off, not wanting to be caught eavesdropping on something like this. *Fuck. Fuck these people, fuck them for being giving and kind, fuck them for taking him out of the rain.* It was so embarrassing, so awful to be gawked at like a Christian charity project. Gypsy fucking orphan, Jesus. They probably half expected him to steal the silver, although to be fair, he had certainly been considering it earlier. He shut his eyes and tried ignoring his angry bladder, scampering back into the room and huddling into the bed with Jamie once more. Jamie wrapped his arms around Lucas's body and made a contented noise. Lucas was exhausted and found sleep quite easily in the cozy room.

He woke up the next morning still cuddled up in Jamie's arms. With a calm little sigh, he snuggled in closer, enjoying the warmth of the blankets and the way the rain sounded as it pelted against the windows. He still had to pee, but it could wait, he was too comfortable and didn't want to move.

Jamie groaned pleasantly as he awoke, startling away from Lucas when he opened his eyes. "Huh? Oh—oh of course, good morning, Lucas! Did you sleep well?"

Lucas nodded against Jamie's chest.

"Want to check if breakfast is ready? Granny makes really nice porridge."

Lucas just nodded, rubbing his eyes. The house smelled wonderful, like fragrant tea and warm, clean clothes, and he couldn't help but relax as he made his way through the tidy home. Jamie let him use the toilet and wash his face, and they both scampered to the kitchen to eat their fill.

"Did you sleep all right, Lucas?" Jamie's granny placed a generous portion of porridge in front of him, with a drizzle of honey oozing down the top, and she'd added some fresh red fruit that he wasn't sure he'd seen before.

"Yes, thank you."

"Lovely. Lucas, would you mind saying grace for us?"

Lucas panicked. Oh Jesus, his family never said grace, shit, okay. "I don't— my family never—" Of course they didn't. They weren't a well-bred godly group of people like the Murrays— fuck!

John smiled at him, warm and sad. "It's all right, Lucas. Eat up, as much as you want."

Lucas was hungry enough that his embarrassment abated a little. He poked the red thing with his spoon before putting it in his mouth. He was suspicious of it but found the little berry to be tart and delicious. Jamie liked his tea with lots of milk and sugar in it. Lucas had always had his black but imitated his host— damn, it was lovely.

"This is really nice," Lucas said after he'd wolfed everything down. "Thank you. I'm really happy right now." His cheeks were red and he felt like he could cry. *Was every day like this for Jamie? Warm and safe and good?*

In response, John tried to pat Lucas's head, stopping when the little boy flinched violently away. "Sorry, son." John muttered. He made a point of always letting Lucas see where his hands were after that.

Lucas wasn't stupid; he knew this couldn't last for very long. But the stupid part of him was imagining what life would be like if the Murray family took him in. If maybe they went to their holiday cottage together. He could play with Fiona, get a kitten and laugh when it chased mice in the field. Jamie could read to him every day, and he'd always have porridge with honey, with berries . . . It was a beautiful dream, but why should they take in a street urchin like him? He had nothing to offer; his own father knew what a useless leech he was, how he'd ruined their lives and kept them all miserable. And his manners weren't good; he saw that now. He couldn't even say grace right.

"Well now, Lucas, do you want to come with Jamie and me while I go shopping for books? It looks like the weather will be a little bit nicer today, maybe we can visit the park as well."

Lucas nodded, not wanting to be alone in the house without Jamie. John found some of Jamie's old clothes, which fit Lucas perfectly, and he marveled at having shoes that didn't get filled with water the moment he stepped outside. They made their way down Grafton Street, wandering in and out of bookstores. Jamie pointed out various things along the way that caught his interest: the new sweeties at the store, the toy soldier set he'd had his eye on for his birthday, a big fat pigeon that was splashing its way through a puddle.

Lucas just stood back and listened, smiling a little as Jamie talked and talked and talked. He was an angel, he really was. The world was brighter for his presence; everything he touched was sweet and good. The picture Jamie painted of Dublin was one he'd never seen before, where even the oil streak in the gutter had incredible and intense rainbow beauty to it. Lucas wanted to get lost in this world. He wanted Jamie to narrate the rest of his life.

John, of course, peppered the experience with little purchases here and there. He bought each of the boys a small bag of sweets, a little metal soldier figurine (Irish class, of course), and mildly suggested avoiding the pigeons for fear of catching communicable diseases. He seemed happy, and kept patting the two boys on the head. Jamie and Lucas trotted beside him, playing with their new toys and laughing all the way down the pavement.

"All right boys, one last stop," John smiled as they walked toward a hole-in-the-wall bookstore just at the edge of town. "Not a lot of people know about this place. The owner has the best collection I've ever seen. I'm going to try and get him to part with a classic I've had my eye on for ages."

Lucas was getting a little nervous; they were getting near the King's Inns, and he knew his way home now. Nothing good happened to him here, nothing ever had. "Um . . . Mr. Murray, I don't think we should . . . "

"Lucas? What's the matter, son?"

"It's just we're really close to where my Da' works and . . . "

John looked at him kindly and fluffed up his hair. "Do you want to go look for him, little one?"

"No! No, it's not that, he's just— he's a bit . . . " He avoided John's eyes, self-consciously rubbing at the bruises on his neck.

"Ah. Well, I think we'll manage all right. You tell me if you start to feel unsafe, okay? It'll just be a minute."

Lucas nodded, keeping an eye on the door the whole time they were in the shop. He knew his father would never step into a book-store, but he was wary all the same. John picked out his books and put them in his well-worn leather satchel, smiling down at the boys. "Shall we?"

Lucas allowed himself to be optimistic. They walked out of the shop together, Jamie excitedly telling Lucas about what delectable feast his granny was going to treat them to that evening.

"Oi!"

Oh no.

"Oi! Hey, you with the glasses!"

John turned around and alarm crossed his face as the drunken figure staggered toward him. His eyes were bloodshot, his hair a mess; he reeked of drink and could barely walk.

"The fuck you doing with my boy?!"

Lucas had always been small for his age, but in that moment, he wished he could just disappear. He hid behind Jamie for a moment. The older boy put an arm in front of him to protect him.

"Ah, is Lucas yours? He was alone in the street last night, so I—"

Mickey's fist collided with John's face, smashing his glasses. *Oh Christ, oh shit, why? Please don't let him be hurt, please!*

"You kidnapped my boy! You buggering pervert, you kidnapped my son! I'll have you hanged for this so I will, you piece of shit!" He pulled Lucas behind him, shielding him from John.

"Da', he didn't!" Lucas protested, trying to hold him back.

Mick flung out his fist and sent Lucas flying, his lip split in half.

"Think you're better than me? Huh? You think you're bloody better than me, you—"

He interrupted himself to vomit on the pavement. He raised his head, hands supported on his knees. Jamie's father looked down at Mick, who turned his attention to his young and battered son. "You think you deserve anything better than what you've been given, Lucas? What a *joke*."

Lucas didn't really cry anymore, but Jamie did. He looked positively petrified. John was bleeding and cradled his face, surely debating what to do. On the one hand, he was terrified of Lucas's brutish father, and on the other, he felt it would be awful to child in the hands of such a man.

Lucas longed to leave with them, to let his father become a fading memory, like an old scar. But the Murrays probably didn't want him, and Mick's pride wouldn't let him give Lucas up to them. The dirty little boy would stay with his own flesh and blood, and the rich educated bastard could go to hell. Lucas knew it was stupid to fight against the inevitable. It was only going to make things worse for him, more dangerous for Jamie and John.

"I'm sorry," Lucas said gently to both of them, bowing his head.

"C'mon Da', let's go home, okay? Mum'll be wondering where we are." He wiped some of the blood away from his lips with his sleeve and managed a small smile for Jamie, but the other boy could barely even look at him.

Lucas and his father marched away from the Murrays, back toward their hovel. Mick dragged Lucas roughly by his arm, ignoring the gazes of people in the street who seemed mildly perturbed by the sight of a small child with blood running out of his mouth.

It was better this way. Lucas destroyed everything he touched, and he wasn't going to do that to Jamie and his family. He didn't belong in Jamie's life, anyway. . . John hadn't tried to intervene on his behalf, and the sensible part of Lucas was glad of it. A part of him was furious, though. How dare such a kind and caring adult not step in to protect him from his belligerent, drunken father? What kind of Christian was he anyway?

The familiar stench of stale urine assaulted his nostrils, and Lucas knew he was home. His father fumbled with his keys, growing frustrated when he couldn't keep his hands steady enough to unlock the door. Lucas tried helping him, and was met with a backhanded slap to the face. His poorly coagulated lip wound erupted fresh, and he backed off, not in the mood for any more beatings.

When Mick eventually managed to open the door, he dragged Lucas inside and shoved him against the wall. He towered over his son, swaying mildly. Lucas tried to imagine him as a reed by the side of the lake near Jamie's house. He knew better than to smile at the image, and kept his face still. He wondered where his mother was . Normally, she would have intervened by now. Maybe she was trying to get the doctor to do something for Jessie.

His father took a moment to collect his thoughts, seemingly trying to remember just what he was so angry about. It came to him, and his whole face brightened "Stayed the whole bloody night with some strangers, did you?" Mick demanded, yanking Lucas's arm so hard he pulled him nearly to his feet once more. "Think you're too good for *me*, eh? Think you can do any better than I did? I was a brat, too, boyo. I had dreams, I wanted a better life for meself, and look where that got me." He spat on the ground and shoved Lucas back against the splintery wall. "Fucked your mother once and now look at me! Me whole life ruined, all my damned money going to feed a bunch of miserable little parasites! And you . . . you started it all, you!

"You want to live with rich people? You think you can escape this life and leave the rest of us behind?"

Lucas was weary; his eyes felt dull. He'd heard it all before. There were only so many times he could be blamed for an entire family's misery before he stopped listening. But blank apathy wasn't the response that Mick had been hoping for, so he upped the ante.

"You think that man wanted you? You think he wanted to waste his time and money on a gutter project like you? The Bible wants people to be charitable, but Christ, Lucas . . . you're even dumber than I thought. Did he bugger you, Lucas? Did you let him? You make me sick."

Lucas wasn't even sure what he was being accused of anymore, so he let the words wash over him. He knew John hadn't wanted him; he knew the whole thing was a stupid dream . . .

"And the boy," Mick started, pulling his flask out of his pocket and downing another a swig of whatever swill he'd managed to salvage that day. "Rich little shit like that . . . maybe I should take him for a night, see how *his* Da' likes it."

Lucas's eyes widened and he stood abruptly, his jaw tight. "Don't. Don't you go near him! I'll stop you!"

Mick smirked. Apparently, he'd struck a nerve.

"Will you, now? A little pissant like you? What the fuck are you gonna do about it?" He cracked his knuckles and loomed over his small son, licking his teeth. "I'll find him, I'll drag him back here, and I'll—I'll cut off his finger to send to his Da'. He'll pay a fucking fortune, I bet. Show him what a friendship with a lowlife like you is worth, eh?"

Mick made his way for the door, and Lucas wasn't sure if he was serious. He couldn't risk it; he couldn't let Jamie get hurt for his sin of kindness. Lucas grabbed a knife off the kitchen counter and hesitated for a moment.

"Da', stop. I'm warning you, leave Jamie alone." His hands were trembling around the hilt of the blade, an impossible certainty coursing through his veins.

"His name's Jamie, is it?" Mick smirked. "I bet he cries easy."

Lucas charged, plunging the blade deep into his father's leg. Mick seemed almost impressed for a moment before he howled in pain, pulling the offending weapon from his sinewy flesh, and letting it clatter to the ground. "You miserable little bugger," he muttered, trying to stanch the bleeding with his hand. "You ungrateful bastard!"

"Stay away from Jamie," Lucas warned again. "I won't let you hurt him." He had never physically resisted his father before. If Mick had ever turned his attention to his mother or siblings, Lucas tended to use distraction tactics, redirect the anger toward himself to protect them. But this was more than he could take. For the first time in his life, Lucas saw his father for who he was: a weak, pitiable drunk who could barely keep himself standing and could only win fights against children. He was pathetic, and Lucas marveled at the clarity.

Mick advanced on Lucas, striking his head against the wall so hard he almost lost consciousness. "Don't . . . don't touch him . . . " He watched his father apply a tight cloth bandage to his leg and stagger out the door. "No . . ."

Lucas tried to follow him, but he was dizzy and disoriented. He slid against the rough wood of the wall and weakly called for his mother. Perhaps she had waited until Mick was out of the picture before she tended to her ailing child, cradling his head in her lap.

"Lucas! Oh, thank God you're all right. I thought . . . "

Yes, his Ma was there, after all. She sniffled a little, stroking the hair out of his face.

"Where were you last night? What did your father say?"

Lucas groaned, running his hand through his hair and finding it caked with dried blood. "Oh . . . oh no . . . I have to . . . " Lucas struggled to his feet, feeling nauseous and disoriented.

"Baby, no," Molly cautioned gently. "I don't want to lose you, honey, please."

Jessie started crying, and a pained expression crossed Molly's face.

"Lucas . . . please don't do anything stupid," she begged, moving slowly to get back to her sick little girl.

Lucas saw his chance and slipped out the door once her attention had shifted, running as fast as his legs could carry him to Jamie's grandmother's house. Deep down, he knew Mick didn't know where Jamie lived but . . . He was a vengeful, miserable prick. It wouldn't take long to locate a rich barrister's house in this part of town.

"Please be okay. Please be okay. Please, please, for the love of Christ don't let that bastard have found him . . . "

He pressed his face to the window and let out a sigh of relief when he saw Jamie, his father, and his grandmother, all gathered peacefully around the dining table. John's left eye was nearly swollen shut, and he had a different pair of eyeglasses on, but he seemed none the worse for wear, really. Jamie was sticking very close to his father, not smiling broadly like he had been for the past day, but not traumatized, at least. Seemed like, anyway. *Thank God.*

Lucas shut his eyes and moved away from the window. His father was an ass, but he was right that he couldn't be a part of Jamie's life. They were from two different worlds. Lucas couldn't even imagine a man like John raising a hand to a woman or a child. And Jamie was better off being away from people like Mick, away from gutter rat charity projects like Lucas.

He threw up in the street as he walked home; his head was hurt much worse than he'd realized. To hell with it, he'd manage somehow. Molly hadn't noticed that he'd left, thankfully, and he curled up next to Becky in the little bed that they shared.

Mick staggered home a few days later, his leg more or less healed, the grudge still fresh in his mind. He blamed the injury and didn't work for weeks; it was a hard bloody winter. Lucas was glad to pick up the slack, and had to take up a route as a newsboy, a chimney sweep, and any job a tiny boy could manage.

Little by little, he tried to put Jamie out of his mind. He wanted to forget about the Murray's house in the country, the picnics with his family, that halo of light that had made the boy's golden hair shimmer under the glow of the streetlamps. Lucas had to grow up quickly, for the sake of his siblings. But he kept Jamie nestled in his heart. The sweet, gentle little boy who had taken him in out of the rain and made him feel safe and loved. Jamie had the kind of life he only dreamed of, the sort of warm security he wanted for his family. Lucas had never dared to keep something like that in his heart before; an ideal to strive for, a dream to hold onto. He wouldn't let that go for anything.

1918

Angela hadn't been lying to him. There was no court-martial, he wasn't hanged, and he wasn't dishonorably discharged. Lucas did everything he could, but in the end, he wasn't given permission to find his best friend's body. It killed him. It fucking killed him to leave Jamie behind.

Jamie, like many others, was laid to rest in a mass grave in foreign territory and was lucky that anyone had bothered to place earth over him at all. Lucas fought them every step of the way, all he wanted was a chance to . . .

"To do what, Lucas?" Angela had asked him after he'd needed to be physically restrained in his bed once more. "To go to some mine infested hellhole, pull back the mud with your bare hands, and . . . and what? Go through all the mangled corpses one at a time until you found Lieutenant Murray? You could try for a hundred years; you'd never find him."

He knew she was right, but on some level felt she must have been exaggerating a little. Surely the bodies of soldiers weren't treated with such disrespect, surely someone would know— he just . . .

"I *promised* him I'd keep him safe, Angie. I *promised* I'd get him home."

He thought of Jamie's body alone in the mud, his lonely spirit wandering the Belgian fields and wondering where Lucas had gone. Christ, maybe he was an angry ghost out for revenge— maybe all he wanted was to throttle Lucas for ending his life. Lucas would have let him though; God knew he deserved it. If he'd only been patient, Jamie would have . . .

He shut his eyes and wondered what would happen if he defied orders and went searching for Jamie's remains. He could see his fingers in the earth, tearing up the soil and digging through the corpses until he found Jamie: mottled, rotting, cold. Lucas felt sick imagining him like that, and wondered if he would have had the stomach to face Jamie now. The hole in his chest . . . his flesh stiff and malodorous, his glassy eyes still open, that little look of betrayal still etched on his face . . . *I'm coming for you Jamie, I'm not going to leave you here, even if—*

"Lucas, you have to let it go." Angela put her hand on his and squeezed gently, pulling him out of his spiraling obsession. "His body is just a body, he's not in it anymore. His soul has left this awful place and is probably watching over you from a cloud in heaven. Please. Please don't do anything stupid."

She was right. She was right. Lucas felt the last remaining part of his heart crumbling as he acknowledged the truth: Jamie was gone. There was nothing meaningful left of him, and no amount of impossible suicidal grave desecration was going to change that. As much as Lucas wanted to punish himself, to at least make it feel like he was *trying* to do right by Jamie, the fact remained that he would never, ever be clean of this heinous deed.

Lucas had been a bit of a heretic for a number of years now, and wasn't sure he believed in God or souls at all . . . but if there was such a thing, he and Jamie would never be meeting one another again. His sin of murdering Jamie had surely condemned him to hell, and he could accept that. He'd made his choice, after all.

He was discharged in due time, awarded a medal for bravery or heroism or some bull he didn't care about.

Angela went with him back to Dublin, but did have her own life to get sorted out.

"Promise me you won't kill yourself as soon as I leave you alone." She pinched Lucas's cheek. "I'll be in touch. I love you, okay? Life is worth living, you are worth saving, and I'll always be here for you." She kissed his forehead and left him alone in the street.

Lucas had two stops to make today, deciding to get the easier one out of the way first.

He made his way to the sadly familiar Henrietta tenements where his surviving siblings still resided. It made it easier to find one another again after the war and everything that came with it, Becky had suggested, if they stayed in the same place.

Lucas braced himself and knocked on the door, completely unsure of where his keys had gotten to. Jessie opened the door and squealed when she saw her big brother.

"Becky! Mattie! It's Lucas! He's back!" She threw her arms around his shoulders and kissed him all over his face.

"Hey there, little fish," Lucas said softly, chuckling. "Miss me, eh?"

Ugh, it felt weird to be here. It hadn't been his home in such a long time but he could hardly go back to Jamie's flat now. It dawned on him that he didn't really have a home anymore.

"Of course, you dafty! We were starting to assume you'd run off and joined the Belgian chocolate-making society!"

"They made me a very tempting offer. But I said no, I have a little sister who needs someone to pinch her cheeks now and again." He pinched her and looked toward the hallway, surprised his other siblings hadn't made an appearance.

"Is Mattie . . . ?"

"Becky's with him. It—it just takes time."

Lucas nodded and followed his little sister to Matthew's corner of the flat, which was dark and smelled like . . . death, an odor Lucas was all too familiar with by now.

He'd heard about what had happened in vague terms. "Caught under heavy fire, Patrick Connolly lost in battle, Matthew Connolly suffered severe injuries to his face and limbs." Lucas had been avoiding this moment, unsure he could bear seeing how badly his brother had been wounded. He'd been so wrapped up in his own grief with Jamie that he hadn't even had time to send a card.

"Mattie? Lucas is here, petal," Becky said gently, opening the curtains for him. "Do you want to see hi—I mean, do you mind if he visits?"

Light bathed the room and Lucas covered his mouth with his hand when he saw just how bad "severe injuries" really were. His brother's face was covered in gauze, a sickly yellow-red fluid soaking through much of it. He'd never see again, they'd told him. The gas had burned his eyes beyond saving, and the last thing he'd seen was his twin brother choking to death. Just peeking out from the borders of his bandages were the margins of normal skin, meshing with the thick and red ruined mess that made up the majority of his face. Matthew's hands were mangled, too, maybe not beyond use but . . . He was seated in a wheelchair, his left leg ending abruptly in a tight mess of gauze and dried blood where his knee should have been.

"Mattie," Lucas managed, his throat suddenly dry. *What on earth could he say to him? 'Looking good?' Christ.* "Long time no see—I mean—"

Matthew managed a little smile. "Lucas, calm down. Life is hard enough without avoiding any words related to vision, yeah? Sit, sit. Let's catch up. I bet you look like shit, right?"

Becky's shoulders sagged a little with relief. Mattie seemed all right with everything, more than all right. "I'll let you boys talk. And yes, Lucas looks like shit," she said pleasantly, going to join her sister by the stove.

"Fuck off, Becks," Lucas muttered, smiling a little anyway. His facial muscles felt tired and out of use, but he had to admit it was sweet to be with family again. Jamie's family would never see him again; Jamie's family would never get to smile like this. *He's dead and it's your fault, you killed him, you killed him, you—*

"Lucas?" Mattie said suddenly. "Can you open the window for me? I hate the way it smells in here."

Lucas nodded, then remembered Matthew couldn't see him. "Yeah, sure." He cracked open a window. *Christ, the alley piss smells better than Mattie's bandages.*

"So . . . " Matthew began, as though used to making small talk to people horrified into muteness by his injuries. "How was the war?"

Lucas laughed a little abruptly, a single cough-like noise that fell flat in the stale air of the room. "A bit shit, honestly. And how was it for you?"

"'Bout the same." Matthew's whole body tensed. .

"Mattie, what's wrong? Do you need an analgesic?"

"I can't. The girls spend enough on me as it is," he hissed, breathing in and out slowly and steadily to calm himself.

A few moments of silence passed between them; Lucas didn't know what to say. Yeah, Jamie was dead. But complaining about that in the face of Mattie's injuries seemed disgusting. Lucas envied Jamie for being gone, for being free . . . but no man envied Matthew.

"Lucas, say something," Mattie implored. "It hurts. Say something. Anything. Take me out of my head for a goddamned second."

"Jamie's dead," he blurted out, mostly because that was the only thing he had thought about for over a month.

"Oh . . . Lucas." Mattie's mouth opened a little, then closed. "How bad was it?"

Was he maimed? Was he burned? Was he cast into blindness and terror before you walked home without a fucking scratch on you?

"It doesn't matter," Lucas said. "I don't know what to say, Matthew. Tell me how I can help you."

"Jesus, Lucas. Just don't . . . don't pity me like this. Be normal with me. Tell me I'm an ugly fucker, tell me nothing changes between us." He laughed; his whole body shook as his laughter gradually morphed into sobs.

Could he even cry anymore? Did he have eyeballs? Little shriveled balls of rubbery uselessness or just empty holes where his smoky gray eyes used to be? He was only nineteen . . .

"I'm scared, Lucas. The world is empty; my body is broken; my twin is gone. No woman's gonna love me like this. They said I'll live; they said the infection probably won't kill me." He hiccuped a little, his mangled hands clawing at the bandages near his face. "Is God punishing me?"

What was his brother thinking? Was the injustice of it all clawing at his throat and threatening to emerge as a scream? *Why me and not you, Lucas? Why me and not you, you abdicating sodomite coward? You shoulda been there, you shoulda been with us and not with him!*

"No, Mattie," Lucas said. "Ma' woulda said He's testing you. You . . . you're lucky to be alive."

"Fuck you, Lucas. You don't believe that."

"You're right." Lucas sat down beside him and put a gentle hand on his knee. "Being alive is fucking hard. I can't imagine how much harder it is for you now. But I've been thinking about mortality a lot recently. We're the soldiers who made it home, Mattie. It's our responsibility to live for the ones who didn't. To keep Pattie and Jamie alive in our hearts because no one else is gonna do it. No one else knows what we know, how they lived, how they died . . . that they mattered."

Matthew was silent as he listened.

"I tried to shoot myself when Jamie died," Lucas added. He hadn't admitted that to anyone, not even Angela. "I had the gun in my mouth. It was out of bullets. I asked my friend to help me kill myself when I woke up in the hospital, too. I know you have it so much worse than I do. I know I shouldn't even be talking about this . . . but I decided to keep living. I don't deserve the peace that an eternity in hell would grant me, I don't deserve to stop suffering. But you . . . "

He looked at his brother. Life felt like a punishment, sometimes. For Lucas, he'd accepted that as penance for his sins, but Matthew hadn't done anything wrong. He didn't deserve to suffer like this. Mattie wouldn't even be able to shoot himself if he wanted to; his hands didn't work right.

"I . . . I can set you free, if you want. I'm already going to hell."

"Fuck you, Lucas. Get away from me," Matthew hissed, wrenching his leg away from his big brother's grip. "What the hell is wrong with you?"

Lucas shook his head. "I wish I knew. I'm sorry, Mattie."

"Rebecca! Get him out of here!" Mattie hollered, hissing in pain as the words left him. "He's a monster!"

Becky turned to face them and gave Lucas an apologetic look. She seemed used to these outbursts. Silently, she guided her oldest brother out of the room and gave him a hug.

"He needs time," she said. "Can I make you some tea?"

"No. I'll be in touch," he lied. How could he face any of them now? His misery paled in comparison to what Matthew was enduring, and the girls were going to be burdened with him for the rest of his life. Now he'd bared his murdering heart to his only remaining brother, and had offered to violate the Fifth Commandment on his behalf. Their lives were dark enough without the shadow of his evil looming over them. Lucas hugged his sisters and collected himself. Then he left, away from his family in the wretched part of Dublin, and toward—where?

He couldn't put it off forever . . . he didn't have anywhere else to go. Slowly, he made his way back to the enormous flat that he used to share with Jamie.

Fuck.

His hands trembled as he put the key in the familiar lock, and he braced himself for the inevitable agony of his home with Jamie . . . without Jamie. He opened the door and it hit him all at once. The place smelled like Jamie; his clothes and books were everywhere. Lucas could almost imagine Jamie waking up, sniffing the air, and wondering where the hell his breakfast was. It felt like life would stop now that Jamie wasn't in it . . . but the world kept spinning, and there was nothing he could do about it.

He went to the table and began sorting out their massive pile of mail. It was pretty straightforward. Lucas didn't get much post, and he'd figure out what to do with everything addressed to Jamie at some point. Strangely, there was a letter for him near the top of the pile, with a neat feminine script playing across the envelope. It wasn't Angela; it wasn't his sisters. Curiosity got the better of him and he tore the envelope open.

Dear Lucas,

Sorry to send you a letter out of the blue like this—my mind is all over the place. If you're reading this, you must be back at the flat. Jamie loved that place, didn't he? Lucas, you're more than welcome to stay in the flat as long as you want, I don't know what else I could do with it. John probably would have wanted to sell it but . . . I can't really put you out like that, can I? Not after the good friend you've been to Jamie all these years.

Oh, Lucas, I feel like I know you. Jamie loved to talk about you whenever he visited home. He thought you were the greatest man in the world. Jamie loved you so much, and I know this loss is likely hitting you pretty hard, too. I'm so sorry, Lucas. I'm so sorry you had to be there, to see it happen. It must have been so horrible for you. I can't even imagine. His superior said he didn't feel any pain—he wasn't lying, was he, Lucas?

There were little tear stains on the document, and Lucas tried ignoring them.

Anyway, sorry to ramble on like this. I'd love to hear from you, to meet you in person, put a face to the name I've heard so much about. You're always welcome in my home, Lucas. I know it's silly, but I feel so close to you, I want to help you if I can. Fiona wants to meet you, too, I think she imagines that you're very handsome—but don't tell her I said that!

Please don't worry about paying rent, the flat is paid for and I'm not losing anything by letting you take care of the upkeep. I hope to hear from you soon. This is such a terrible time for our country. Every single street in the village has a black banner in one of the windows. I hope they all died for something.
With all my love,
Anna Murray

Lucas shut his eyes and crumpled the paper up, guilt and love and regret nipping at his soul. He didn't deserve Mrs. Murray's kindness, her generosity, her love. He didn't deserve to live in the space he shared with Jamie, in this beautiful apartment that had given him the happiest years of his life. He pulled out a plain piece of paper and sat down at the desk.

Mrs. Murray,
Sell the flat. I don't need it. Jamie didn't suffer.
Lucas Connolly

1928

Lucas went to bed early that night, not wanting to sit with Jamie for any longer than he had to. He had never admitted to anyone that literally—and directly—Jamie Murray's death had been entirely his fault. That he was in every sense of the word a murderer, and the architect of his own misery and loneliness. How could he ever admit that to the increasingly dissatisfied spirit that endlessly haunted him? Jamie *hated* being dead. Lucas watched from the corner of his eye as Jamie moved to pick up a book and his hand whizzed right through it.

"Damn it!" Jamie growled, his aura flashing crimson. "How long does it take to get used to being a ghost?"

"I dunno. With Mattie's injury it was over a year, I think. I guess he didn't lose his whole body though."

"It's not funny."

". . . I know it isn't. I'm sorry, Jamie."

". . . It's not your fault, Lucas. Get some rest."

He pulled the covers over his head, not sure if Jamie was going to sit and watch him sleep or—or whatever the hell a ghost would do to occupy its time in the late hours of the evening.

"Lucas?"

Christ. For fucking Christ's sake.

"What is it?"

"I really am sorry about before. About doubting you."

Lucas peeked over the edge of the blanket and saw Jamie's forlorn expression. "It— don't worry about it, Jamie. It must have been a tremendous surprise for you to find out I was 'like that.'"

"Doesn't matter. I know you. You deserved better than how I treated you."

"Jamie, come here," Lucas offered, moving the covers aside like it made a difference. "You can sleep here with me if it's not too weird for you now. I forgive you; I love you, and I want to help you."

Jamie swallowed. "It's not too weird for me. Is it too weird for you?"

Lucas smiled. "Nah. Besides, even if you wanted to fool around, it's not like it's possible with your little impairment."

"You're such an ass." Jamie smirked and moved toward the mattress all the same. It took him a moment to figure out how to lie down effectively, since he went through the whole bed if he wasn't paying attention. It would have been funny if it wasn't so sad. Lucas smiled at his efforts.

"We used to do this all the time, eh?" Jamie offered, settling inside the mattress but under the covers as much as was possible. "I loved being close to you. I always felt safe with you."

"Me too," Lucas whispered. "I bet the other guys talked about it, you know. How close we were." *How often we slept in the same bed.* Once again, he found himself wondering if Jamie was real, if all of this was just a figment of his mind as it slowly self-destructed. Jamie was still so agreeable, but at times Lucas wondered if he was just saying things that his own mind wanted to hear. It didn't matter if he was real, it didn't matter. He was never going to get another chance to make things right like this again if he lived to be a hundred.

Jamie reached out his transparent hand rested it over Lucas's shoulder. "I hated to see you the way you were when I first got here. Not to toot my own horn or anything, but you seem a lot more vibrant since I've arrived." He chuckled. "I want to help you, too. And I forgive you for when I died. Hopefully that sinks in eventually and we can move on. We'll need to figure out what other things I can help you with so both of us can find peace."

"You can absolve me all you want, Jamie. It's still my fault you died. I don't want to argue about it."

"Okay. We can come back to that one." He looked at Lucas's face for a good long while. "Do you want me to kiss you?"

Lucas's eyes widened, and he licked his lips without thinking about it. "No."

Jamie nodded and rolled over, staring at the ceiling. "Guess it wouldn't feel like anything to either of us."

"Probably not," Lucas said quietly. "Jamie? Do you want to see your family again?"

"My . . . is my mother still alive?"

"I don't know. She sent me a letter right after you got killed. I visited her once, a few years ago. Angie arranged everything. I must have it around here somewhere; her address would be on it." Mrs. Murray didn't seem like the type of person to sell a house to which she had an emotional connection. Jamie had grown up in that house, and John had lived and loved them all of those years there. Lucas would bet a fair bit of money that she would have stayed put.

"What about Fi?"

"I'm not sure, I think she lives in Dublin. I figure once we find your mum, we can ask her about Fiona. Seeing her would be good for you."

"What was the letter about?" Jamie asked, resting his arms behind his head. "Did you like her when you met her?"

"She said I could stay in the old flat. She wanted to know if you suffered. She wanted me to visit her. I said no to all three questions.

When I finally met her, she was kind and lovely. I didn't want to impose on her for too long, though."

"*Did* I suffer, Lucas? I don't remember it at all."

"You were shot in the heart; you never knew what hit you. I was with you 'til you passed."

Jamie rolled over and looked at Lucas.

"Then what happened?"

Lucas shut his eyes.

"I put my gun in my mouth and pulled the trigger. I was out of bullets. I almost killed a guy trying to get your gun to finish the job. They overpowered me, and I don't know why they didn't kill me. I woke up in casualty clearing a few weeks later. I don't remember anything from before that." He felt his pulse quickening and wondered if Jamie could see the steady violent beat of his heart.

Your blood was hot and salty, it was on my hands, it was sticky, and it made it hard to do anything. I killed you. I killed you, and I watched you die.

"I'm so sorry, Lucas," Jamie whispered. "To leave you like that." The spirit was silent then, and Lucas continued to be astounded by his beauty. This was what an angel looked like, surely.

"Okay. Let's go see my mother; I think it'll be good for both of us. We can get up early tomorrow and try and dig out that letter together."

Lucas wasn't sure he was ready to face Anna again, but it seemed like it would give Jamie closure. "Yeah. That's a great idea."

"Can we see your family, too? I've missed them so much."

"Sure, Jamie. I don't see them very often, though. Jessie's got the kids, and Becky's got her hands full with Mattie . . . I don't like to impose."

"The war really damaged us both, even before it was over. I think seeing them all will help bring you peace. Little by little, I want to set you free," Jamie reasoned. "Jesus Christ, Lucas. I wish I could touch you."

He reached out a hand and rested it against Lucas's cheek. Despite not being able to feel it, Lucas found himself nuzzling the air in an attempt to get closer.

God. This was torture.

"I wish you could, too. I wish things were different for you." He knew the apologizing was getting old, from both of them. It wasn't productive, and it wasn't going to solve their problems. "Worst case, we can try to find an exorcist and try and banish you to heaven that way," he joked, hoping it wouldn't come to that.

"Lucas, it's okay, honestly. It's frustrating, but it's like any disability, really. I'm sure it just takes some getting used to. I promise you, this is better than being dead. Hell, it's better than being alive was, some of the time. I have more clarity now, I'm not afraid anymore. Near the end . . . it was getting bad, wasn't it?"

Lucas swallowed. "Yeah." He reached over and tried to brush some of Jamie's shimmering golden hair out of his eyes. But of course, he couldn't. "It was really bad."

"I know I wouldn't have made it as long as I did without you, you know. You did so much for me, and I don't know if I ever really thanked you."

Jamie looked up at him, and Lucas wondered if the offer for a kiss was still open.

"You don't need to thank me, Jamie," Lucas assured him. "Your friendship was the most precious gift anyone ever gave me. You were the greatest part of my life. I would have done anything for you. I still will. Hell, you think I would have tried to get my shit together if I didn't think it would get you to heaven? I'd do it again; I'd do it all again."

The image of Jamie's face as the life drained from his eyes conjured itself unbidden to the front of his mind and cursed him. *Not here. Not now. Not while fucking Jamie needs me.*

Lucas . . . ?

His head flopping to the side, his eyes glazing over, the horror of that smile still playing on his lips . . . *Jamie . . . ? Jamie!*

"Lucas?"

His sharp silver eyes darted up to Jamie; he must have looked like he'd seen a ghost.

"Sorry." Christ, how embarrassing. He hadn't meant to get into a fucking flashback while Jamie was with him. "I was thinking about things I would have done differently. I was thinking about how you died."

"I can't even imagine watching you die. It must have been so horrible."

Oh, Jamie.

You have no idea.

1918

Lucas didn't leave the flat for a few days after he sent off the letter to Mrs. Murray. He felt like he was underwater, like he was slowly freezing to death. He couldn't really hear anything, feel anything. No hunger or fatigue, just emptiness. Regret. He went into Jamie's room and thought about cleaning, about dusting the place, washing the sheets . . . but he couldn't bear to do it. Each wash would lessen Jamie's smell a little, remove his little touches here and there, and a large part of Lucas felt like he didn't deserve to disrupt this sacred place. He went out only once that week, to buy some flowers to put into a vase in Jamie's room.

He sat on the floor facing Jamie's bed with his head in his hands. Why . . . why had he done it? Why had he shot Jamie? His eye twitched all the time now, it was his curse to forever relive that awful, awful moment. He had been so certain that the army would have him shot for murder but . . . it never occurred to anyone that Lucas Connolly would have laid a hand on Lieutenant Murray. Why would he? They loved each other; they were like brothers.

Lucas?

That look of betrayal in Jamie's eyes as the gun came out—the confused little smile like he couldn't believe what was happening. In his last moments, even as he was dying . . . Jamie trusted Lucas with all his heart. *You'd never hurt me, Lucas, not you, never.* That stupid idiot!

Lucas was weeping, he realized quite suddenly. Hot tears had been streaming down his face, snot running from his nose and over his lips. What the fuck was wrong with him? He never cried; he hadn't even cried when he had known the war was over . . . Had he? Peace had settled in around him, and the consequences of his choices had come to light. Never hearing Jamie's voice again, never making him laugh again. Their beautiful, peaceful home empty and gone, Lucas's life in tatters. Jamie was never coming back, it was Lucas's fault, and he was going to spend the rest of his life alone.

Jamie haunted his every waking moment, his dreams, his nightmares, there was nowhere to run. He'd taken care of most of his remaining duties, and he had to face his demons, whether he liked it or not.

For the better part of the last two years, Lucas had been watching Jamie lose himself to the darkness inside of his mind. He blamed himself for his father's death, for Lucas's involvement in the war, for failing to live up to his own expectations.

The guilt had slowly seeped into his consciousness and started poisoning him, compounded by the very real shell shock that had taken hold of his sanity. Jamie probably could have gone home on sick leave, but how could he leave the others behind? How could he let something as simple and weak as his mind overcome his duty to his country, his men?

Maybe that was part of the problem, that Lucas himself had become blinded to the reality that Jamie was flagging and suffering. Jamie's dreams had become bigger than Jamie himself was, and over time those dreams had lost their clarity: help Ireland, avenge my father, be a man, a hero, someone my mother can be proud of. Survive, survive, survive.

Gradually, Lucas started to forget what Jamie's smile looked like, what his laugh sounded like. Little by little, the war chipped away at the things that made him *him*. By the time Lucas realized just how bad the damage was, he feared it was too late to get him back. His episodes of intense fear and delusions were getting more frequent and longer, it was only a matter of time before he killed the wrong person . . . before he got discharged as a coward. Lined up and shot by the crown that he hated. Was that why Lucas had done it? To protect Jamie from a court-martial?

No. Unequivocally, no. That thought hadn't been in his mind at all, had it? Odds are they never woulda shot him over this, right? Certainly, protecting Jamie from legal action wasn't grounds to fucking put him down.

Jamie was charmed; he'd have managed somehow; he was so handsome, so poised, so likable . . . even a British court would have taken pity on him. Had it been Lucas's fear of losing Jamie altogether? A selfish wish to keep their bond pure, their memories untarnished?

No. It had been that last little smile. That beautiful, serene face when they'd held each other that last time. Lucas had barely gotten Jamie out of his own head that day. He was losing him. Jamie had smiled, time had slowed, and . . . Lucas wanted to set him free. Let him go when he was still lucid, when he wasn't afraid— when all that existed in the world was their friendship and the love between them.

Free him from the hell that Lucas was still trapped in, where his father was still dead, his comrades missing limbs, his mind about to shatter into pieces. Stop Jamie from slipping further away from him, preserve the memories they had before—before he . . . let him die as a man, with his dignity, his intelligence, and his humanity intact. Lucas hadn't been thinking, really, it had been a spur of the moment decision. Give Jamie peace, let Jamie rest, let Jamie go.

Lucas had never thought about hurting Jamie before, his whole damn credo was to protect the idiot. But in that moment, death was a mercy and existence was a punishment. Lucas realized that the only thing he couldn't protect Jamie from was the darkness of his own broken mind.

Lucas's body shook, the muscles in his abdomen ached as he doubled over with agonized sobs. He gasped for air, hiccupping with grief as the truth assaulted him: that if he had only been patient . . . Jamie could have come home.

He'd be here with me, he'd be a mess, but he'd be breathing, and we could fix his problems together. I'd stay with him; I'd never let him go.

Lucas had given up on him too easily, but it had been two fucking years, two years of watching the man he loved suffer and crumble. He couldn't watch Jamie lose any more of himself, right? That smile . . . that beautiful smile that he hadn't seen in years. The smile that said, "I'm happy, I'm comfortable, I'll be okay. Thank you, Lucas."

He couldn't — he should have waited, he . . . *Lucas? Why? Why?* Lucas screamed into his knees and covered his head with his arms.

If Jamie had lived, he would have heard Lucas's cries, he would have come running and put his arms around those narrow shoulders and held him until he was calm enough to talk. Lucas could almost imagine his fingers clinging to the fabric of Jamie's shirt, burying his sopping wet face in the crook of Jamie's neck and muttering unintelligibly about how sorry he was for everything. Jamie would stroke his back, his lips nearly touching Lucas's ear, whispering that it was going to be okay. And Lucas would believe him, since Jamie was never wrong about anything.

Lucas looked up from his knees to the empty apartment around him. All he could hear were his own shuddering breaths. Jamie wasn't coming to hug him; Jamie wasn't coming to tell him it had all been some terrible mistake. Jamie was dead. He was dead and buried in a mass grave in the middle of Belgium.

Go to the bathroom, Lucas. Get the razor. Make it quick, open your wrists . . . it'll be over soon.

Yet his penance forbade it. Lucas had stolen Jamie Murray from the world, and his curse was to wander the earth as a miserable husk until he died of natural causes. Death at his own hand was too easy, too gentle.

He slept on the floor in Jamie's room, just wanting to be close to him in these last days and hours before he left their past behind. It didn't take much to pack his life into boxes; it wasn't like he had much going on anymore. Lucas placed his meager possessions into a rucksack and walked into Jamie's bedroom one last time. He thought about taking some memento, something tangible he could hold on to when the days dragged on together, when it was hard to remember what he was living for anymore.

The army had probably sent Jamie's identification tags and medals to his mother, along with his father's pocket watch that he never went anywhere without. Lucas felt like a grave robber as he opened Jamie's drawers and closet, trying to find something suitable— well, acceptable, to take for himself. Nothing valuable, nothing too personal, he knew he didn't deserve it, but he also knew that he needed it if he was going to survive.

At the back of the drawer of Jamie's desk he found a button that had fallen off one of Jamie's shirts. Perfect. Jamie had been hopeless at sewing, and Lucas wondered why he hadn't repaired it for him. Maybe there hadn't been enough time, maybe Jamie had never thought to ask. Lucas held the button in his fist and brought it near his heart.

I'm with you Jamie, I'm with you, and I'll never let you go for as long as I live.

It took only a small amount of time for him to find the shirt the button belonged to. He held it close to his face and breathed in deep, savoring the familiar scent of Jamie's skin as the soft fabric kissed his cheeks. Vaguely, he imagined himself reuniting the shirt and the button. He used that thought to justify taking the garment as well.

Lucas packed the last dregs of his life with Jamie into a little suitcase and left the flat behind him. He never looked back; he couldn't afford to. His blood was ice, his chest was empty, and Lucas Connolly was glad of it. He slid the little button into his pocket and marched out into the world, directionless, reckless, and alone. The people around him seemed to have no faces, the sky had no color, and the earth had no music. This was life without Jamie, and he swallowed.

Better get fucking used to it, Connolly.

1923

"Jesus, Lucas, we've got to get you out of this flat for a few days, eh? Get your mind offa things," Angela suggested, dusting his one shelf and opening the window to let some air in. "Tell me how to help you." Five years had passed since Jamie's death. The seasons were changing, and Lucas's mood began to dip, as it always did near the anniversary.

"You can help me by not bringing it up," Lucas protested, although it never did any good. Their friendship did seem healthier when she let the matter of his obsession with Jamie drop. *No, that's not fair.* Lucas knew his stupid obsession was the root of the problem, though he doubted he'd ever fucking deal with it in a meaningful way.

Angela ignored him and began tidying up a little bit of the clutter that was so prevalent in his apartment. She stumbled on an old box of documents and sifted through it little by little. "Lucas? What's this letter?" Angela asked, holding up a familiar envelope without opening it. It was just as well she didn't, or Lucas probably would have lost his temper with her.

"It's a letter from when we got back from Belgium. Jamie's mother sent it."

"You didn't tell me that! Can I open it?"

Lucas sighed and folded his arms on the table, resting his head in the nook of his elbow and peering up at her. God, she was annoying. "If you want."

Angela opened and scanned the letter quickly, her expression softening. "What a sweet woman. Did you go visit her?"

"No. I wasn't up for it."

"Did you reply at all?"

"Yeah, I did. Nothing special really, just . . . cutting ties. I left the flat, and I dunno if she wrote me again after that." He shut his eyes and tried not to think about it too much.

"Lucas! This is perfect! You can go visit Mrs. Murray! Reach out to the one other person on earth who went through the same pain that you're going through. Who knows, maybe you can help each other! She sounds sweet, Lucas, I'm sure she'd be thrilled to see you."

"Angie, I don't think she'd want to see me after all this time, she doesn't even know what I look like. I doubt she even remembers writing that letter."

"Five pounds says she does. C'mon Lucas, I bet she still lives at this address. I'll buy the ticket for you; I'll even walk you to the railway station. What do you say?"

He groaned. "I'm wondering why this matters to you at all."

Of course he wanted to see her, but how could he? He'd flat out murdered her son. No. He couldn't. But nothing had changed in five years. Lucas was still the same miserable git he'd been when they'd stepped off the plane at the end of the war. Maybe Angie was right.

"Because you're a mopey old fucker, and it'll be well worth the price of the ticket to get you off your ass this Christmas! Save me the trouble of checking you haven't died of alcohol poisoning every day until the seasons change."

"You're too kind, Angela," he muttered as he fingered the button in his pocket. Lucas did manage a small smile, though. Maybe this wasn't such a terrible idea. Mrs. Murray did seem like a kind, gentle woman. Enough time had passed that Lucas had started to hate himself a little less, that he was hungry for more connections to Jamie as the sharp details of his memories started to fade.

Angela got him the ticket, as promised, and wished him all the best. He took a page from Jamie's book and assumed things would just work out okay— even if he didn't have any accommodation or maps or any real semblance of how the hell he was going to find Anna Murray in a village he had never been to before. Armed only with the envelope, he made his way through Waterford. He asked a number of people for directions, and gradually he was able to find a sweet little cottage with an immaculate white mailbox out front which proudly read "Murray."

Okay. Okay. The mother of the man he loved; the one person left alive who could even come close to understanding his grief. Someone who would probably never tire of hearing about Jamie, someone he felt he could love, maybe. Anna Murray was a chance for a new start, possibly even absolution. But he'd murdered her son. *Fuck.*

He took a deep breath and knocked on the door.

An older woman answered, wiping her hands on a pink frilly apron that went down to her knees. Her hair was graying, but he could still see the brilliant gold that Jamie had inherited. There were subtle smile lines around her eyes, which were so familiar that they almost moved Lucas to tears. She didn't look terribly excited to see Lucas, and he found his mouth dry.

"Can I help you?" she offered, cocking her head to one side. He could smell a pie baking in the house. A geriatric, grumpy-looking cat weaved between her legs, its erect fuzzy tail curling around her calf.

Lucas had had a whole speech prepared in his mind. He'd been planning on telling her about his friendship with Jamie, about how he'd loved him so dearly, about how sorry he was that he'd been such an ass in his letter, but . . . His mouth couldn't quite form the words.

"Y-yes." He managed, pushing the letter toward her chest. "I know this is completely out of the blue, Mrs. Murray but . . . I—I really wanted to meet you."

She frowned, not putting it together until she took the letter and scanned it briefly with those beautiful, beautiful eyes. Jamie's eyes.

"Lucas?" she whispered, taking a small step forward as she burst into tears. "Is it really you?"

He nodded, unsure what to do. Jamie's mother made the decision for him, and pulled him into her chest, hugging him as tightly as she could. "Lucas . . . Lucas! I'm so glad to see you, come in! Please, come in. Let me make you some tea! Oh, I must look like such a fool, I'm just—this is so unexpected."

She took him in, and Lucas wondered if she was disappointed by what she saw. He was hardly the beautiful soldier from Fiona's imagination, the hero from Jamie's stories, the decent chap that John had told her about. He was an undersized, underfed, ill-bred scoundrel who had wasted the past five years doing nothing.

Lucas followed her into the home, moved to the point where he was finding it difficult to speak. She was just like he'd imagined her from Jamie's stories—she was warm, she was gentle, and he loved her.

"I'll put the kettle on, please make yourself at home," she offered. "How do you take it, Lucas?"

"Black is fine," he assured her, his eyes wandering over to the mantle over the fireplace— photographs. There was a family photo from when they were all younger. He recognized John, and little Jamie . . . oh *Christ, he was so cute back then.* The way Jamie looked at his father in that photo, the love and admiration in his eyes. Lucas touched the frame and smiled, missing them both with all his heart. Right beside it, a photo of Jamie in his military uniform. He looked so hopeful, so happy, so strong.

Lucas turned away, unable to take all this at once. He was glad, in a way, that he'd avoided seeing Anna Murray in the first few months after Jamie's death. A little shrine to Jamie's memory like this, he probably would never have left her living room. That, or the guilt of being near Jamie's mother might have driven him to madness all the sooner.

The cottage was clean and warm and the carpet felt thick under Lucas's shoes. The rooms were well lit, cozy yet decorated with care . . . God, he would have killed to grow up in a home like this. But he was glad that Jamie had grown up here, that he had spent the best years of his life feeling secure and loved and valued. He returned his attention to the mantle where Jamie's pictures were displayed so proudly. Jamie's mother had his medals in a special case, along with, his identification tags. Lucas felt closer to her than he had let himself feel to another human being in a very, very long time.

"Ah, I love that photograph," she smiled, handing Lucas a perfectly steeped cup of black tea. "Jamie was so proud when he first enlisted, you know? He was so excited to make the world a better place, he tried to make me feel less worried. I was so scared for him, and Fiona was terribly cross." She laughed, shaking her head as she brushed a bit of dust off the frame. "I had this awful feeling that he wouldn't . . . " Her smile vanished and she took a moment to collect herself, taking a deep breath and allowing her smile to emerge anew. "Sorry, Lucas. I shouldn't bring up the worst parts of the past like this. It's not every day that you come all the way to Waterford! How long are you here for?"

"I'm not sure, Mrs. Murray. I just . . . " He didn't want to lie to her, but how could he possibly explain? "It's almost the anniversary of Jamie's death, and I've been thinking about him a lot. I thought about the letter you sent and I . . . "

Wanted to reach out because you're one of the only people on earth who went through something similar. Someone who felt the world end and their heart die when Jamie's stopped beating.

Mrs. Murray sat down on the couch and shut her eyes. "Come sit with me, Lucas. I'm not as young as I used to be."

He obediently sat beside her and waited to hear what she had to say.

"These last years have been very hard on me. After John died, I never thought I would recover. And then to lose Jamie just two years later— There were weeks, maybe months at a time, where I wouldn't leave this house. I found my strength in Fiona, bless her. And of course, Jamie and John wouldn't be impressed with me if I just cooped myself up here for the rest of my life. They would have wanted better for me."

On some level, Lucas knew that Jamie wouldn't have wanted him to suffer in his masochistic little hell for the rest of his life, either. But Mrs. Murray had committed no sins against Jamie, and she deserved better than Lucas did.

"He loved you so much, Mrs. Murray. He never said one bad thing about you."

Lucas squeezed her hand. She smiled and squeezed back.

"He never said one bad thing about you, either," she said. She looked at the photo and set her teacup down. "I see him in my dreams sometimes. He's always just beyond my grasp— bathed in sunlight, his face obscured a little . . . He sounds like he's underground, and I run and run but I can't ever reach him." She fiddled with the little frills on her apron. "He was always just out of reach, wasn't he? Even when he was little."

"Yeah." Lucas put his teacup down, too, and wondered if he would have lost Jamie in one way or another if they'd both made it back home together. If Jamie's trauma would have made them drift apart, if

he would have found a wife, and if she would have found their close-
ness inappropriate. He licked his lips. "How is Fiona?"

Mrs. Murray's face lit up. "She's wonderful. She lives with her
husband in Dublin; he's a barrister like John was. They're actually in
that old flat of yours, you know? I couldn't bring myself to sell it, but
luckily, they've made good use out of the place." She smiled. "She has
a little boy; he's turning one in December! He's such a darling thing.
He's called 'little James,' and he brings me so much joy. She'll have to
be careful, or I'll kidnap him one day!" she laughed. "Oh, Lucas, you
should see little James though, he's the spitting image of Jamie when
he was a baby. He'll be nothing but trouble, I keep warning her. I keep
trying to get her to move here but her husband's work is rooted in
Dublin."

Lucas smiled and imagined him, blond and perfect, with fat pink
cheeks and a mischievous smile. He thought it was so sweet that Fiona
had named her firstborn son after Jamie . . . In some way, Jamie could
live on.

Mrs. Murray met his gaze and her eyes sparkled. "What about you,
Lucas? Do you have a family?"

"Sort of." He wondered if she was getting perturbed or disgusted
with the way his expression warmed whenever he made eye contact.
Jamie had gotten a lot of his features from his father but his eyes, those
beautiful icy oceans that he'd fallen in love with . . . there they were,
clear as day. "I still have three siblings after the war. There's Jessie—
she's got a sweet little niece for me to terrify. Becky— whose husband
treats her like the princess she is—she looks after my brother Matthew.
He was crippled at the end of the war. I lost my brother Patrick in
battle." He didn't want to mention the siblings he'd lost as a child. Mrs.
Murray didn't need to hear about how hard his life had been. "I never
wanted to start a family of my own. It's hard. My mind is still deeply

troubled after everything and . . . I don't do well in crowds, with people. It's easier to be by myself."

"I can understand that," Mrs. Murray assured him. "But you don't have to be alone." She touched his hand. "Stay with me for a little while. I want to know you; I want to feel closer to Jamie. Fiona . . . it's so hard for her to talk about him, it's still so painful for her to even think about it. She almost never speaks about him or her father, and sometimes I feel like it's just me with my grief."

"Mrs. Murray . . . " Lucas wondered if he'd found a kindred spirit. He wondered, too, if maybe he would get lost in her, sink into the gentle tar that was Jamie's past, and never, ever leave.

"So, stay with me, just for a few days. We can talk and get to know each other. And who knows, maybe this is the start of a beautiful friendship? Please call me Anna."

"I can't impose—you just met me! I might be a murderer, for all you know."

Mrs. Murray chuckled at that, shaking her head. "Well, I'll do my best to keep all my deadly weapons out of reach, and you can try and control your homicidal urges for the weekend. Sound fair?"

"Yes." Lucas smiled gratefully at her, but in his heart, he was torn. He wondered if all of this was a terrible idea. Still, Angela had been right about one thing: he felt a lot warmer and happier than he had in a very long time. He silenced the voice at the back of his mind that wondered how he was going to mess this all up. This was a good start, and he was determined to make the most of it.

1913

"Jamie?" Lucas asked casually as the two of them walked beside the River Liffey. Jamie's classes had just let out. "Have you ever told your father that I'm . . . you know, 'Lucas from when you were little'? Or the, well, unique circumstances under which we reconnected?"

Jamie stretched his long muscular arms up over his head and cracked his neck slightly. "I may have mentioned that we were old friends, yes." He grinned. "And I don't see any reason why he needs to find out that you and I found one another once more in a seedy Dublin tavern."

"You don't need to hide it," Lucas muttered. "Your Da's probably better off knowing the sort of bloke you're spending time with."

Jamie smiled and clunked his arm across Lucas's shoulders, bonking their heads together. "He knows everything he needs to know, Lucas. Which is that you're lovely, reliable, hilarious, and can handle yourself just fine if we end up in a large-scale bare-knuckle fight. He knows that I care about you, that I respect you, and that maybe you didn't have the best start in life, but you make the most of what you're given. And besides, you already know what an insufferable prick I am, but you still choose to spend time with me. You cannot imagine how valuable a trait that is in a friend."

"Not to mention the fact that you're a smarmy, know it all, chatterbox, blanket-hogging idiot who's somehow managed to get both my sisters and my mother to fall in love with you in a matter of months," Lucas teased, barely resisting the urge to nuzzle Jamie's neck.

"And you give it to me straight, Lucas! Most of the people in my life are too polite or too stuck up to do that. I know you're being honest with me. I know that I can trust you." Jamie's smile was warm, it was welcoming.

"Well, as much as you can trust someone who tried to rob you," Lucas pointed out, a harsh blush springing to his cheeks.

"To be fair, though, you've had loads of chances to try and rob me since then and you haven't even tried at all," Jamie rebuked, squeezing his shoulder. "How's your family holding up?"

Lucas frowned a little at the question. It was embarrassing, it was sweet, it was fucking irritating that Jamie made him feel so much so easily. "Good, thanks. I've been able to get work pretty regularly recently, so it's been good. Plus, the twins are finding odd jobs here and there, and Becky's doing housekeeping jobs where she can get them. I suppose that's the point of having a whole pack of children, eh? Eventually they do all the work for you, and you can sit back and relax."

He bit his lip.

"Jamie? Actually, I wanted to take you out to supper tonight."

Jamie met his eyes.

"Aw, Lucas, you don't have to do that. Honestly, your poor mum feeds me often enough as it is."

"I want to, though. I owe you for that first time." It was import-ant to Lucas to do this, to not be in debt to Jamie. He still felt awful about trying to rob him, and a large part of him couldn't believe that a friendship had managed to grow out of that initial introduction.

"You don't, Lucas. You put me up for the night and you made sure I got home alive. I'm not going to hold that over you."

"Please? It would mean a lot to me." Lucas wondered if he looked too earnest, too desperate. He'd been saving up for this for a long time.

" . . . All right, boyo. What do you fancy?"

"You pick. That's part of the fun of being taken out, I thought."

"Well, there is a new fish and chips shop I've been wanting to try near the campus," Jamie said after a moment's consideration.

Of course he'd pick that. This sweet, sentimental bastard. Lucas smiled and imagined them growing old together, sitting on a porch in the country drinking beer, Jamie's hand on his knee . . . *Stop it. Idiot.*

Lucas followed Jamie's lead and they approached the shop. It smelled delicious— salty and fresh and warm, and Lucas could feel himself salivating from the moment they walked across the shop's threshold. He ordered them each a one and one and carefully counted out his coins. He wasn't good at math, and he had to dig around in his pockets to even produce the correct amount. The cook was not impressed, and neither were the people who had lined up behind Lucas.

"James!" one of them called out, roughly grabbing Jamie's sturdy shoulder. Lucas was focusing very intently on making correct change and didn't react to his intrusion. "Lad, you should have said you were going out for supper tonight! You could treat us! Just our luck to be stuck behind this shifty bastard, eh?"

Lucas's shoulders sank. He pulled his cap down and hid his eyes, hot embarrassment pricking his ears and making the bile rise up in his throat. Christ, why did this have to happen in front of Jamie, of all people? It was so fucking humiliating. It wasn't like he could get into an honor brawl over some snide remark in a chippy, could he?

He felt a heavy arm fall across his shoulders and looked up to Jamie in shock.

"Take that back," Jamie said. "This is my best pal, and I won't let you talk about him like that."

The boy held his hands up in surrender and exchanged a knowing look with his companion before addressing Jamie. "Sorry, Murray, I didn't know."

A pause.

"Why are you—I mean how do you know this . . . person?"

Lucas was obviously not from the part of Dublin where the university students spent their time. His clothes were old, tattered, and out of style. His hair was overlong, he was quite thin; muscles ropy from his years of working and fighting to survive.

"We met last year, he showed me around Dublin and made sure I settled in okay. He's a wonderful guy." The smile was missing from Jamie's eyes, and Lucas just wanted to leave.

"O-okay James," the boy said incredulously, as his friends were either hiding snickers or gawking at Lucas. "I guess we'll see you around. Unless you want to . . . grab food together as a group?"

"No. Lucas and I have plans already," Jamie spat.

Lucas snatched up the food as soon as it was ready and held it close to his chest. He grabbed Jamie's wrist and marched him out of the shop. Jesus Christ, that was awful. He never wanted to see those boys again. Jamie'd risked his stupid social status for him, Jamie had stood up for him . . . Lucas was furious and in love, and *ugh*, it was supposed to be fucking battered cod and greasy spuds, not fucking fodder for the greatest romance in the history of the world.

"You didn't have to do that," he muttered, pushing Jamie's share toward him. "Those guys are gonna hate you on Monday."

"No one talks to you like that when I'm around. They don't know you; they don't know anything. They think they're kings of uni, they think they can do whatever the hell they want. Bunch of rich fucking nobs who never worked a day in their lives." He frowned. "You think poorly enough of yourself as it is without strangers making assumptions about you."

"Still, you're supposed to be making connections for your career and everything, right? You don't need to risk your reputation because of me." He met Jamie's gaze . . . Christ, what a man.

"Maybe some things are more important than reputation. Maybe some friends aren't worth having. Maybe I don't like hanging out with a bunch of stuck-up pricks who try to trick me into buying them shit and who only want to spend time with me when they need something. I won't associate with anyone who thinks I'm too good for you, or anyone who treats you with disrespect. My father taught me that I should only do things that I can live with. You're ten times the man those guys are. They make me sick."

Lucas swallowed and impulsively hugged Jamie tightly to his chest. "No one has ever, *ever* stood up for me like that. I don't think you know how much that meant to me."

"Oi, oi, you'll squash the food." Jamie chuckled, patting Lucas on the back. "Do you want to go back to your place and eat this? The wee ones will be dead cross if they find out we got fish and chips and didn't share."

"Yeah. That's a nice idea." Jamie was full of those, it seemed. "I'll walk you back to the dorms after we finish. I don't want you getting stuck in the wrong part of Dublin by yourself if I can help it."

"Nah . . . I don't want to go back tonight." He paused expectantly, and then when Lucas said nothing, added, "I'd rather stay with you again, truth be told."

Lucas cocked an eyebrow at him, as always scanning the man for sexual intent, finding none. "You stay over often enough and I'm gonna start charging you rent, pal."

"I'll get us all breakfast then, is that fair?"

"Not really, staying at my house is horrid." Lucas understood the appeal, though. His siblings loved Jamie, so he'd get coddled and cuddled and spoiled like he did at home. If Lucas had his way, they'd spend every night together.

"I hate the student halls. My room is drafty and lonesome, and I don't sleep well there. When I'm with you, Lucas, I feel like I'm home, somehow. Please? I'll share the blanket better this time, I swear."

"Okay," Lucas whispered, a small smile creeping to his face.

He was finding out very quickly that he couldn't deny Jamie Murray anything.

They went to Lucas's flat and doled out the food, which made Lucas very happy because they'd all sleep so much better with full stomachs. They all climbed into bed after the sun had set, and Lucas thanked his lucky stars that a weirdo like Jamie Murray had come into his life. He woke up in the middle of the night and noticed Jamie was seated at the only window in the flat, his expressive eyebrows knitted together as he thought long and hard. Jamie noticed Lucas's presence all of a sudden and offered him a warm smile.

"Welcome back," Lucas quipped, leaning on the wall and peeking out the window as well.

"You hush." Jamie chuckled quietly; neither of them wanted to disturb the rest of the Connollys. Lucas loved making Jamie smile for real, loved how close they'd become. He fucking lived for moments like this.

"You'll catch your death out here," Lucas mused, hugging himself with his thin arms. "Can't sleep?"

"I was just thinking about something my father said. About the

WILD WITH ALL REGRETS

kind of man I want to grow up to be, the kind of life I want to live. He always said a man is judged equally for his actions and inactions. What do you think he meant by that, Lucas?"

Lucas was struck by the sincerity of the question, the genuine curiosity in Jamie's eyes. As though Lucas was worth asking, like his answers were worth listening to. As though Lucas could ever come up with something Jamie hadn't already gone over and discarded in his head a hundred times over. "*Tch.* Don't ask me, you're the one in university learning how to weave words into money." He felt his cheeks flush red, and worried that Jamie would see the limits of his mind.

"No, really, Lucas," Jamie encouraged, touching his shoulder. "I trust your opinions. I want to hear. What do you think he meant?"

"I guess . . . that . . . you can spend your whole life avoiding shit, and that kinda cowardice or laziness can make you look as bad as if . . . as if you did bad things all your life, or something. Someone who watches evil unfold carries some of the burden of guilt because . . . he could have made the world better and didn't?" He felt like an idiot.

"I think so, too." Jamie's breath ran out in a steady white stream of condensation against the window in the chilly air of the flat. "I want to be a man of action. I want to be able to sleep at night."

"And yet here you are, awake," Lucas teased.

"You know what I mean. Like with those guys today— I'm glad I spoke up. I'm glad I didn't just let that slide because I don't want you to think I don't hold you in high regard." He smiled. "I want to live my whole life like I lived today. Making the world better in my own way, like you do."

Lucas leaned against Jamie's shoulder and said nothing, enjoying the comfortable silence that settled between them.

"Jamie?" he said softly, after a pause. "I'm really happy. I like being with you. I like this." It was perhaps the most emotive he had ever been in this house. His heart was racing as he awaited Jamie's reply. There was a very good reason Lucas didn't express himself well. Getting rejected by Jamie at this stage would probably kill him.

But Jamie was merciful. He met Lucas's eyes before casting his gaze out over the misty cityscape just visible out the window. Without a second thought, he smiled and squeezed Lucas's hand.

"I love this."

1928

It didn't take long for Lucas to dig up the letter that Mrs. Murray had sent him all those years ago; he'd barely accrued any possessions in the last decade. Objects with no connection to Jamie had little value to him, and he cast most of them aside. He put the letter down on the table so Jamie could read it, wondering how he would react to seeing his mother's hand, the way her tears had smudged the ink . . . if he would be angry that Lucas had rebuked her so coldly . . . that they'd left things so badly last time.

"God, I'd know her handwriting anywhere." Jamie seemed relieved. "Let's go visit her!" he beamed, and Lucas prayed that she hadn't passed away in the last five years. He hated to disappoint Jamie, he hated when the world was anything but kind to him.

"I don't know. When I saw her last, we didn't part on good terms. I want to write her first. I think that would be the best way to do it," Lucas requested, and luckily Jamie agreed.

Lucas wrote a hasty letter with his apologies and sent it off to Mrs. Murray. After a few weeks it was back in his hands, a large "return to sender" stamped on the front of it.

Jamie swallowed, obviously worried. "You don't think . . . you don't think anything happened to her, do you?"

"I doubt it, maybe she just sold the house and is living with Fiona now." Lucas thought for a moment, then his eyes lit up. "Fiona! Jamie, your mother told me she was living at the old flat! I'm sure we'll be able to find her, then we can see your mum as well."

Jamie smiled.

"And you know that the best part is?" Lucas asked, reaching out toward Jamie's shimmering form.

"Tell me."

"Fiona has a little boy named after you. Maybe the five of us can meet up in the city center and, I dunno, make things right. I think getting back in touch with your family is a really good idea, I know it'll help you figure out why you're here."

Lucas headed down to their old neighborhood that very day, not wanting to make Jamie wait to see his loved ones. He owed him that much. Jamie was very well behaved on the journey, seemingly lost in thought as they made their way down the familiar streets. Lucas just watched him, love in his eyes. He'd missed this, he'd missed doing things to make Jamie happy. Nothing else made him feel as fulfilled or alive.

Lucas had tried to make himself look presentable for Fiona. He was wearing Jamie's old jacket and had combed his hair, shaved his face . . . he cleaned up all right, he supposed. At least people weren't giving him funny looks on the street anymore. Maybe that was the confidence, the happiness, the sense of purpose of having Jamie back. He felt like he had a place in the world again, felt like a normal human being again, just taking solace in Jamie being physically closer. Of course, if Jamie left again, then . . .

Gradually, they arrived at their old building, and Lucas took a deep breath to ground himself. Christ in heaven, what was he doing here? Fiona was going to think him mad. But he'd come this far, right? He couldn't turn back now. What the hell was he going to say to her?

Hello ma'am, you might not remember me since we've never met, but I used to share a flat with your brother who died ten years ago? He's a ghost now; we need some closure.

"Lucas, it's okay, my sister is really sweet and gentle. I'm sure she'll know who you are, I'm sure she'll be glad to see you." Jamie rested a glowing hand on his shoulder. "Don't worry. I'm with you."

Lucas nodded and knocked on the door, smoothing out his hair and praying she wasn't home.

A stunning young woman answered his knock, looking irritated at the unwelcome disturbance. Her hair was the same shimmering gold as her brother's. Her eyes had the same brilliance but none of the warmth.

Jamie didn't seem to mind; his spirit was practically littering her apartment with sparkles of delight.

"Holy hell." He grinned at his sister, looking her up and down. "She hasn't changed a bit, look at her! I—I'm so glad we came." She was beautiful, she looked so healthy—and better still, she was pregnant.

"Well? What do you want?" She looked down at Lucas, seemingly having inherited some of the favorable height genes in the Murray family from John.

"*Ah* . . . my name is Lucas Connolly. I was Jamie Murray's friend before—before he—before the war." Lucas swallowed. "I . . . um, your mother might have mentioned me— I'm sure Jamie did, when he was alive. . . "

Her eyes narrowed. "Yes. I assumed never contacting you was a reasonable course of action considering I have no interest in meeting you."

This was going great.

"Ah, well, my apologies for disturbing you. But I was hoping you could give me your mother's contact information? I miss her terribly, and I'd really like to see her."

"No." Fiona crossed her arms, her eyes suddenly a bit shinier and redder than they had been a moment ago.

"What do you mean, 'no'?" Jamie asked, letting out a frustrated noise when Fiona predictably ignored him. "Damn it! What does she mean, 'no?'"

"Why not?" Lucas asked.

"Because she died six months ago, you insensitive prick."

Oh God, he was too late. What the hell was he going to do for Jamie now? How could . . . he'd just ignored her and neglected her for five fucking years when she needed . . . God, no. No! He stole a glance up at Jamie, who looked distraught, completely unraveled. "How—I . . . I just . . . " He was stuttering, despondent, deflated. A shell of the ghost that he normally was, which was in and of itself a shell of the man he had been ten years ago.

Lucas wanted to reach out to him, to comfort him, but how could he without seeming to be a madman? He reached out a hand, then hesitated. No, he had to remedy the Fiona situation first.

"I'm so sorry, Miss. I didn't know," Lucas offered. "I'd like to pay my respects then, if that's okay."

"What in the world are you telling me that for? Do whatever you want." She turned and started to close the door.

"Hey," Lucas started, putting his foot in the doorframe to keep her there a little longer. He wasn't happy, he didn't like to be so pushy with women, but Jamie needed this. "I'm glad to have met you. Jamie only ever said good things about you. I feel so close to you—I've always wanted to meet you, that sweet little sister from Jamie's stories."

She looked away. "And you're *the* Lucas. The one who dragged Jamie off to war and got him killed." She glared at him.

"I didn't—I never!" His face was bright red; astonished at her bluntness. She couldn't know, could she? *You did get him killed. She knows.*

She knows and she'll tell Jamie, you fucking idiot. He shook his head, it wasn't possible. "Jamie wanted to go to war on his own, even Mr. Murray couldn't stop him! I did—I did everything I could to protect him."

Lucas's voice was small. Jamie stood beside him, keeping a hand on his shoulder.

Fiona hesitated a little. "I know. I'm sorry. I'm still really angry." She looked at him and crossed her arms over her stomach. "Can I make you a cup of tea? It can't have been easy for you to come see me like this."

Lucas's shoulders sagged with relief. Good. Maybe she knew her anger was misdirected. Maybe she actually could provide a little closure for Jamie. "Yeah, I'd like that."

"Careful though, the wee one's running around causing trouble. He's too much like Jamie," she grumbled affectionately.

Jamie's facial expression was mixed . . . pained, delighted, remorseful, exuberant. His mother was dead, but his wee nephew was a comfort, surely.

Lucas smiled at him, trying not to make it obvious that he was interacting with a figure that no one else could see.

"Little James, right? Mrs. Murray loved him so much."

"We mostly just call him Jamie now, to be honest," she said, smiling. "Jamie! We have company, sweetheart!"

A beautiful blond boy came scampering out of Lucas's old bedroom, apple-cheeked and beaming. He was near enough identical to the photograph of Jamie when he was a boy, and it made Lucas's heart melt when he saw him.

"Jamie? This is Mr. Connolly. He was friends with your uncle before he passed away."

Little Jamie clutched his mother's skirt with one hand and peered at him, shyness seeping into his confidence. "Uncle Jamie's friend?"

"Mmhm. Grandpa and Grandma liked him, too. Do you want to say hello?"

He nodded and stepped forward, extending his hand like a proper little gentleman.

"Hullo. It's nice to meet you, I'm James Regan. Most people call me Jamie, though."

Lucas knelt down and took his hand, giving it a nice firm shake. "A pleasure to meet you, Jamie. My name is Lucas Connolly, and most people just call me Lucas. What kind of things do you like to do?"

Little Jamie looked to his mother for guidance, and she shrugged, giving him a somewhat uneasy smile.

"I like to play," he muttered. "I'm going to my room."

Jamie crouched down beside Lucas, staring at the little boy. His expression was a mix of awe and despair . . . He'd lost so much; he'd missed *so* much.

The whole family had been altered irrevocably from their grief. The gentle girl from Jamie's stories had grown into a woman whose life was peppered with relentless, unimaginable losses.

One by one, the important people in her life had died off, from pointless conflict, stupidity, or illness. The life she'd made for herself was beautiful, fulfilling and perfect; she had a husband who loved her, a beautiful growing family, a large comfortable flat. Of course she didn't want some gutter trash digging up old memories, forcing her to deal with her anger and resentment.

Lucas didn't care for her very much either, but she was the only link to Jamie's family left in the world. He met Jamie's eyes and nodded, willing to weather the storm to help him find his freedom. Fiona looked small somehow as she sat on the couch and sipped her tea. She was as beautiful as Jamie had been, but Lucas could almost see the lengthy tirade of long-stifled anger hammering away at the back of her teeth. To her credit, she took a deep breath and centered herself. "Mr. Connolly, why are you here?"

"I wasn't lying to you earlier. I did want to find out how to get in contact with your mother."

"And the second part? Wanting to know me because Jamie and I were so close? I can tell a lie when I hear one." She crossed her arms. "So, what's the game this time, Connolly? Worm your way back into this flat, get close to little Jamie, see how much of the past I've kept boxed up so you can spirit it away to your hoard?"

"With all due respect, Miss Murray—"

"Mrs. Regan."

"Mrs. Regan, I don't understand where this hostility is coming from. I've never even met you before today."

"No? You said earlier you already feel so close to me after a few conversations you had a bloody decade ago," she said.

Lucas narrowed his eyes. This fucking bitch was nothing like Jamie.

She poured a bit of milk into her tea. "Maybe I feel close to you for the same reasons. Maybe I spent the better part of five years listening to my brother ramble on and on about how great you were, how you were teaching him how to fight and gamble, how you were going to go to Germany and save the world together.

"Maybe I see some socially inept little pauper trying to squeeze his way back into the family he helped to destroy. Maybe I see a man who had an unhealthy obsession with my brother and can't move on after ten goddamn years! Maybe I see what love and attachment can do to people, maybe I think my mother would still be alive if she'd never met you, that *certainly* my brother would still be here if not for you."

"Mrs. Regan . . . I never—I didn't mean to—I tried to help him . . . all I ever did, I did to protect him."

Fiona stood up at that, her fists balled, tears welling in her eyes.

"You're the one who encouraged him and let him do whatever the hell he wanted! You're the one who said he should take that year off at university! You're the one who went with him and kept him there after our father died! You watched him deteriorate and didn't fucking get him sent home before it was too late!" she spat, her whole body trembling.

"You're the reason my brother is dead! You're the reason my mother's misery consumed her, the reason she started drinking again! You destroyed this family! You took my brother away from me!" She had tears in her eyes, her face was red. "We needed him! *I* needed him! And you—and you—!" She turned away, her breaths coming in soft hiccupping gasps.

Jamie was hovering beside her, tears in his eyes. "Fi, I love you, I'm so sorry I left you, I didn't—I never would have—you were right, you were right all along, and I shouldn't have joined up." He was almost shouting, but of course she couldn't hear him. He swore loudly and kicked the air, deeply frustrated by his lot in life . . . or death.

"Lucas! Tell her!" he implored.

"Jamie . . . says he's sorry, Mrs. Regan. He says he loves you; he says you're right."

She took a step back, eyes wide.

"What the hell are you talking about? How can—you're insane! You're completely off your nut!"

"No, Mrs. Regan. Jamie's spirit is here with me, and he wants to talk to you."

Unlike Angela, Fiona did not want to test if Lucas was crazy or not.

"You're sick. You're sick in the head, and if you don't get out of my home, I will call the police. I never want to see you again. Do you understand me?"

He nodded; he didn't want to fight. She was never gonna understand him, and . . . Christ, maybe she was right. Maybe he was completely insane. Anna Murray had nearly said as much, hadn't she? He shut his eyes and tried to still his aching heart. Why did it hurt so much, still?

Fiona's expression softened. Like maybe she understood that Lucas was truly mentally unwell.

"I had to let go of my father," she said, "and I had to let go of Jamie. It was the only way I could function. I think the fact that you're still *this* obsessed with him after all this time is really, truly disgusting. I can't imagine what you thought you would get out of this visit . . . I got rid of most of Jamie's things when my mother died." She avoided his eyes.

"I don't want my home to be a tomb, I don't want to live for the dead. Jamie is gone and he's never coming back. Get used to it and get the hell out of my life."

She shut the door in his face and Lucas walked back to the flat in silence, Jamie floating wordlessly beside him. It was a little disconcerting; Jamie had gone quiet like this right before he was about to snap, back in the trenches . . . Lucas hoped things were different now. They got to his flat and Lucas lay down on the couch, not sure what he could say to Jamie. 'I'm sorry your mother is dead, and your sister wants nothing to do with us . . . but at least I suppose that's a form of closure for you?'

Jamie floated to the corner and stared out the window. "Life's moved on without me. My father died, and I wasn't there to protect him. My mother died because she couldn't bear the pain of my death. My sister wishes she'd never known me . . . she hates and resents me for following my stupid goddamn heart all the time."

He looked over to Lucas.

"And I destroyed you, too. Everything I touched, I ruined— unless they were smart enough to cut their memories of me out like a cancer."

Jamie put his head in his hands. "What was the point of my life? I might as well have died in the womb!" His shoulders were shaking.

Lucas ran over to hold him in whatever way one could hold a spirit. "Jamie, no, your life had meaning, you meant everything to me, you know that," he repeated softly, a chant or a prayer to stop Jamie from losing himself to his fears once more.

"I shouldn't have died out there, I should have come back home . . . I don't . . . I almost made it back, I almost . . . fuck! Fuck!" Jamie's shaking worsened, his eyes weren't focused, his hair had somehow become disheveled . . . no. Not this again.

Lucas tried to grab him, but of course, it was impossible.

"Jamie! Goddamn it Jamie, look at me," he snapped, his own voice cracking. "For Christ's sake . . . Jamie . . . "

Their eyes met, and Lucas saw a flash of Jamie, normal Jamie, hiding behind the fear and desperation. Lucas had fallen back into using the same words he'd used during the war to get Jamie out of himself . . . maybe it would work again.

"She said I'd be alive if it weren't for you . . . she—she said I would have made it back . . . "

Lucas managed a smile, reaching out a hand to feign clasping his shoulder. "No, Jamie, no," he said softly, his eyes never moving away from those near-transparent blue irises he loved so much. "I've got you, Jamie. I've got you."

Jamie's brows were furrowed, his eyes darting from side to side as he racked his memories. "I was with you, you were holding me—we were in the trenches; we were safe from . . . from bullets . . . " Jamie's eyes widened. "You . . . " He trembled, his mouth dropped open, and his expression turned manic.

Lucas's eyes widened, too. He didn't like the look on Jamie's face right now.

"You . . . you were there when I died. We were together—we were in the trenches. You kept me calm, you kept me safe, but . . . that last time . . . it . . . " His throat bobbed; his pupils were blown wide. "It was you. You had me, you held me, you tried to keep me calm . . . and then you shot me, Lucas. On purpose. It was you. It was *you!*"

Jamie's eyes flashed scarlet and he pushed away from Lucas, a burst of white-hot energy surrounding his form. There was a hole in his chest, right where Lucas had shot him, and fresh blood leaked down his uniform. A dribble of sanguineous saliva fell from Jamie's mouth, and he rose up, somehow bigger, brighter, and deadlier than he ever had been. Lucas backed himself against the wall, hyperventilating as he watched the truth hit Jamie all at once.

"You lied to me! You fucking shot me in the goddamn heart, you watched me die! How!? How could you, Lucas?!" Jamie paused, his eyes full of tears. "Say something!"

Oh Jesus, oh fucking Jesus Christ. No, no, no, no, no, no, not now, not now, Jamie please, please, please don't—stay with me. I need you to stay with me Jamie, please, please, please don't— if you're gonna kill me then— I'd rather that than losing you— Jamie, Jamie, fuck, fuck, fuck, fuck!

"Jamie—I—you don't understand—it—I just—"

"It was you. You killed me. You killed me and condemned me to this hell," he whispered, shaking his head. "You fucking *murderer.*"

"Jamie—no!"

In a flash of white light, Jamie disappeared from the flat without a trace. Lucas shielded his eyes and his face, expecting to be burned or blinded or . . . or to receive some kind of punishment for his part in Jamie's death.

Jamie should have killed him, but . . . no, that would have been too easy, too merciful. He looked down at himself, disgusted that once more he was fucking unscathed. Jamie had left him once again, in a colder, darker world. *Jesus, Jesus Christ, no.*

Lucas tried standing up straight, but his legs wouldn't support him.

"Jamie! Jamie, please!" he cried out to an empty flat, no doubt alarming the neighbors. "I'm sorry, Jamie! I—I'd take it back if I could . . . " he whispered, sliding his back down the wall and shaking his head.

He wouldn't leave me— he wouldn't hurt me—he—he wouldn't!

And that nasty voice which sneered from the back of his mind bared his teeth. *You stupid fucking bastard. He probably thought the same about you.*

What had he done? He'd only just gotten Jamie back . . . his life had felt right and . . . they were gonna fix everything, right? They were gonna get him to heaven. How could anyone *possibly* be foolish enough to destroy a second chance like this?

"Jamie . . . "

He couldn't lose him again; not like this.

The world was gray and empty once more, and with a clarity that almost startled him, Lucas knew what had to be done. His resolve hardening, his mouth dry, he picked up the pieces of his heart and took the first step toward absolution.

1914

Lucas got up a lot later than he normally did, feeling disgusting and hung over from the night before. He heard someone messing about in the kitchen and braced himself to face Jamie once more . . . damn it, he wasn't ready for this. Lucas was still fucking angry with his flatmate, and as soon as he saw that stupid handsome smile, he knew everything was gonna be forgiven as usual. Lucas wasn't ready not to be angry anymore, and it wasn't fair that Jamie knew all his damn weak spots.

"Morning, prick," he started, running a hand through his hair. He froze, however, when he realized that it wasn't Jamie in the kitchen at all. His face turned bright red as he recognized Jamie's father fumbling with the kettle. "Ack, Mr. Murray, I'm so sorry, I didn't know it was you." He wondered if it was possible to die of embarrassment. "Sit, please. Let me make you some tea."

John chuckled and waved his hand. "It's fine, Lucas, you don't need to make a fuss over me. I came over uninvited, after all." He smiled and pushed his glasses up his nose. "Now where is that 'prick' son of mine, anyway?" he teased.

That gave Lucas pause. His heart started beating faster and he stopped filling the kettle. "I'll check on him."

He made his way to Jamie's room and politely knocked on the

door. Hearing no response, or even the semblance of a response, he knocked a little harder and tried to swallow his panic. "Jamie, you smarmy git, I'm gonna come in if you don't stop me!"

He didn't want to, he didn't want to see fucking Maggie's stupid tits out, but . . . he opened the door with a flourish and his stomach dropped as he realized the room was empty, the bed unslept in. It wasn't like Jamie not to come home, he liked sleeping in his own bed when he could . . . The man was a creature of comfort and habit, after all.

Lucas's adrenaline spiked; he imagined the worst. That goddamn woman was a serial killer, she preyed on stupid men like Jamie and ate their entrails for fun. He shouldn't have left him, he should have stayed and made sure he got home okay.

John approached from behind and put a gentle hand on Lucas's shoulder. His panic must have been apparent. "He's a grown man, Lucas," he said kindly. "Come have breakfast with me. He'll make an appearance whenever he finds his way home."

Lucas followed Jamie's father back into the kitchen and tried to start making breakfast. All he could think of was headlines in the paper tomorrow—

Bright and handsome university student found murdered in back alley, apparently abandoned by flatmate. Maybe there'd be a photo spread of Jamie's dismembered remains, with a normal picture of his face for contrast. Oh God, why hadn't he just stayed with him? She was some slag in a pub, it wasn't like she meant anything to Jamie anyway. Jesus. What if he—

He couldn't keep his hands steady, and he swore as he burned himself on the stove. John smiled sadly at him, sitting him down at the table. "Allow me. I'll make you my famous Irish breakfast à la John."

Lucas nodded dumbly, his head in his hands as he imagined the worst. Their last night together . . . if only he'd known, he wouldn't have wasted it being angry and jealous. Everyone he loved died, everyone he touched ended up bitter or gone.

"Lucas." John's steady voice pulled him out of the dark corner of his mind. "Why don't I tell you about Jamie when he was younger? He'd always get into mischief, and I used to worry myself half to death about him." He smiled. "The boy's blessed, I tell you. He can charm himself out of any brand of trouble. He always comes out of things with a smile."

Lucas looked up, his gaze traveling as it always did to the thin scar over John's left eye. "What was he like?"

"Oh, where to start?" John put his cup of tea down in front of Lucas and offered him a warm smile. "Once, he wanted to get a birthday present for little Fiona . . . he must have been about twelve, then. He looked and he looked until he found the perfect gift—a feral cat." John laughed and cracked some eggs into the frying pan. "The damned thing nearly scratched his eyes out, but you know Jamie . . . a little desperate violence was never going to put him off. I thought he'd been through a thorn bush when he came home, took me ages to clean all the cuts out . . . but he never cried, he never gave up. Fiona wanted a cat, and he was determined to get one for her. He fed the little monster every day for two weeks, being bitten and scratched all the while until it finally followed him home. You never met a more ornery beast in your life, Lucas."

Lucas could imagine young Jamie trying to make friends with an angry cat . . . his little skinny arm dangling a precious bit of cod out toward her, his complete lack of awareness of the danger of a cat bite. Still, maybe John was right. Jamie was charmed, he could win *anyone* over, miserable beastie or not.

John pressed a sausage into the hot oil, and it sizzled; the whole flat was filling with a beautiful aroma. "That cat . . . she hated *every-one* except for Fiona in the end. Fi named her Cuddles and spoiled her rotten. She's still alive, you know? Stopping Fiona from finding a boyfriend to this day. Maybe I should get that dreadful cat a can of fish one day, as thanks. Never have to worry about burglars when she's on the prowl."

Lucas idly wondered how different his life would have been if he'd had a man like John as his father. Someone loving, warm, attentive, someone who embraced him for who he was instead of . . .

"And you know what a terrible swot he is, right?" John continued, drawing Lucas back out of the spiraling negativity that so often consumed him when Jamie wasn't around. "When he was about eleven, he got so engrossed in reading at the library that he didn't realize they were closing, and he was locked in the whole night. He didn't have many friends, and this sort of thing happened from time to time. His mother and I turned the village upside down looking for him but . . . the next morning, Anna was crying her eyes out over breakfast, he walked in like nothing happened, with an armful of books and a smile on his face. He'd had the time of his life, actually."

Lucas chuckled, looking up at John. "He's an idiot."

"The point of the story, Lucas, is that he'll always make you worry, and he'll always break your heart a little, but . . . he gives you that damned smile of his and makes it all worth it, somehow. Jamie's no fool. Hapless, yes. Careless to the point of negligence, perhaps, but he's smart enough to know how to take care of himself. After all, if he wasn't being so careless and ill-prepared back in the day, he never would have met you now, would he?"

John put a generous plate of food down in front of Lucas and patted him kindly on the shoulder.

"So relax, let him be an idiot, and wait 'til he comes back to you.

If he loves you, he'll always come back. Now eat up, you know how much I'd like to get a little meat on your bones." John sat across from Lucas, popping a corner of toast into his mouth.

They ate together quietly after that, and John was good at keeping conversation going when Lucas wasn't really feeling up to it. He'd only really known Jamie's father for a couple of years, but each time they interacted, Lucas liked him more and more. John treated him with respect, like an adult, like an equal. Lucas was glad that Jamie'd had such a wonderful Da' as he was growing up. John could almost make him forget about the fact that Jamie hadn't come home that night, a feat that was in and of itself astonishing.

They finished eating and John made a move to help with washing the dishes.

"Don't you start with me, Mr. Murray," Lucas warned, a smile playing on his lips. "You are not allowed to cook my breakfast *and* clean up after me. My mother would box my ears if she heard I let you do that." He wondered if John would like his mother, but suspected she wouldn't live long enough for them to find out one way or the other.

"All right, all right, I hear you." John held up his hands in surrender, chuckling softly and picking up the newspaper.

"What are you doing here, anyway?" Lucas asked, not meaning to sound rude.

"What, besides checking on my only son and a property that I own?" He laughed, peering at Lucas over his glasses. "I wanted to drop off some new books that I thought you two would enjoy. Plus, it's always a pleasure to see you, my boy." He gently patted Lucas on the head and fluffed his hair affectionately. "It's nice to see Jamie has a friend who cares about him so much."

Lucas smiled and scrubbed at the plates, satisfied with the answer.

A key turned in the lock and Lucas's ears perked up. He practically dropped the dish he was holding and ran to the door, swinging it open before Jamie even had a chance to take the key out.

He looked disheveled, hung over, like he needed a bath, and Lucas had never been happier to see him.

"Heya," Jamie said softly, sheepishly running a hand through his hair. "Sorry I lost you last night."

Lucas looked at him. He was here, he was whole, oh thank God, thank God he was okay. Lucas wrapped his arms around Jamie's body and held him close, not even minding the foreign smell of perfume that had sunk into his clothes.

"You didn't. You never could."

Jamie's strong arms returned the embrace, and Lucas's fingers tightened in the soft fabric of his jacket. "I hate you, you cock." He muttered, and Jamie chuckled against his ear.

"I love you too, Lucas."

As Lucas pulled away from the hug, he kept his hands on Jamie's arms and looked into his eyes. "Now go wash up, you smell like a drunk whore."

Jamie laughed and gave him that beautiful smile, and all the anger and insecurity melted away from Lucas's heart. How could he do anything but adore this man?

1923

"Let me give you the grand tour!" Anna Murray beamed at him, showing him around the sweet little cottage. She showed him John's old study, Fiona's old room (which had been converted into a nursery—at Fiona's request), the garden, the kitchen; everything was immaculate, cozy, and well loved. Even the damn furniture matched. It was so fucking sweet how much care this woman put into her home.

Lucas imagined Jamie growing up in a house like this, coming home with dirt on his knees, a smile on his face. Mrs. Murray would catch him by the arm, hold him back, and make him wash up before he tracked mud everywhere. And Jamie would laugh, obey, and chatter cheerfully about what he'd learned at school that day.

Lucas imagined him being tucked into bed by his mother, a handmade quilt up to his chin as he snuggled into the sheets, trying to get comfortable. John would come in and read him a bedtime story, maybe a chapter from the newest adventure book that had captured his fancy. *Good.*

"And last but not least, Jamie's room." Anna paused at the threshold, a look of hesitation on her face. "I kept it just the way Jamie left it. You can go in, but please . . . try not to disturb anything."

"Mrs. Murray—"

"Anna," she corrected.

"Anna, I would never, ever disturb Jamie's things. You have my word on that." Lucas bowed his head; this place was sacred to him.

"I know, I just . . . " She touched the spine of one of the books on the shelf and sighed. "It's all I have left of him."

Lucas swallowed and rubbed his fingers over the little button in his pocket. "I know how you feel. I'll be careful, I promise."

"Let me at least get you settled first, then you can have at it." She smiled. "You can stay in the guest room; it has a little bathroom attached. I've got towels, some spare clothes, and we can pick up anything else you need in town. What can I make you for dinner?"

Lucas chuckled. "Anything is fine, Anna. Don't go out of your way for me, I'll be happy with whatever you make." He reached into his pocket and got some money out, handing it to her. "Let me help pay for the groceries, at least."

"Lucas, I won't hear of it. You're my guest, start acting like it." She laughed, shaking her head. "I'll come check on you later, just relax. You can go into Jamie's room whenever you want."

Lucas was grateful for the privilege and took some time to settle down in the guest room before he intruded onto Jamie's sacred space. He helped Anna prepare their dinner, set the table, and he found it terribly easy to settle into a little domestic routine with her. They got along well, and Anna had no shortage of stories about Jamie, which always left Lucas with a smile on his face.

Gradually he felt comfortable enough to venture into Jamie's old room. It didn't smell like him anymore—of course it didn't—but there were pieces of him here which didn't exist anywhere else in the world. His old collection of books and toys, his spare clothes, his military uniform . . . Anna had taken such good care of everything.

Lucas carefully lay himself down on the bed and shut his eyes. This was Jamie's bed, in Jamie's home, where Jamie had lived and loved and grown into the man Lucas adored with every cell in his body. The smell of Anna's cooking wafted in from the kitchen, and he wondered how in the world he would ever convince himself to leave this haven. A little paradise that brought him so much peace. Why had he waited this long to get in touch with Mrs. Murray?

Lucas's self-hatred had dwindled in this cozy nest, but it flared now, and there was his answer. He had robbed Anna of her only son; he had prevented Jamie from living out the rest of his days in peace and happiness . . .

"Lucas? Sweetheart, what's the matter?" Anna asked at dinner that night, noting the very obvious change in his countenance.

"It's nothing," he muttered, then looked into her eyes and sighed. "I just— in a lot of ways, I blame myself for what happened to Jamie. I feel like being here with you has been so wonderful for me. I'm not worthy of being happy with you like this."

Anna nodded and reached over the table to touch his forearm. "I blame myself a lot for what happened, too, that I wasn't a stronger figure in his life, that I didn't try harder to stop him from enlisting . . . " She shook her head. "But it's not productive or healthy for me to dwell on the past. Fiona always scolds me for getting lost in how painful everything was. I told you, right? She hates to talk about Jamie, or her father . . . she was so young when we lost them both, and it all happened so suddenly."

"I know." Lucas swallowed. "Jamie was so, so broken up when we lost Mr. Murray. I can't imagine how hard this has been for you."

"Thank you, Lucas, I appreciate that." She took a sip of her tea. "After Jamie died, I very seldom left the house. I stayed in his room, I cried, I cuddled up with his jacket and I wished that I'd never loved him as much as I did. That things could be different, or that I could die and be with him again. Fiona had me assessed by a doctor. It wasn't healthy, the way I was. I drank too much. I won't touch the stuff anymore."

Lucas squeezed her hand, moved by how similar their experiences had been. He imagined Anna writing a letter to him, reaching out for a human connection while she reeled with the loss of her only son . . . how awful she must have felt at Lucas's chilly, impersonal response. He was an ass.

"After John died, I had to take on most of the family responsibilities, including the finances. It was difficult, I almost lost our home. Fiona's husband—her boyfriend at the time—helped us both through the worst of it; he's a good man. I thought I'd finally recovered, but then"— she sniffled—"he almost came home. He almost made it back to us. If he'd just managed to hold out a few more weeks . . . if they'd sent him home after his shoulder injury instead of back out to the front lines."

Jesus Christ, it was so strange and awful to hear these things out loud after all these years. They were the same. Lucas found himself trembling and was glad that Anna had her head in her hands. "Anna—I—"

"I'm sorry, Lucas," she said after a moment. "It's been a long time since I let myself feel these things. It's been a long time since I've had anyone to talk to about them."

"Me too," Lucas admitted. "I can't talk about Jamie to my family since my brother is in such bad shape. Everyone thinks it's strange how much time I still devote to missing Jamie." He looked at her. What was she going to think? What was she going to say? He'd never even admitted this to Angela.

"I loved him, Anna. I loved him with all my heart, and my life is in tatters without him. I don't know what to do with myself, I never have. He's been the most important person in my life since I was sixteen years old and. . . Fu—my God, why doesn't it get easier? I wonder if I can move on—and then I wonder, do I want to?" *How can I let go of someone I loved so much? What kind of man would I be?*

Anna leaned over the table and hugged Lucas. For a moment the world stood still as they shared in their grief together. Lucas had found a kindred spirit, and he wondered if Anna felt the same way.

They spent the next few days and weeks together in and out of Jamie's room, reliving the good memories and the bad ones. Lucas was obsessed with knowing the details of Jamie's life, and Anna was obsessed with knowing the details of Jamie's death.

"Please, Lucas. Please tell me what happened. None of the officers would tell me the truth," she begged him one night as they finished a bottle of wine together. He'd been resisting answering her questions, dragging out every detail of Jamie's childhood before he dared traipse through the bullet-pocked landscape of his last months on earth. "Do you really want to know?" he asked, his eyes dark. "You want to know everything?"

"Yes, Lucas. Please."

Lucas shut his eyes and nodded.

"Jamie had . . . really, really severe shell shock. He was sent to medical for it once—actually, I . . . *I* had him sent there. He resented the shit out of me for it, but he seemed better. He got really good at hiding it after that. He was erratic, he was unpredictable, he was sometimes a danger to himself and others. I did everything I could for the better part of a year to keep it hidden, to keep him out of trouble. He was an officer, it . . . it mattered so much to him to stay steady. I could see when he was about to get panicked, I could pull him out of it, I could keep him calm.

"But little by little, I started to lose him. Jamie felt so awful about what happened to his father; he agonized about how he kept surviving when other good men didn't. His mind was breaking, and I didn't know what to do. It was so bad that I was worried he would be shot for cowardice if I reported him again, and he didn't deserve his reputation to be destroyed over something like this. He wasn't a coward, he was just—traumatized beyond reason.

"The day he was killed . . . He had a fit of panic, a really bad one. I had been injured and he completely flipped his lid; he was terrified, couldn't be reasoned with, he couldn't think straight. To the point that he started threatening his own men with a gun."

Anna covered her mouth, her eyes wide.

"So . . . I wrestled the pistol off him, I took him aside and I held him until he calmed down, like I always did. I almost didn't get him to calm down that time. I thought he'd finally snapped. They might have court-martialed him, they might have had him executed, but . . . "

Lucas looked at Anna and wondered if she would still love him if he revealed the truth of what had happened. No one else knew, no one in the world.

"I got him back. He was there, and he was at peace, and we were holding each other and smiling . . . and then . . . he was shot in the heart. He was gone so quickly, he never knew what hit him. It all happened so fast."

Lucas's words were tumbling out; he could scarcely stop himself. "His blood was all over my hands and my face, and I held him in my arms until his body went slack and, and I screamed. I tried to kill myself, I couldn't see anything, couldn't do anything . . . I don't remember much after that. They had to sedate me for weeks. His body was buried there. I never saw it again. He hated it there so much— I tried to get him back, I tried to take him home, but they wouldn't let me. They wouldn't fucking let me. I left him to rot out there, alone."

Without a word, Anna Murray went into her bedroom and shut the door behind her. She didn't come out for the rest of the day.

Lucas made her tea and tried to get her to eat, but the food went untouched.

"Mrs. Murray?" he called, knocking gently. "Anna, please come eat something."

Lucas wasn't sure what to do. He was good at cultivating grief. He was good at making misery grow and flourish. Helping someone through their grief, being a shoulder to lean on in a time of need . . . no one had needed him for that since Jamie died.

Lucas listened to Anna's sobs for most of the night, wondering why he always left a trail of bitterness and resentment in his wake. It was another day or so before she finally emerged and met his eyes. Anna was tired and unkempt; she looked like she'd been crying. There was sorrow and hesitation in her eyes, and her lip quivered as Lucas watched her struggle to find the words.

"Lucas . . . I think . . . I think maybe this isn't going to work," she said, after a pause. "I care about you, I treasure you as a person, and—and I'm so glad that Jamie had a friend like you. Lucas, I can't live in the past like this. You loved Jamie so much—but since you've been here all I do is think about my son, and how much I loved him, and how much I miss him. I can't do this, it's not good for me, and it's not good for you, either."

She took his hands and looked into his eyes. "Jamie would have wanted us to live. He would have wanted us to be happy. And I don't think I can do either of those things if I'm always reliving the parts of my life where Jamie was alive. I have little James now, and I have to be strong for the only family I have left."

Lucas swallowed and nodded. Of course. Of course, the only person on earth who could possibly understand his grief thought he was too broken, even for her. He was so sick. He was so damaged. Even now, all he could think of was Jamie. He'd be so disappointed in

Lucas. *"How could you upset my mother like this, you ass? What the hell is wrong with you?"* Jesus. Jesus, it hurt. He prayed he could keep it off his face.

"I understand. I'm so sorry, Anna."

"Please don't be sorry," she insisted, cupping his face in her hands. "I know your heart is in the right place, but I don't think we're good for each other. We both needed him too much. We both loved him too much. It's too easy to get trapped in the sticky black grief that's encasing our hearts. I need to heal. You need to heal. We both need to move on, and we both need to live.

"I'm the one who's sorry," she continued. "I'll write you; I promise I will. And maybe one day we can grow as people enough that we can think about Jamie and smile instead of . . . " She drifted off, her shoulders shaking and her expression dark. "Promise you'll write me back."

"Of course I will," he lied. He couldn't bear to speak with her or write to her. He was broken, right? She'd already cut him to the quick, tossed him out like the trash he was. A dense miasma of anger and agony was blurring his vision, and he forced himself not to blame her for her choice. *Fucking bitch.*

No. No, no. She was right. As much as anger and bitterness would have been easier, she was right. Lucas looked into her eyes, those beautiful, perfect eyes that he never thought he'd see again, and forced an empty smile to his face. "I'm glad I knew you," he managed, and turned on his heel so he could leave her behind.

The rejection was profound and agonizing, and he wondered how he'd explain this to Angie. Even without knowing his secret, Anna had rejected him. Lucas's heart was in tatters as he walked, and he wondered if it was possible to die of loneliness.

1928

Lucas stood perfectly still in his flat, mind reeling. Jamie was gone. Jamie was gone again, and it was all his fault. He supposed it was only natural for Jamie to figure it out eventually . . . it was only by some miracle of blessed chance that Jamie had managed to avoid remembering the truth of his death for as long as he had. Lucas had vowed to spend the rest of his life in lonely penance, and Jamie had made it quite clear that that wasn't good enough. Jamie's was the only opinion that really mattered to Lucas, and Jamie had spurned him, rejected him, cast him aside like the filth he was. His sin was beyond redemption, and it was only fair that his life would be forfeit.

How could he make up for this? He could devote his life to per-forming good deeds, he supposed— try to save Ireland, enrich orphans, protect victims of domestic or sexual brutality. No. There was dignity in that, there was the chance for a long and healthy life; exactly the thing he'd stolen from Jamie. Suicide had always had a certain allure for him, yet somehow it didn't feel powerful enough. He would die with his secrets locked in his heart; no one would know the truth of the matter, there would be no justice for James Murray. There was only one option, then. To confess, to shout from the rooftops the gravity of his crime— *I killed the only man I ever loved, I robbed the world of sunlight.* He would be tried, maybe, he would be convicted, and he would die for his sins. A life cut short; his secrets revealed . . . how fitting. How sweet.

He marched himself to the nearest military headquarters and asked to speak to a senior officer as soon as possible, although he didn't want to explain further than that at the moment. When pressed, he explained that he was a veteran of the Great War and had some important information about some of the later battles he'd fought in.

Lucas was seated in an uncomfortable wooden chair and given a cup of tea while they dug up someone to talk to him. Although meeting with some random honorably discharged soldier from a decade ago was hardly a priority, it seemed.

A tired looking major showed up eventually, and Lucas couldn't help but smile a little. The Irish Free State military; Jamie would have loved to see this. He was led to a small room near the back and again told to take a seat.

"My name is Major O'Sullivan. I was told you had some intel for us?"

Lucas hesitated, and he could see the man's back stiffen a little. He was a stout fellow, wearing thin wire glasses like John used to have, and his hair was a neatly combed nest of salt and pepper.

"Well? What is it?" he demanded, crossing his arms.

"I . . . I murdered my commanding officer in Belgium. His name was James Murray, he was a Lieutenant, he was killed on October 14th, 1918, in the Battle of Courtrai. I shot him in the heart, and I watched him die. He was Irish."

Lucas peered up at the Major, who was giving him a very incredulous look. "I can't live with the guilt anymore. I can't prove it. No one can prove it. But he wasn't killed in action, he— I murdered Jamie." He put his head in his hands. He'd never said it out loud before, and the wave of cathartic relief that washed over him was almost painful in its intensity.

"Murray?" O'Sullivan narrowed his eyes. "James Murray, you said?"

"Yes, sir."

" . . . John Murray's boy?"

Lucas's mouth went dry. He'd known John had still had some connections in the army when he'd died but . . . "Yes, sir."

O'Sullivan swallowed and shook his head, his eyes dark. Lucas looked up at him, uncertain. "Why are you telling me this, Connolly? Why now?"

"I don't know what else to do—I can't go on like this. I don't deserve to be free after what I did. I don't deserve to live. I have to pay for my crimes. Please."

"And why— why would you murder Lieutenant Murray?"

Lucas met his eyes and swallowed. "He was losing his mind. It was . . . it was supposed to be a kindness. I was wrong. I shouldn't have done it, and I've regretted it every moment of every day since I pulled the trigger. I want to make it right." A stray tear ran down his face and he wiped it away angrily. "Please . . . "

The Major shook his head and exited the room, locking the door behind him. He returned a little while later with another officer in tow, who asked Lucas to stand up so he could be handcuffed and taken into custody. Lucas did as he was told and kept his head down, unsure if what he was feeling was solace. He'd wanted this, right? Wanted to cast himself into the fires of judgment, to pay for his crimes? He tested his wrists against the cold tight metal and swallowed his fear. *This is your redemption, Connolly. Jamie despises you. Be a man, stop being afraid.*

Still, it was only natural to want to bolt at the thought of being imprisoned and executed. He was put into a small holding cell at the back of the military office, and idly wondered if his father had ever spent the night in a place like this.

Time ticked by slowly, and every moment that slipped by he

watched and waited for Jamie to come back to him, like he always had in the past. A grin on his face, a glint in his eye . . . *C'mon, you daft bastard, I'll get you drunker than you've ever been in your life as payback for killing me, you bloody wanker.* And Lucas would smile, and the world would keep turning like it always had. He'd have to explain to Jamie that he was in prison now, that he had confessed to a murder, that if all went according to plan, he'd be dead by next year. But each time he opened his eyes, Jamie was still gone.

He had no idea how much time had passed before Major O'Sullivan called him into his office. "Mr. Connolly," he started. "Your case is an interesting one, a difficult one. You are to be court-martialed, and you will most likely be convicted and sentenced to death. Do you have any questions about that?"

Lucas just swallowed. "No, sir. Thank you, sir."

He deserved this. He deserved everything he was getting. This was better than suicide; this was better than a life in prison. The whole world would know he was a monster, and Jamie would get his vindication. How sweet, how fitting, that Lucas would die at the end of a rope for Jamie's sake. The thought brought him comfort in the dank of the cell, helped him while away the hours as he awaited justice.

The cell he was kept in was small and cold. There was a tiny window that looked out over a courtyard, but Lucas didn't bother enjoying the view very often. He imagined most men in this room had been panicking, or distressed, or praying to God that they might be able to make it out of here alive. Lucas had almost forgotten how to feel anything except emptiness and despair. Then Jamie had come back and brought light back into his universe, made him remember joy and hope and worry. And now what did he have?

The empty chasm left by the death of possibility. The knowledge that he and Jamie might have been lovers, that Jamie had seen his soul and rejected him. His siblings, his memories, even Angela, none of that could make up for the black void that Jamie's choice had left in his soul. He was worse off now than he'd ever been in his life, and as much as he feared the unknowable future, he was glad that at last his miserable life would be at an end.

Jamie left of his own volition, with hate in his heart and fire in his eyes. Lucas's heart had died when Jamie's stopped beating. His soul had died when Jamie forsook him, and all his body had to do was catch up with the rest of him.

The heavy sound of a metal key in the lock of his cell awoke him from his stupor, and he looked up at the brusque guard who had disturbed his tranquil misery.

"Connolly. You have a visitor."

Angela brushed past the man and into the cell, throwing her arms around Lucas's shoulders. She pulled away and slapped him once across the face, then paused, considered her options, and slapped him again with her other hand.

"You idiot! You complete fucking lunatic maniac!" she cried. Her face twisted up with anger. "What the hell did you do?"

"Ange . . . " Lucas started, but he couldn't meet her eyes.

"Officer, can you give us some privacy, please?"

The man nodded and locked the cell behind him, his heavy boot-steps thudding along the corridor at a respectful distance.

"Lucas . . . What the fuck happened? You confessed to a fucking murder?"

"How did you find out?"

"My Da's a retired colonel, stupid. But that doesn't really matter right now. Christ. Lucas, they'll hang you for this." She clutched his shoulders and made him meet her eyes. "Why, Lucas? Did . . . did *Jamie* tell you to do this?"

"No, Angie. He . . . he's gone, he left." He saw the desperation and anguish in her eyes, and he regretted causing another human being more pain. Everything he touched turned to ash, his whole life was just a string of failures and regrets.

"Oh . . . Lucas." She hugged him, and he nudged his face into the crook of her neck. He reluctantly wrapped his arms around her soft body and scrunched his eyes shut, trying to stop himself from feeling anything.

"Is it true? Did you really kill Jamie?"

"Yes."

"Why, Lucas? Why?"

He shook his head and started trembling. He didn't want to relive that moment again and again. That was what the damned court-martial was for. Angela was smart enough to figure it out on her own, anyway.

She held him and cried with him; they were beyond needing words to understand each other. He was going to be killed, she was never going to see him again, and he would reject her help if she tried to offer any.

"Lucas . . . you daft fucking cunt of a man," she whispered, dripping her snot onto his shirt. "I'm gonna tell your family where you are."

"No, Angela."

"Yes, Lucas! It's your family, for Christ's sake! They deserve to know you're not gonna make it to Christmas this year since you're being executed for a war crime!"

"It's not technically a war crime," he said, petulantly sticking his tongue out. "It's a military crime."

"You pedantic fucker— you stupid, wretched man. Of course, I'm gonna tell them, they need to see you, they need to be with you if they . . . " She buried her head in his chest. "Why didn't you come to me first? Why do you hate yourself so much?"

Lucas laughed a little, and he thought of how much he loved her. "There's a very long story to answer that question, Angie." He met her eyes and managed a smile. "You've been watching me self-destruct for the better part of a decade. And c'mon, Ange, you knew this wasn't going to have a happy ending. Irish love stories never do."

She laughed a little, too, and hugged him nice and tight. Her eyes were red and puffy, and Lucas thought she looked beautiful. "I wish I could have helped you, Lucas. I wish I could have made things better for you."

"You did, Angie. You always did. Right now, I know it doesn't seem like it, but this is the right thing for me to do. All the time I've been running from what I did to Jamie . . . I need to tell the truth, I need to face the consequences, and if they hang me for it, well, an eye for an eye."

She wiped her eyes and kissed his cheek. "I'll talk to my father. Maybe I can do something to help you. I don't care if you want me to or not, I'm gonna fucking try to help you because, God help me, I care about you, and I'd prefer you not to be dangling by your neck."

"Ange . . . " he started, but decided there was little point in arguing with her. He'd committed at least three capital crimes that he could think of. He seriously doubted that some retired old man could get him out of trouble. His best chance was claiming madness, but he didn't want to go down that route. Jamie had learned of his deeds, and Jamie had judged and forsaken him. The whole world would know what a monster he was, and there was no turning back from this choice.

Good.

Angela squeezed him, she kissed him, and she promised him she'd visit again.

" . . . I'm sorry, Lucas. I should've— maybe I should've let you end it in Belgium." Her face scrunched with pain, and she turned away from him. "Spared you from all of this."

"Ange . . . "

"I'm so sorry."

"Angie?" He called, and she looked at him, her eyes red and her cheeks stained with tears. "After . . . after they . . . will you take my ashes to Courtrai? So I can be with . . . "

She hugged him again, nodding against his neck as she cried. "Of course, Lucas. Of course, I will."

He watched her go and settled down with his back against the wall. He was lucky to have people who loved him, he decided.

The day of the court-martial came and went quite quickly, although most of his days seemed to go that way now that the light had vanished from his life once more. If he could feel anything, he would have thought it was funny how little he cared about the outcome of the trial.

He was treated roughly by the man who had been tasked with bringing him to the hearing, but Lucas didn't resist as his hands were chained together for the short walk over. He was unceremoniously pushed into a stiff wooden chair in the center of the room, surrounded by a small panel of military personnel. The lighting was sparse yet oppressive, so it was hard for Lucas to make out the features of the men deciding his fate.

Major O'Sullivan was seated in the middle of the table, and he looked over some papers at Lucas.

"Lucas Connolly, you are being charged with murder, attempted murder, mutiny, misconduct toward your superior officer, and falsifying records."

He put his papers down and met Lucas's eyes.

"You confessed to the murder of your superior officer, Lieutenant James Murray of the Thirty-Sixth Division, Royal Inniskilling Fusiliers, during the Battle of Courtrai, correct?"

"That's right." His voice was small, and he looked down at the chains that kept his hands close together.

"Do you have anything to say in your defense?" the Major queried, his voice carrying an odd mix of hostility and boredom.

"No."

There was a bit of commotion at that, and Lucas fielded a number of questions about his motivations for his actions, his confession, everything. He'd been playing the moment over and over in his head for the last ten years, and barely heard the questions as he responded.

"Did you kill Lieutenant James Murray?"

"Yes."

"Do you regret it?"

"Yes, every day. Every fucking second."

"How long had you planned this murder?"

" . . . I hadn't. It was a spur of the moment— he was so frightened and damaged . . . there was this one second where he was okay and . . . and I . . . "

"Mr. Connolly, answer the question."

"No. It wasn't premeditated."

"Why now? Why confess now?"

"I can't live with the guilt."

"What's changed?"

" . . . Jamie would have wanted it this way. He probably can't rest if I'm free. Please end this."

He wondered if he sounded cold as he spoke, but he was no longer capable of conjuring emotions, not even for this. The questions

petered off and the deliberation began. The men of the court-martial
sent Lucas out of the room to discuss matters. They pulled him back
in about fifteen minutes later.

"The case was a difficult one, Connolly, as we cannot prove that a
murder even occurred . . . this is why the attempted murder charge
was levied against you," Major O'Sullivan started, pushing his glasses
up his nose. "However, even the intent of physically harming your
superior officer is a serious offense, and whether or not your bullet
was the one that actually ended Lieutenant Murray's life is a bit imma-
terial, isn't it?"

"I killed him," Lucas responded firmly, defensively, almost pos-
sessively. "I had the gun pressed against his uniform. I couldn't have
missed, I shot him through the heart— he trusted me, I loved him,
and he trusted me—"

"Shut up!" O'Sullivan snapped. "It doesn't matter. There is no one
to verify your account one way or the other, and this is where the dif-
ficulty lies. I did find myself wondering, was this confession just the
whim of a madman bent on his own destruction? Suicide by military
tribunal to absolve your soul of the sin of self-harm? No. No, you're
a coward, but not like that. I've spoken to some of your former squad
mates about you, and all of them attested to your irrational attachment to Lieutenant Murray. Most of them sounded astonished that
you'd confess to something so heinous. They didn't believe it. But I do.
And I'm not about to let some pissant, indigent trash get away with
murdering an Irish officer of James Murray's caliber."

Lucas stared back, unflinching. He was not afraid of this man. He
was not afraid of death.

"There was not enough evidence for the murder charge, Connolly.
You cannot be held directly accountable for that. Everything else,

however? Your confession is proof enough. It is therefore the decision of this court that you are found guilty of all remaining charges."

Major O'Sullivan paused, watching Lucas carefully. "We hereby sentence you, Lucas Connolly, to hang by the neck until dead. And consider yourself dishonorably discharged."

Lucas bowed his head for a moment and let the information sink in. Absolution wore glasses and spat when it spoke . . . this was justice, this was the right thing to do. He looked O'Sullivan in the eye and thanked him, ready to face his death head on.

God help me, God forgive me. Jamie . . . Jamie please, forgive me.

He tried to ignore the sick feeling in his stomach as they marched him back to his cell. He'd wanted this, needed this finality, this hand of justice to vindicate Jamie. So why was he so afraid? He cursed his fucking coward heart and shut his eyes. This was for Jamie, like everything else in his life.

1916

"You're lucky, one inch over and that shrapnel woulda taken your eye out," Lucas's nurse informed him, holding him down with one firm hand. She probed around in his wound with long metal forceps that he prayed had been cleaned recently.

"And there you go." She plopped the little piece of metal into a small dish and presented it to him, obviously pleased with herself. Her honey brown eyes gleamed behind her glasses, and she muddled around her makeshift workspace looking for implements of further torture. "Now, I'm gonna need to clean this wound out, and then we'll stitch you up. How much of a wimp are you? I can get you some liquor for the pain, if you need it."

"Not too much of a wimp, but I wouldn't say no to a drink," Lucas decided. He came from a long, proud line of alcoholics after all. Shit, he hoped to hell that Jamie was coping okay without him.

The whole thing had been so idiotic. A bomb had completely missed all of them and cast off several shards of metal in their general vicinity. Lucas had shoved Jamie out of the way and taken a tiny hit in the forehead, which tore open his skin and left him bleeding profusely all over his face and into his eye.

"Lucas!" Jamie had just about tackled him to the ground. "We need a medic! Someone get a fucking medic!"

"Jamie— Jamie I'm fine, it's—"

"Jesus. Lucas, I've got you, okay? I've got you, you're gonna be okay. I've got you. How many fingers am I holding up?"

"Two. How many fingers am I holding up?" Lucas made a vulgar hand motion, which didn't lighten the mood as much as he had hoped.

"Lucas . . . Why did you push me out of the way? I don't—I don't want you getting hurt on my behalf. You could have been killed— I— for me you— I can't— Lucas I can't— Jesus."

Lucas felt fine, honestly, but there was an excessive amount of blood running onto Jamie's hands. The bright Lieutenant was close to tears by the time a medic arrived.

"It—it's a head wound. He's lost a lot of blood—I—"

"Aye aye, Lieutenant." A medic whose name Lucas had never learned tugged him out of Jamie's arms. "Not too bad, yeah? Can you walk?"

"Yes. I'm fine, honestly."

"Good lad. C'mon then, let's get that face patched."

"Take care of him!" Jamie called. "I—Lucas I'll be here, okay? Come back soon."

"I'll be okay," Lucas had promised, taking Jamie's hand and giving it a squeeze. Normally, he would have bumped their foreheads together, but it didn't seem hygienic. "You hold down the fort while I'm at medical, yeah? I'll be back before you know it."

He hadn't liked the look of his nurse when he saw her; she seemed too cocky. She had a broad smile and an easy laugh that seemed terribly out of place while men choked and died around her. But in time, her bedside manner grew on him. She put him at ease and kept his mind off the throbbing pain in his forehead.

"So, tell me about yourself," she said, swabbing an overly generous amount of a miserable, stinging liquid into his open wound and causing him to hiss in pain. "My name is Angela Robinson, a pleasure."

She passed him a bottle of whiskey and he took a long swig before she did anything further.

"Ugh. Lucas. Lucas Connolly. You're a brute with that cotton swab, honestly," he informed her, laughing a little. "How long have you been out here?"

"Long enough that I'm bombproof, a status for which you might consider aiming?" she teased, meeting his eyes for a second. "Hold tight, there's a little tiny fragment still stuck here . . . okay, I'm sorry in advance for this."

Lucas shut his eyes against the pain, Jesus Christ it felt like she was scraping against his skull as she tried to dig it out. "Fuck! Hold up, hold up." He needed a breather, and she gave him one. "You're strong."

"I'm all right. You're not as brave as I was hoping," she said with a wink. "So, what happened?"

"Bomb went off, I . . . I dunno, I probably jumped in front of it, I didn't want my pal getting hit."

"Your pal should get you a beer," she laughed. "Got it. Cheeky little bugger, that!" She showed him the minuscule bit of metal and plopped it down with its brother in the kidney-shaped dish. "Okay, I'll just go over it once more with the sodium hypochlorite, then we'll stitch up. You tell me if you need to stop. Guess worst case we can leave you with a gaping motherfucker of a wound." Angela grinned at him, and he found himself grinning back.

"As much as I'm sure that would increase my rugged appeal, I think you'd best close it." Lucas decided that he liked her. "I don't want my skull to fall out after all."

She flooded the wound with painful cleansing fluids and got her stitch-up kit ready. "Okay, this is gonna be shitty, but I'll go as quick as I can. You just talk, you keep yourself distracted. Tell me about this buddy of yours—not a lot of men out here I'd take a damn bomb for." She smiled and grabbed his skin with her forceps again, driving a curved needle through it.

"Ach! Shit! He—he's called Jamie, he's my best friend, we share a flat in Dublin . . . or we did before all this started. We've been friends for years, I dunno what I'd do without him."

Angela gave him a warm, gentle look. Lucas wondered if it was obvious from his face that he was in love with Jamie.

"And how's he taking your infirmity?" she asked gently.

"He's a wreck, I need to get back as soon as possible," he admitted, smiling just thinking of it.

"Aw, that's adorable! Maybe after the war is over you can get married," she teased.

Christ. Was it so fucking obvious? Shit.

"I'm just joking," she added.

Lucas avoided her eyes and said nothing.

"You must be very close, though . . . it's good to have someone like that. It's good not to be alone when you're out here."

Lucas sighed and tried to relax a little. "Yeah. I only signed up because I knew he'd get himself killed if he came out here by himself." Damn it, he wasn't normally this talkative about Jamie . . . then again, most people didn't really care about what he thought or said or did. It was sort of nice to have someone besides Jamie to open up to—hell, it wasn't like he was ever gonna see this crazy woman again. "You all on your own out here, I take it?"

"Yeah, my fiancé is stationed out in Germany, so . . . " Angela carefully kept stitching up Lucas's face. "I guess it's for the best, he's nothing but a distraction. His name is Euan, and he's positively dreamy!" Angela blushed and shook her head. "Okay! You're all set. That'll be twenty francs."

"You're off your tits if you think I'm gonna give you twenty francs for digging around in my skull!" He chuckled, wondering if he could find a mirror to assess the damage.

"Oh, come now, I did such a nice job! Ten francs."

"I'll treat you to a beer when I get my next leave, fair?" He gingerly touched the skin over his eye and determined it probably wasn't *too* mangled.

"Yes. And you can bring Jamie! I'd love to see what all the fuss is about."

Lucas wondered if Angela had managed to figure him out. Most of Jamie's friends ignored him and most of Lucas's acquaintances didn't dare ask about the beautiful rich blond boy who'd pulled him out of the slums. He wondered if his love was obvious, if his propensity toward men was obvious . . . it certainly had been to Father Doyle.

"He'll probably try to sleep with you. He has a way with nurses," Lucas warned, giving her a wink.

"He'll have to be pretty bloomin' charming to get my knickers off! My feminine virtue is promised to another, such as it is. Eh, we'll see how it goes. Worst case, you protect me from a lapse in judgment, as continuing recompense for fixing your face up. Yeah?"

Lucas laughed. "You're on, Angela. I'll come find you in a few weeks."

He was in good spirits when he went back to the bunker, even though his head was throbbing away. Most likely, he could've gotten a few days leave out of an injury like this, but he didn't want to make Jamie worry.

But of course, he had been worrying, and almost as soon as Lucas was back to the trenches Jamie ran up to him and threw his arms around his shoulders. "Oh, thank God you're okay . . . when I saw all that blood . . . " He shook his head. "C'mon, you can sleep in my quarters until your head is feeling a little better. Got to take advantage of the officer's perks every now and again, eh? . . . are you okay? No—no brain damage?" Jamie forced a laugh.

"No more than usual, Jamie. They said I'd be fine. I'll just have a scar."

Jamie's mouth twitched but he didn't say anything.

Lucas followed wordlessly and plopped down on the bed as soon as they were alone. He really was exhausted—drained from the blood loss and the pain in his head—but he'd stay awake until Jamie was feeling a little more secure.

"So . . . how bad is it? My face completely ruined? Will I ever get married, do you think?" Lucas offered, trying to keep things light.

"Eh, I haven't kicked you out of bed yet, have I?" Jamie laughed, sitting down beside him. "Women think scars are sexy anyway."

"That right? Good thing you don't get injured that often, any more sex appeal from your end and we'd never be rid of 'em. You're already bloody catnip with that Lieutenant stripe on your shoulder," Lucas teased. "Anything interesting happen while I was gone?"

"Not really, I've just been . . . well . . . worrying." He met Lucas's eyes and bit his lip a little. "I . . . fuck, Lucas."

Jamie had been doing a little better with his fears recently, and Lucas hoped this wasn't the beginning of another mental decline. They seemed to get worse and worse each time he lapsed.

"It's okay, Jamie. It doesn't even hurt. You know how bad forehead wounds can look, but they're never that serious."

Jamie took his hand and squeezed it. "Lucas . . . I dunno if I say this often enough . . . you're my best friend, and I love you, and I cherish you. You're my heart, Lucas. If I lost you—if anything happened to you here—I don't know what I would do. You're one of the most important people in my life and . . . and I was so scared today."

"I'm not an idiot, I know you're only here because I'm here, I know you'd be safe at home with your family if I hadn't . . . " He shook his head. "I'm sorry, Lucas. I'm sorry I brought you here, I'm sorry I got you hurt, I'm sorry you almost got blinded because of me." Jamie's broad shoulders were shaking, and Lucas sat up and pulled him into a warm embrace.

"You *are* an idiot. I'm here because I love you and I cherish you, too," Lucas said, glad that Jamie's head was tucked into his chest so he wouldn't be able to see the way his cheeks were reddening. "We look out for each other, and we protect each other. We always have, and we always will. There's nowhere in the world that you could go that I wouldn't follow, and I like to think the reverse is true as well. We're stuck with each other, through thick and thin, and that's the way it should be."

Jamie pulled away and smiled, those beautiful blue, red-tinged eyes shining in the dim light of the bunker. "Yeah. You're right."

He sat up next to Lucas on the bed and let their shoulders touch. Lucas very much appreciated the silence around them. It wouldn't be long before the shelling started again, after all.

"Lucas?" Jamie asked eventually, his eyes drifting to the angry swollen wound on his friend's forehead.

"Yeah?"

"What do you think happens when you die?"

That gave Lucas pause. He'd been a goddamn atheist for as long as he could remember, but he doubted that was what Jamie needed to hear right now.

"I dunno, Jamie. My mother always said that the righteous go to heaven . . . I don't think you have too much to worry about on that end. As for what I think . . . it's not an easy question. Every religion says a different thing, doesn't it?" He squeezed the Lieutenant's hand.

"Yeah. It's not easy to parse the truth if no one can agree on it." Jamie squeezed his hand back. "I've been wondering recently if heaven is just a nice story they tell people to keep them calm and happy until the end, like farm animals. I've been thinking about my father and what his last moments were like. Whether he felt fear, if he's in heaven, if his soul has just vanished. I can't bear it, Lucas. And today . . . I was thinking what would happen if you died. You know I'm not having the best time out here; I know I've made you put up with more than your fair share of bull." He sighed, running a hand through his beautiful golden hair.

"If I lost you, Lucas, I don't think I could make it to the end of the war. Whatever grip on reality I have, I would lose it if I lost you here. It's at times like these that I try to think about heaven, try to convince myself that it's real and we both deserve salvation. I need to believe that death isn't the end, that there's a means to find your loved ones again in the afterlife and make up for lost time. I like the idea that we'd be able to meet up again, go sit on a cloud together and watch the world go by for the rest of eternity. I know how stupid that sounds . . . "

Lucas shook his head and put an arm around Jamie's shoulder.

"It's not stupid at all. Tell you what, whichever one of us dies first can pick out the cloud and wait for the other one to join him. I promise you, Jamie, I promise you—if there's a heaven, and if by some miracle I make it there when I die, I will find you and we'll be together always."

Jamie smiled and gently bonked their foreheads together.

"Ow! You tit, my scalp got poked by a crazy woman all afternoon, as you may recall!" Lucas laughed, nudging Jamie with his forehead all the same.

"Shit, sorry, Lucas." Jamie laughed, too, and Lucas thought of how easy it would be, how natural it would be, if he could just close the few inches that separated them and kiss Jamie like he wanted to. His lips were so soft, so pink . . . *Kiss me Jamie, please, please, no one will ever know, it's just us.*

But of course Jamie didn't do that, and of course, Lucas didn't either.

"You dafty," he said instead, his voice warm and gentle as he imagined them on their little cloud in heaven, watching the world turn without them.

1929

Apparently getting Lucas executed was proving to be a bit of a faff—they had to have the hangman sent over from Britain, and he couldn't come until after Christmas. Frankly, the details were all a little tedious from Lucas's perspective. Angela had told his siblings what was happening to him, but only Becky had been able to come visit . . . maybe that was for the best. Jessie was pregnant, Mattie wasn't in any state to travel, and besides, Lucas didn't really want to see any of them.

Angela had come back once or twice as well, but Lucas could see how hard it was for her to sit with him now that he had the execution hanging over his head. Two weeks, they said. Sitting in his prison cell at Mountjoy was akin to being with a corpse, and he didn't blame Angela one little bit for not being able to handle the loss. It was better this way; he was glad to be alone. Being with people who loved him only weakened his resolve and gave him a reason to keep on living, not that it made a fucking difference now. He wanted to go to the gallows with his head held high, with bravery and dignity. His family would make that all the harder.

He stopped waiting for Jamie to come back as well, but he couldn't stop the way the bile rose in his throat each morning when he woke up, searching the room for a ghost who had long since forsaken him.

He hadn't even managed to get Jamie to heaven, hadn't freed him or helped him. He'd just lost him. Again. Christ, if he couldn't help Jamie then paying his penance was for the best thing for him. He had to keep telling himself that.

He'd been offered a priest, who came to meet with him once before the execution was to take place. "Death will be swift and painless," the man assured Lucas. "Pierrepoint is a professional. Your neck will break in the fall, and you will be killed instantly. You won't strangle to death. You won't feel anything."

"But how does it work? Why would that kill you instantly?" Lucas found himself wondering.

"The theory is it damages the nerves in the neck and shocks the system. You won't be aware of what's happening. Total brain death will take a little more time, but you won't be aware of it. It's very quick, please don't be frightened."

Lucas wasn't frightened. He told the priest he wouldn't need any last rites. He was ready to go as he was.

In a way, prison was quite liberating. Considering that Lucas had spent the last ten years pining, agonizing, and regretting nearly every decision in his past, having that weight off his shoulders now seemed a real blessing. One of the guards had told him that part of being a prisoner was reflection, penitence, trying to make come to terms with the sins of his past.

So he stared out the window and thought of Jamie. Of his beautiful soul, the life that Lucas had stolen from him . . . how just it felt to finally begin to make things right. It had nearly killed him to lose Jamie all over again, but it was clear now that that had been the push he'd needed to atone once and for all.

As the weeks passed, the feeling became more and more natural. It was such a simple pleasure to be able to breathe without having a sinking feeling in his chest. Yet even with his burden lifted, he could not ignore the niggling regret still nipping at his heart. That Jamie had left him before they could make amends. That Jamie's spirit might linger on ever after: angry, vengeful, and lonely.

Lucas found himself praying each night— to God, to Jamie, to any higher power that would listen.

"I'm sorry," he'd whisper. "Please. Please, forgive me. I'm doing everything I can to make it right."

It was a beautiful clear night in January, and Lucas stood at his window as he begged for one last chance. His lips moved silently; his brow furrowed in concentration. There wasn't much time left, and he didn't want to face his Maker without first finding peace with Jamie. He wasn't expecting forgiveness, but he at least wanted the chance to apologize.

"Lucas?"

He spun around, his eyes wild. His voice, he'd know that fucking voice anywhere. Lucas scanned the room, hyperventilating.

"Jamie!?"

"Lucas."

And there he was, shimmering softly in the sunlight, a sad expression crossing his face. He was dressed in his army uniform, the hole from the bullet still present over his chest, but the blood had largely vanished. Jamie put his hand forward and rested it on Lucas's shoulder, the light of his aura white and gentle.

Lucas fell to his knees in front of the apparition and clasped his hands together.

"Jamie, I'm so sorry. I was wrong, and I can never take it back, I can never make it better, but—"

"Lucas stop, it's okay," Jamie said gently, moving to embrace him as best as he could. "I'm still bloody furious with you, mind. But I gave it a lot of thought. After I remembered what happened, how I died . . . I couldn't stand to look at you or be near you."

He sighed. "I was so angry Lucas. I was so angry, and I felt so damn betrayed but I—I don't have it in me to stay mad at you forever. I wish things were different. I wish you hadn't . . . but you would never, ever do anything to hurt me. I know you, Lucas Connolly. I know that you did what you did out of love. I tried to put myself in your shoes, tried to imagine if I were slowly losing you to paranoia and fear, if I had to watch you slowly fall apart every day— shit. If you were suffering the way that I was at the end. I don't know what I would have done, Lucas. I don't think I could have taken your life, but I understand why you . . ." He made a gun with his fingers and mimed shooting himself in the head.

"Jamie . . . " Lucas whispered. "I don't deserve your forgiveness. I was wrong, and I'm making things right now."

"You don't have to, Lucas. I forgive you, and I love you. You never abandoned me, you never let me go. You have my blessing to live, happily and freely."

Lucas laughed, putting his head in his hands. *Why now? Why was this happening now, when it was too late? Oh, Jamie . . . you beautiful, kind, gentle fool.* "Okay. Thank you, Jamie." He had returned with a single goal in mind, to absolve Lucas, to free him . . . *fuck.*

It was too perfect, wasn't it? Lucas wondered if this made it more likely that Jamie wasn't real, that his own mind had re-conjured him in his last weeks for a final absolution. Then again, Jamie'd never had it in him to harbor resentment or anger for long. It was in his character to return. He hadn't been expecting Jamie to absolve him so completely— to just forgive him outright, to want Lucas to find a better life for himself, to live long, well, and happily. Why had he come? Why now, when it was too bloody late to— how could he fucking face death like this? How could he die knowing he and Jamie could have had a life—well, something like it—together?

Jamie frowned, taking a moment at last to peer at his surroundings. "Lucas? I have to ask . . . What the hell are we doing in a prison cell?"

Lucas met Jamie's gaze and smiled. "It doesn't matter." He reached out and touched the space Jamie's hand occupied. "Let's just say I have some debts to pay."

"Lucas?"

He shook his head. "Don't worry, Jamie. Don't worry. I'll be all right, okay? It won't be long; I'll meet you back at the flat when it's over."

"You want me to . . . leave?"

Lucas kept smiling. How could he force Jamie to watch his death? How could he stay strong in front of the man he loved?

"It was lovely to see you, Jamie. I'm so grateful. I'm so glad."

Jamie frowned, his eyes shifting slightly like they always did when he was putting something together in that brilliant mind of his.

"Lucas . . . ?" he said softly. "You're not ever getting out of this cell, are you?"

Lucas opened his mouth to lie, but somehow couldn't form the words. He shook his head and looked down at his knees.

"No. No. You didn't. You didn't, right? Please, Lucas."

"Jamie . . . I—I had to confess. To—to your murder." He managed a rueful smile. "They . . . um . . . they're putting me to death at the end of the month."

Jamie's eyes widened and he shook his head violently. "Lucas. Lucas, no. I— I had to come back to you but I never . . . oh God, Lucas."

"It's okay, Jamie. I had to make things right. I stole the sun from the sky, and it's time I paid the price for it."

Jamie's tears ran down his face, sparkling as the sunlight went through his shimmering form. "You idiot. You didn't have to do that."

"I did. And there's nothing I can do about it now." Lucas reached out and cupped the spot where Jamie's cheek was. "This is probably why you're here, Jamie. To absolve me, to set me free. You've brought light back into my life in a way I never thought possible, and you helped me come to terms with my sins and my crimes. Jamie, I want you to leave me here. I don't want you to watch me die, I want you to go to heaven like you deserve and . . . and . . . "

"I'm not leaving you here, Lucas. I won't leave you to die alone, I won't do it. You let me die as a man, Lucas. You let me keep my humanity, my dignity . . . you made sure I wasn't alone, you made sure that even in my last moments I felt safe and loved. You would never, ever hurt me, Lucas, I know that. Let me be here with you."

"Jamie, stop." Lucas felt his resolve waver, he imagined spending the rest of his days with Jamie's spirit at his side; he imagined the life they could have built together. There were no more secrets, there was no more anger or resentment. They could be happy like this, they could live like they always wanted. . . . Couldn't they? How long would it last? How long before Jamie grew resentful of being a spirit? Could he really, truly forgive Lucas so easily?

The cool stone walls seemed to be closing in around Lucas, and the bars on the window cast black metal shadows over the floor.

"Jamie . . . I'm glad you're here."

"I'm with you," Jamie assured him, taking a seat beside him on the floor. "I'm with you and I'm staying beside you, whatever happens."

The morning of his execution was a clear one, a beautiful one. The sun was shining, there wasn't a cloud in the sky, and the dew on the grass in the courtyard had beautiful little crystals of ice that had formed in the chilly temperatures of the evening.

Lucas took a deep breath to center himself . . . he was ready for this; it had been a long time coming. He shaved his face and washed his body, wanting to look presentable for the devil when they finally met face to face.

Lucas had requested his last meal a few weeks ago, and at around noon one of the guards brought him a nice fresh order of fish and chips with a cup of black tea. It was a meal that reminded him of Jamie, of better times that had long since passed but . . . he could barely stomach even a few bites of the stuff.

Jamie normally would have prodded and teased him, would have said to eat up, that he'd need his strength, but not today, not today. Instead, he watched Lucas sip his tea and tried to keep the conversation light.

"Do you remember when I first moved to Dublin, Lucas? I went to some random little pub, and in a city of nearly five hundred thousand people, we found each other. Even now, Lucas, I was trying to visit my parents' graves, to see Fiona again but . . . I kept drifting back to you if I wasn't paying attention."

He laughed, and Lucas smiled over the deep brown liquid in his mug.

"I was wondering how you found me here, actually."

"I'm sure it's an interesting discussion for a theologian, but there's a light in your heart, Lucas, and it's like the North Star to me. I often sort of wondered if we were, well, destined to be together. That must sound so foolish."

Lucas smiled and reached for Jamie's hand, hardly minding the cool feeling of the stone floor he collided with instead. "It doesn't, Jamie. You are my sunlight." And he liked to imagine the same was true for Jamie. God, if only they could have had more time, if only things were different. He couldn't afford to have regrets now, though, and he steeled himself so he could be brave when the guards came to escort him to the gallows.

They chatted about this and that, like nothing was wrong, like they had all the time in the world, until a clock chimed somewhere in the distance, signaling the last moments of Lucas's earthly existence.

"Connolly. It's time."

Lucas stood up on shaky legs and ruefully offered his hands to be bound for the short walk over to the execution grounds. Jamie floated beside him, silent but desperate, anguish written over his face. Lucas looked at his friend and offered a small smile, not wanting to talk, not wanting to lose his composure now. He wanted to stay strong in front of Jamie.

He tried to keep his eyes on his feet as he walked, but curiosity got the better of him. He spotted Angela among the spectators, and there were his sisters . . . Even Mattie was there, tears running out of his eye sockets as a very-pregnant Jessie spoke softly in his ear.

The guards walked Lucas up the steps on the scaffold and one of them shoved a rough fabric hood over his head. Darkness enveloped him and he started to tremble, his steely resolve all but a memory now that Jamie had come back to him. He didn't want this, he didn't want to do this, he wanted to live his life, he wanted to be with Jamie, help his siblings, drink with Angela . . . he didn't want this, he didn't—

"Lucas," Jamie's voice sounded suddenly, calling out to him in the darkness. "I'm with you. I'm with you, and I love you, and I'm not letting you go on your own, okay? I'll wait for you; we'll find each other again. It's not the end. It's not the end."

"Jamie," he breathed, tears in his eyes, "I'm so scared."

"I'm with you, Lucas. I'm always with you."

He felt the noose fall heavy around his neck and his breath hitched. He was going to die, he would lose Jamie again—there was no afterlife, this was all just a hallucination, he'd never see him again, he'd lose him all over, no, no, no! He wondered if his terror was obvious to the people watching. He wondered if O'Sullivan and the others were glad that his last moments would be as horrifying and frightening as Jamie's had been. It was *justice*, he reminded himself, but that didn't make it any easier.

Jamie's voice was in his ear all the while: "I love you, I'm with you, you're not going alone. I'll find you when this is over, and we'll be happy, I promise."

Lucas tried to be brave, he tried to remind himself why he had done this, how he had gotten himself here. *No regrets, steel resolve, do it for Jamie, don't let your sisters see how awful this is, don't let them see how frightened you are, please, please, for once in your goddamn life be strong.*

He heard the lever on the trap door click into place, the sounds of his sisters crying somewhere out in the distance. His heart raced, his breath coming in unsteady puffs as he relished his last access to oxygen. He wondered if his tears were soaking through the execution hood, he wondered if his cowardice was obvious.

The hangman threw the switch, and Lucas cried out for Jamie. The word was strangled by the fabric, and he wasn't sure if anyone had heard him. For one swift moment, the earth fell out beneath him and suddenly he was falling and then—a white flash and he felt no more. He wondered if this was what it felt like to die . . . if time was slowing, his brain shutting down, releasing euphoric chemicals, and pleasing memories to make passing easier.

His body was weightless, his hands unbound, and the world around him vanished. A great empty void, shadows of oblivion.

There was nothing. And then there was Jamie.

From the corner of his eye, he could see a warm and brilliant halo of light. His angel stood before him dressed in white, his eyes sparkling, and a beautiful smile on his lips. Lucas reached out to Jamie and walked toward him . . .

Jamie's hand was warm, it was solid, and his strong fingers closed around Lucas's. They could touch again, there was weight to him, there was heat.

"See? We always find each other again," Jamie said with a grin, a golden-white aurora dancing behind his head. "I missed you," he whispered, "are you all right?"

Lucas smiled back and nodded, the world at his fingertips and the weight lifting steadily off his shoulders. Somewhere at the back of his mind, he reminded himself that most likely, this was just the process of his brain shutting down— that his mind was being flooded with merciful euphoria that made everything seem okay.

But he pushed that thought away and locked eyes with Jamie.

For once, he was at peace. For once, he was happy.

It didn't matter if it was real. It was real to him.

Acknowledgments

I would like to thank my mother Sonia for all her help and support in writing this book. I would also like to thank my dear friends, who patted my head when I needed it and helped me become a much stronger writer. Lastly, I want to acknowledge my husband Greg, who is sweet and lovely, and always able to put a smile on my face.

About the Author

Photo Credit: David John Headshots

Emma Deards grew up in New York City and earned her undergraduate degree at Barnard College at Columbia University , where she studied Japanese literature and biology. She was then accepted to The University of Edinburgh, where she completed her veterinary degree. She remained in the UK afterward, and since then has split her time between her day job as a vet and her secret passion: writing. Emma has authored a number of humor articles for *In Practice*, a veterinary magazine, and was the recipient in college of two writing awards: the Oscar Lee Award and the Harumatsuri Award.

Wild with All Regrets is her first book.

SELECTED TITLES FROM SHE WRITES PRESS

She Writes Press is an independent publishing company founded to serve women writers everywhere. Visit us at www.shewritespress.com.

The Island of Worthy Boys by Connie Hertzberg Mayo
$16.95, 978-1-63152-001-3
In early-19th-century Boston, two adolescent boys escape arrest after accidentally killing a man by conning their way into an island school for boys—a perfect place to hide, as long as they can keep their web of lies from unraveling.

Boop and Eve's Road Trip by Mary Helen Sheriff. $16.95, 978-1-63152-763-0
When her best friend goes MIA, Eve gathers together the broken threads of her life and takes a road trip with her plucky grandma Boop in search of her—a journey through the South that shows both women they must face past mistakes if they want to find hope for the future.

Center Ring by Nicole Waggoner. $17.95, 978-1-63152-034-1
When a startling confession rattles a group of tightly knit women to its core, the friends are left analyzing their own roads not taken and the vastly different choices they've made in life and love.

Entangled Moon by E. C. Frey. $16.95, 978-1-63152-389-2
Long ago, Heather left her old life behind, and now she has everything she ever wanted. But when a woman she helped fire is murdered, it sets off a chain of events that jeopardizes everything, and she and her childhood friends must once again band together—to take on this new threat, and to face the events of the fateful night that has shaped all their lives.

The Sound of Wings by Suzanne Simonetti. $16.95, 978-1-64742-044-4
What if a stranger held the secret to your past that would change your life forever? In this masterfully crafted tale of love, friendship, betrayal, and the risks we take in the pursuit of justice, three very different women's lives come together in unexpected—and life-changing—ways.